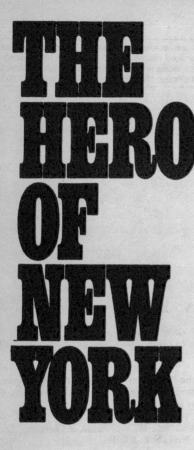

THE HERO OF NEW YORK

T. Glen Coughlin

ST. MARTIN'S PRESS/NEW YORK

THE HERO OF NEW YORK

Published by arrangement with W. W. Norton & Company, Inc.,
500 Fifth Avenue, New York, N.Y. 10010

Library of Congress Catalog Card Number: 85-8791

ISBN: 0-312-90730-3   Can. ISBN: 0-312-90731-1

Printed in the United States of America

First St. Martin's Press mass market edition/July 1987

10 9 8 7 6 5 4 3 2 1

FOR NEW YORK CITY COPS,
THEIR WIVES, AND THEIR CHILDREN

Special thanks to my parents for understanding; my cousins, Jim, Lumpy, Disco Pete, Higgs, and Guy for friendship; my little sister for listening; and Laura for love

Thank you, Yaddo, for believing

THE HERO OF NEW YORK

CHAPTER 1

When my father came in, I was lying on the living room couch, a pillow under my head, trying to absorb three chapters of accounting for a test on Monday. I called hello to him. He headed into the bathroom without a word. It was almost one o'clock in the morning. My mother and sister had gone to bed after the news. It was a Saturday night in October. Outside there was a yard full of leaves that needed raking.

We lived in a large blue-shingled house on a block with twelve other houses in a suburban town that was one hour from New York City, if you caught the express train, and it was on time. I'd say it was a nice house, nothing too spectacular. It had a den full of books that no one read, a finished basement, and a big, square, old-fashioned kitchen that had a new, square, white refrigerator that made its own ice.

I closed my book, deciding it was too late to study. "Dad, do you want coffee?" No answer. I heated a pot of leftover coffee anyway. Somehow I had become addicted to coffee. Six cups a day was a good day. My mother was trying to get me on the decaffeinated stuff. No beans, I told her. The wind knocked a branch against the kitchen window, and I jumped. The house was cold. I put my father's jacket over my shoulders and stood watching the blue flames under the pot. It took me a moment to realize that there were dried blood stains covering half the coat.

"Dad, what happened?" I asked, knocking on the locked bathroom door. Dad was a City Detective and this wasn't the first time he had come home bleeding. Once someone hit him across the face with a chain. It almost ripped through his cheek.

He opened the door and said, "It looks worse than it is."

"That needs stitches." There was a gash as thick as a cigarette that snaked from his hairline to his eyebrow.

"You sound like your mother." He pushed past.

In the kitchen he poured himself a glass of whiskey and sat heavily at the table.

"What happened?" I asked.

"The Jews," he said with disgust. "You should see my car." He drove an eight-cylinder Buick Electra. He polished it every Sunday. In the glove compartment there was a toothbrush for dashboard cleaning in traffic jams. "Those crazy Hasidim stormed the precinct house. There must have been two thousand of them, and I'm not exaggerating."

Dad worked in the Borough Park section of Brooklyn, a sixty-block area housing over thirty thousand Lubavitcher Hasidim. Many of these Jews had blood ties to the European ghettos of World War II. How they wound up in the middle of black Brooklyn would probably be news to God himself. No, their black suits, derbies, beards, and earlocks didn't exactly jibe with the neighborhood.

The Hasidim and blacks were neighbors and strangers. The tension was high. Blacks claimed they were being forced out of the area because Hasidim were buying up property and organizing their political stance. When Hasidim moved, they moved together. Hasidim claimed they were easy prey for muggers, robbers, and burglars and blamed these crimes on the black community.

I knew this because for twenty-one years my father had worked at the 74th Precinct. A few times I had gone through the streets of Crown Heights, Brooklyn, in the passenger seat of his patrol car.

Dad drank the whiskey straight and told me the story.

"There were only nine of us in the station house," he explained. "I was getting off work, checking out my chart for the next tour, when one cop comes running in yelling, 'There's six blocks' worth of Jews headed for the station house.'" A drop of blood fell from his head and landed on his white shirt. "Shit." He unbuttoned it and tore it off. He was a big man with heavy, muscular arms, huge, round, sloping shoulders, and short, thick legs. He looked impossible to knock down.

"Anyway, they stood in front of the precinct house yelling, 'We want more police!'" Dad put his shirt in the kitchen sink and turned the cold water on. "This isn't going to come out," he said.

"What were they protesting?"

"A Jewish jeweler was robbed and shot by two spades fifteen blocks from the station house. They got nothing. The poor old guy was observing the Sabbath so he had no money on him." Dad sat and poured another glass of whiskey, then got me a glass. "They pushed into the doors of the precinct house until it was wall-to-wall people. Files were turned over; all the papers on the desks were thrown in the air. When a brick came through the window, I knew it was time to get the hell out of there." He poured me a shot and refilled his glass. "I got pressed against the wall. Charlie, you wouldn't have believed it. Those people were going crazy." He flattened his grey hair. "I pulled my nightstick and they began screaming, 'Nazi! Nazi!' "

"Did you hit them?"

"Hit 'em? One of them spit right in my face. Do you know what that feels like? Someone spitting in your face because you're a cop? Yeah, I hit 'em. Look at this." He pulled his undershirt over his head. There were purple bruises on his chest. "And all the time that they're pushing and punching the shit out of me, I could feel my gun pressing into my stomach." My father prided himself on never shooting his gun, never once in twenty-one years. "But, oh God, I wanted to pull it so bad," he said.

I had on a grey sweatshirt and there were half moons of perspiration under my arms. Two round fluorescent bulbs lit the kitchen from the center of the ceiling. There were no shadows.

"The sad part is the car," said Dad. "I got out to the steps swinging everything I got and I see about a dozen of them standing on the goddamn hood, jumping up and down like it was a trampoline. I went through them swinging my way to the car and one of them snaps off my aerial and whips me on the head with it." He pointed to his forehead. "I grabbed that piece of shit off the car, and Charlie," he lowered his voice, "I don't know. I know I shouldn't have, but I pounded his skull on the curb with the whole goddamn lot of them pounding on my back. I got up and took them on, the whole damn crowd of them, and I," he held his breath, "I . . ." He made a fist. It turned deep red. Blood trickled from a knuckle. "I did some damage," he said.

"You didn't kill anyone?"

"Maybe. I don't know."

"You think you killed someone but you're not sure," I mumbled. It wasn't hard to believe that my father could kill someone with his bare hands. In the army, during the Korean War, he boxed at 198 pounds: fifteen fights, twelve knockouts, three wins by decisions. He could have turned pro when the war ended, but he met my mother and, I guess, needed a steady income.

I had seen him hit someone at a little league baseball game and I have never forgotten it. The bases were loaded and I was catching. We had a good pitcher. That day the ball was coming in like a Lear Jet. I knew if it hit me I was a goner. Those pitches could crack a jock cup or take a toenail off right through a rubber-tipped sneaker. I caught only because no one else would and no one else could. The outfield was covered by three kids who came to practice without mitts, and, when they remembered them, they wore them on their heads. So, that game, my father kept yelling, "Get in front of it, Charlie!" Woosh, the pitch came in. I did all I could to get out of the way. The ball hit the backstop and ricocheted into the weeds behind the bleacher. I didn't know it, but one father from the other team had quickly slipped the ball into his pocket. Everyone was stealing home while I searched for the ball. One smart-aleck kid did a crab-walk down the base line.

When everyone had scored, the guy dropped the ball back into the weeds. My father had seen him. Dad charged over and began yelling, "You dirty son of a bitch!"

The guy pushed my father's finger out of his face. "Oh, calm your pits," he said. Dad swung and connected. The guy danced back a few steps, spun, and landed in the infield.

Dad sat across from me rubbing the bruises on his chest. He had enough hair on it to carpet a Chevy van. "I can remember when two guys got into a fight and fought clean," he said. "Who the hell ever heard of biting an ear off? One of them tried to bite Phil Marineo's ear off."

"Who's Phil Marineo?"

"You know him," exclaimed Dad. "The cop we met at the Quarter Deck Bar. He was one of the police reinforcements today."

"Oh, yeah," I said. I had never heard of Phil or the Quarter Deck.

"Well, some Jew-nigger tried to bite his ear off," he nodded knowingly. "You know, you don't have to be black to be a nigger anymore, either."

I was getting sleepy and Dad was getting drunk. I wouldn't go to bed until he went. Whenever he drank, he liked to talk. He sat there holding the small glass in his big hands, looking at me.

"Do you remember that fight I had in Mundo's Clam Hut?" he asked.

"No," I said, remembering it. I'd heard all of his fight stories.

"Sure you do," he said. "You were only a little boy then, but you were old enough to remember."

"Yes, I remember."

The blood was drying on his hands. He got up and opened a window. Night sounds of passing traffic and blowing leaves came in.

"Tell me what you remember," he whispered.

"I'm not really sure I have all the facts straight." It was in the afternoon. He had stopped on his way home from work and picked me up at my grandmother's house. He had on his uniform and was carrying his .38 Special with the mahogany handle. "You kicked a guy's ass," I said.

"That's all you remember?"

"It was a long time ago," I said.

"God, I remember it like it was yesterday. Mundo's was my hangout. Ten cents a beer, two cents for all the peanuts you could eat."

I didn't correct him, but he had the wrong place. The bar with the peanuts was called Rocco's Tavern.

"You and I were sitting at the bar," said Dad. "And some white—nigger stood up and said, 'I'm not drinking with any fucking cop.' Now you remember? I told him to watch his mouth. That nobody used language like that in front of my boy. Nobody! Maybe I'm wrong, but I never let anybody, no matter how big or strong or bad he thought he was, get away with that, especially in front of my son." His eyes flashed with anger. "I beat the living crap out of that creep and I want you to remember it."

"How could I forget."

"And that was a fair fight," he said, not listening. "Nobody tried to bite anybody's ear off and nobody jumped in. And let me tell you something, nobody had the balls."

"Come on, let's go to bed," I said.

———————

Sunday morning my mother flipped when she saw my father lying in bed next to her with a freshly scabbed slash on his forehead. "You were fighting. You were drunk and you were fighting," she said.

I came out of my bedroom. It was the next room over. Across the hall was Louise's room. She had a "Keep Out" sign and a square of cardboard that read "Beware of Girl" taped to her door. To the left was our guest room. Besides Dee, Louise's girl friend, who usually wound up sleeping with Louise anyway, we had never had a guest.

"Did you see his head? Charlie, did you see it?" asked Mom, sitting up in bed.

"Yeah." I buckled my belt and sat on the edge of their night table. Dad rolled over and propped himself up on his elbow.

"Charlie, take her downstairs and tell her what happened. I tried to tell her last night. Do you know what she said? 'Mmmmm!' "

"I was sleeping."

"Mmmmm. I come home bleeding and she says, 'Mmmmm!' "

My mother was slim and had real blonde hair at the age of forty-eight. Sitting on the bed, she pulled her blue robe on, stood, and slipped her feet into matching slippers. I was always real proud of the way she looked. When kids had started that 'My father's stronger than your father,' I'd always throw in 'My mother's prettier than yours.' She was a real no-nonsense mother. She let me do what I wanted. I can remember walking home from kindergarten on the first day of school holding a map she had drawn. It wasn't far but at six years old it seemed like around the block in eighty days.

In the kitchen Mom made coffee in a Mr. Coffee coffee-maker. We had always been an instant family, until last month when my mother won the machine at "Wednesday Night At The Bingo" held in the church basement. She was very involved with the parish. Sometimes she went to Mass twice a day and then did some house cleaning or gardening at the rectory. "You don't get enough work here?" I'd say. If my father heard me, he'd jump down my throat. "You should have half the grace your mother has," he'd bark. I think he figured her prayers would save him from hell. Neither he nor I ever went to church. Louise went on Sundays and usually never got there. I'd see her standing in front of the deli drinking a Yoo Hoo and unwrapping a Scooter Pie. Her collection money never made it either. I couldn't say a word. I had done the same thing.

We listened to Mr. Coffee spit the brown water into the pot. "There was trouble at the precinct," I said, acting bored. "The Hasidic Jews broke into the station house and somebody hit Dad in the head."

"With what? A knife?"

"No, a stick," I said quickly. "Some kind of sharp stick." I was going to let Dad explain. My mother wasn't the hysterical type, but she could be very emotional. I could just hear myself, "Well, he thinks he killed a guy, but don't worry."

"He should have gotten stitches. It's an inch wide."

"It's about a quarter of an inch."

"Someone should have looked at it."

"I told him that last night."

Dad never liked doctors. Once he had stepped on a rusty nail. It went through his shoe and almost through his foot. He hopped into the house, blood seeping out of the hole in the rubber sole. Mom wanted to rush him to the hospital. He told her that he would take care of it, that he had stepped on plenty of things worse than nails. Over the tub, he sat and cleaned the cut with peroxide, put a towel between his teeth and dug around for dirt. Grimacing he said, "I'm saving a good fifty dollars."

Two days later the foot began to swell. He couldn't get his shoe on. Still, he wouldn't see a doctor. For hours he sat soaking it in Epsom salts and hot water. Finally, the swelling subsided. "You don't run to the doctor for every little thing," he said.

My mother unhooked my cup off the rack and put it on the table. She had long slender arms. Sometimes my father called her Flamingo. He even invented a special drink for her called the Pink Flamingo. "I bet he got that in a bar fight," she said. "I've known him too long to believe that story." She was a pretty smart cookie. "That's all he told you?"

I held up my cup. On the side in brown letters it said, "Give Me A Break." We all had our own cups. Louise's said, "I've Had a Hard Day." My mother's cup said, "Satisfaction Guaranteed." Dad bought it for her after her "Don't Call Me, I'll Call You" cup broke. She had dropped it during an argument about my dropping out of college. I was majoring in business administration and getting bored into a coma. Another important reason for throwing in the towel was that I was failing almost everything. During the argument she had been trying to point at me and hold her coffee cup, and "Don't

Call Me, I'll Call You" had become history. Dad's cup said, "The Boss." Everytime he got a new cup he bought the same thing. It was a family tradition.

Mom went into the living room. I heard the front door open with a tug. It stuck so badly in damp weather that we had to pry it open with screwdrivers. My mother was as strong as she was wiry. On grocery day she was a triple bag carrier. Even if there were only three bags in the trunk of the car, she took them all in one trip. In the summer she liked to ride my ten-speed bike. She filled the thermos with juice, put sweat bands on her wrists and head, and off she'd go, her long legs pumping, her finger tips gripping the lazy bar handle brakes.

Mom came back into the kitchen holding the Sunday newspaper as if it had diphtheria. "It's front page news," she said.

"Mob storms 74th Precinct," declared the headlines. There was a blurry black and white photo of the Jews standing on the steps of the station house. I read the story to my mother:

Riot at the 74th Precinct
Between Jews and the N.Y.C. Police

Yesterday the 74th Precinct in the Borough Park section of Brooklyn was the scene of a club-swinging, rock-throwing riot as hundreds of Hasidic Jews, outraged over the fatal shooting of Norman Coleman, stormed the police station. Policemen on duty tried to quiet the angry mob, but violence broke out as the mass pushed up the steps and spilled into the precinct house.

The clash, a terrible reminder of the riots of the 60's, left 82 people injured, 56 of those police officers. Many of the bruises were the result of hand-to-hand combat between police and the Jews. At least 25 policemen and

6 Jews were wounded seriously and were transported to Maimonides Hospital by ambulance. Blood ran down the face of Sidney Cantor, one of those seriously injured, as he told reporters that he sustained his head injury from a "police nightstick." Cantor claimed that it was the policemen, not the Jews, who started the clash. "Without police protection," Cantor went on to say, "we Jews are as powerless as those in the concentration camps."

The Jews demand more police protection. The brutal shooting of Norman Coleman, a frail 76 year old jeweler was in midafternoon and just 20 blocks from the station house. Many Jewish community leaders justify the $25,000.00 dollars damage to the 74th Precinct by holding up the Holy book Coleman was carrying at the time of his death.

Police Officials claim that there are at least two suspects connected to the murder of Coleman. 30 Detectives have been assigned to the investigation. Although no arrests were made during or after the storming of the 74th, the Mayor has ordered an investigation into the actions of the Jews as well as the policemen.

I looked at my mother and opened to page two. The reports of the storming went on and on. The mayor had stood on the station house steps shouting in English and Yiddish, trying to calm the crowd. "There will be an investigation," he said. "But, the question is, do we ever do ourselves a service by coming in and tearing up the place?"

My mother waited for my reaction.

"Holy shit," I said. "You better show this to Dad."

CHAPTER
2

I stood at the front door looking out the slatted glass.
The clouds were moving fast and the leaves were falling. It was about noon. Mom had gone to Sunday services. Louise was taking a shower. Dad stood on the lawn, hands in his pockets staring at the Buick. The beautiful car was a wreck. The top and hood were caved in, the windows were broken, and the doors dented. It was cold and he wore only a tank top. A dog trotted sideways down the walk and sniffed at a tree. I came out of the house and called the dog. He ran across the street and up a driveway. Dad just stared at the car, moving the muscles in his arms. They tightened and relaxed like large snakes.

The car was an Electra 225, long and low, built when

gas was thirty-four cents a gallon. It had every option, including rear footstools. Neither rain nor snow had ever dried on the black paint. If Dad was caught in a storm, he wiped the hood and fenders, then knelt and dried the fender wells before shutting the garage door. Remember the expression, so clean you could eat off it? Well, you could have done open-heart surgery on that engine. Dad had even put red and green felt rings on the battery terminals and pin striped the air cleaner.

I stood next to him. "They really did a job on it."

He nodded and gently touched the gash on his head.

"You should have gotten stitches."

"All right, all right, give it a rest." It was the first thing he had said since reading the paper. When he had seen the headlines, the blood drained from his face. He took the newspaper into the bathroom and locked the door.

The sun popped out. Tiny glass cubes glistened on the dashboard and seats. The side windows had cracked into ice-like webs and the windshield had shattered. "A mess," I said. "A real mess."

Dad pulled the door. It squeaked open and the window fell between the door and the step plate. It smacked on the cement driveway, almost landing in a perfect square. "Sons of bitches," he said slowly. "Get me the vacuum."

We cleaned the car. I knew he was so worried about his job, about the man in critical condition, that he had to keep busy. He kept looking up the street when he thought I wasn't watching. I was pretty worried, too. He could lose his job, his pension, and, even worse, go to jail.

I brushed the large pieces of glass into a dust pan and

he vacuumed the splinters. I got a sliver stuck in my finger. I pulled it out and the cut bled. Dad watched me and said everything with his eyes. He was scared. Plain and simple fear.

With a hammer he chipped out the glass still stuck in the window frames. He worked slowly like an artist shaping marble.

"How much will it cost to replace the windows?"

"That I don't know. The only thing I know is someone is going to pay."

"Aren't you cold?"

"No. Believe it or not I'm sweating. My blood pressure is so damn high that I don't get cold anymore. I had it checked in one of those drug store computers. 170 over 120." He laid the hammer on the roof and pulled out his wallet. "If I can find it I'll show you the diagnosis." He gave me a card that said, "Dangerously high. See a doctor."

"You better go see a doctor."

"First I'm going to try another machine."

I didn't want to press him. He opened the hood and hammered out dents. The banging sound echoed against the houses across the street. He was a good, all-around fix-it man. The depressions popped out under the pounding of the rubber mallet. The paint chipped and cracked in large pieces as the metal stretched back to shape. It would be rusting tomorrow. He backed up, looked the car over, and shook his head.

We went for a ride. Dad drove right down Main Street, and people pointed and smiled curiously at the windowless Buick. The wind stung my face and whipped my hair around. "Are you doing anything important today?" asked Dad.

"No."

"Good." He gave the car the gas. "Let's go to Brooklyn. I have to look up a few friends and then we'll go over to the station house and show them the car."

I smelled trouble. "What friends?"

"Friends, just friends."

"Forget it. Take me home. What are you going to do, beat up more Hasidic Jews?"

"Don't do me any favors. I couldn't care less." We were already in the middle of town. The diner went by on my right, the funeral home, hobby shop, a pizza joint. The movie house was coming up. "Let's go to the movies." The marquee said, *The Post Man Rings*. It was a half-price joint and never had enough letters for the long titles. "*The Post Man Always Rings Twice*," I said. "I know you didn't see that." Jack Nicholson was one of my favorite actors.

"I'm taking you home."

He was such a stubborn bastard. I thought of myself sitting at home all day wondering what the hell he was up to. "I'll go."

He slapped me on the thigh. He had this crazy smile on his face. It scared me. I didn't want trouble. When it came to fighting, I never trusted myself. I was not only afraid of getting hit, I was afraid of hitting someone. I've had my share of run-ins, but by the time I finish talking, counseling, and cajoling, the guy usually wants to buy me a drink. But today, the truth scared me. If my father fought, I'd fight. It was something I knew without knowing how I knew it.

On the parkway the wind was strong. "It's like riding on my old Harley," shouted Dad.

"Do you know how to spot a happy motorcyclist?" I asked.

Dad pulled into the third lane. "No."

"By the flies in his teeth."

Dad smiled. "You're hot shit."

I was flushed with warmth. It was amazing how a stupid compliment like that could make me feel good. "What do you call a hooker with a runny nose?"

"What?"

"Full."

Dad got a kick out of that one.

"What does Miss Piggy douche with?"

"What?" He was already laughing.

"Hogwash."

"You're sick," he laughed and turned on the radio.

The music was like a slap in the face. "What's the matter, you didn't like the jokes?"

"Go ahead. I'm enjoying them; I just want to listen to the news."

I was wondering how the radio was playing when there was no antenna. Looking out the back window, I saw a wire coat hanger stuck in the broken aerial.

We slowed at the parkway exit. To the right, tall brick buildings, all with the same metal terraces, towered above the small stores and houses. "That's the Carver Projects," said Dad. "It's full of welfare niggers and junkies. It has its own police force and the highest crime rate in Brooklyn. Used to be a garbage dump, used to be kind of nice looking, you know, with all the sea-gulls and weeds. Now it's welfare niggers."

He was always talking about welfare niggers, street niggers, park niggers and a slew of others. "There's plenty of white people on welfare," I said.

"Name one."

I didn't know anyone on welfare.

"No such animal."

I let him win. He was full of shit anyway. When the Jacksons moved onto our block, Dad carried on for a month, threatening to sell the house, claiming we wouldn't be able to leave the doors unlocked. Then last summer, he and Mr. Jackson went to a dozen Yankee games together. "He's not your average black man," Dad had said.

We made a few turns and slowly doorways, stoops, and sidewalks came alive with people. Graffiti-sprayed plywood squares covered the windows of burned-out apartments. Abandoned cars rested on their rims, stripped or black from fire. Dad stopped the car. "I'm going to run in and pick up some beer. Do you want anything?"

"You're blocking the street."

"If a cop comes, tell him your father is a detective."

"You wait and I'll get the beer."

He slipped me a twenty.

When I came out of the deli, traffic was backed up to the intersection. The corner was locked. Horns were blaring. "Blow it out your ass!" yelled Dad. I hopped in and we zoomed down the street like a getaway car. He lit a cigar and opened a beer. "I don't take any shit around here. I've been on these streets since '62." He tossed the six-pack on my lap.

Someone yelled, "Billy!"

Dad waved and pulled to the curb. "This is the Plaza," he explained quickly. "It's a drug strip. I used to work undercover here, but everyone got to know me."

Undercover? My father? Undercover in a black neighborhood?

A man with a gray bozo afro and large crooked teeth stood smiling with his hands on his hips. "Holy moley," he said. "What happened?" He patted the car and leaned through the windshield.

"You didn't hear."

"No." There was a can of Colt 45 in his pocket that was slowly pulling his pants down. I wondered if he was an informer or an ex-con. I also wondered how the hell my father knew him.

"The Jews used it for a soap box during the storming," said Dad. "I'm thinking about donating it to their Holocaust museum."

"They're crazy. Crazier than us niggers," he laughed.

"Joe, meet my son, Charlie." We shook hands through the windshield.

"Just thank the Lord you look like your mother," he winked.

A crowd was gathering around the car. With no windows I felt as if I were sitting in the street. "This still might make one ass-kicking pimpmobile," said Joe. "A little chrome work, spokes, a touch of velvet. Shit, how much do you want for it?"

"I'm suing the city. If they can't fix it, I want a replacement."

A guy with a paper clip in his ear and metal rake in his afro knelt next to my door. "You got a dollar?"

"No." I had my shoulder against the door and was ready to shove it open, hopefully sending the guy for a loop.

"Don't bullshit. I know you got a dollar."

I pulled the handle up. The door was locked. Plan B. "Dad, this guy wants a dollar."

My father smiled, taking out his wallet. "No problem." He flashed his badge. "Get the fuck out of here."

The guy put his palms up and backed away.

"He's a junkie," said Dad. "They're afraid of every-thing except needles."

Pulling away, Joe kicked the car and yelled, "I'll give you fifty dollars."

"I used to work with him," said Dad.

"He's a cop?"

"Yup."

"Doesn't look like one."

"Not supposed to."

Dad lead-footed it through the streets, weaving around traffic like a stock car race driver. He was really some-thing, drinking a beer, puffing on a black two-inch cigar, the ashes whirling in our faces. The stogie was flat and soft as hot tar. It was clamped in the left side of his mouth and he had to keep one eye almost closed because of the smoke.

For a few weeks in high school, I kept a cigar stuck in the corner of my mouth. But I couldn't get used to them. In the mornings my throat felt like I had just gargled with Love Canal mouthwash.

"I'll take you over to the station house," he said, motioning for another beer. We swung around a cor-ner. "How you doing, honey?" he yelled to a woman in a yellow mini-skirt. "That's Sandy. She has more crabs than Jones Beach."

"How would you know?" I liked to put him on the spot.

"I used to go crabbing there." He pulled his cigar out. "It's a goddamn joke, for Christ's sake."

A block later we were pulled over by a patrol car. "You really did it now," I said.

"License and registration," said an Irish cop who was trying to grow a mustache.

In one hand, Dad crushed his beer can. "What's the problem?"

"For starters, where's the windshield?"

"It's right here." Dad reached as if to touch it. "What the hell? Charlie, where's the windshield?"

I couldn't believe he was joking at a time like this.

"All right, mister, out of the car."

"What's your name?" asked Dad. "You must be new."

"Come on out!"

"Because mine's Patterson." Dad pulled out his gold detective badge and hung it on the door sill. "I work over at the seventy-forth."

"Michael Connelly," said the cop. They shook hands. "What happened to the car? It looks like a bomb hit it."

"A new air conditioning system. My son thought of it." They laughed and Dad explained the whole story. "And the city's going to pay," he said. "That you can bet your life on."

———————

It was dusk when we trotted up the stone precinct house steps. Dad was pretty drunk. He walked as if he had something very important to do. He swung the heavy door open and I hurried in after him.

At a tall wooden desk that was built into the wall sat two gray-haired policemen. "Hey, Bill," one called.

"Hay, that's the first stage of horse shit," answered Dad.

We passed four men handcuffed to a heating pipe. I'm sure if they had tried they could have pulled the plumbing right out of the wall. They were dressed in colorful suits and their shoes shone even in the dim light. "Cigarette?" asked one of the men.

"No, it's a cigar." Dad threw his butt at their feet.

I followed him up the worn slate stairs. The wooden banister was as smooth as glass. The lime-green walls were chipped and the window at the landing had so much grime on it, I could barely see the rectangular wire pattern beneath the glass. I pressed to the wall as a red-eyed prisoner came slowly down the stairs with a cop holding him from behind by his handcuffed wrists. The place was like a war zone.

On the third floor, end of the hall, Dad barged into a room marked "Detectives."

"Heil Hitler!" shouted Vince from behind his desk. "That's what the guys downstairs are calling you. Charlie, did you know your father is famous? He holds the record for civilian complaints. Eighteen in one day."

Vince was my father's partner; a bald, smiling man who got drunk once a month in our kitchen.

Dad grabbed him by the arm and pulled open the blind. "You see what they did?"

The Buick sat across the street like a wounded animal. "I see nothing," said Vince with a German accent. "I was only following orders."

There was a holding pen made of thick iron wire in the corner of the room. It went from the floor to ceiling like a monkey cage. Inside were two teenagers, staring across the office. They held the metal mesh as if they were hanging from it. I felt their eyes on me.

"They're wanted in six robberies," said Vince. "We picked them up last night on a weapons charge. I'm waiting on a gun trace."

"Big time tough guys," said Dad.

"Fuck you," mouthed one prisoner. He began to shake the cage. "And I'm telling you, you're violating my rights."

THE HERO OF NEW YORK

"He's on smack," said Vince. "He thinks he's got rights."

"I know my rights!" he screamed.

"You don't know shit," said Dad.

"Pigs. You think you're so fucking smart. You come in here and I'll kick your ass." His eyes shone through the metal grating. "Big mouth motherfuckers." The quiet prisoner leaned against the wall and slipped to the floor. "You think because you got a gun you're a big man."

"Shut up," said Vince.

I stood there as if someone had given me a shot of novocain. I had forgotten what my father's office was like, the type of people he locked up. A long time ago he told me, "Just remember, I don't lock up the good guys." I turned my back to the cage and faced a wall full of "Wanted" bulletins. There must have been over a hundred little black-and-white mug shots stapled to the description sheets. Names like David Berkowitz and Charles Manson came to mind. But those sickos seemed a million miles away. Names like Winslow Tylor, Byron Blakely, George Johnson, and Tyrone Butler stared from their mug shots and sent chills up my spine.

"That's our hall of fame," said Dad.

I spun around. "They look like some mean dudes."

"They're not so tough."

I did everything but look at the cage. The adjacent wall had composite sketches of men and women. I searched the drawings as if I expected to find my own face. I came to the end of the wall and sat on a radiator under an open window that was working overtime, sending heat into the brisk Brooklyn fall.

Dad sat at a desk reading some kind of stapled report. I didn't know if it was his desk. There was no name

plate or pictures of the family. "Who caught the Pace
Liquor store case?" asked Dad.

"Larry picked it up. He hasn't made a collar in two
months. He needs it. He's a nervous wreck, thinks his
wife is trying to kill him. I swear to God he's gone
bananas. Yesterday he told me she asked him to paint
the house, but he's afraid to go up the ladder when
she's home."

Dad ripped up the papers he was reading and tossed
them in the metal pail next to the desk. "Larry always
was a nut," he said.

I knew Larry. During the summer, he came to a barbeque at our house. He was a real quick talker with a
nervous mouth. His lips stayed in gear even when he
was listening. He was the only guy who had come
without his wife, so we sort of hung out together. The
whole afternoon he kept telling me what a great guy
my father was. "I'm two weeks on the job." The words
came like bullets out of a machine gun. "Two weeks.
And your old man comes over and says 'You better wipe
your ass, pull your pants up, and start acting like a
detective.' I gave him the who-the-fuck-do-you-think-
you-are look and he says, 'I'm telling you this for your
own good. They'll have you for fucking lunch.' For
fucking lunch, that's exactly what he says." I felt real
bad for Larry. Some guys shouldn't be cops. He should
have been a coin collector or a hotel clerk.

The radiator was too hot to sit on so I went over and
sat on a folding chair next to Vince's desk. The prisoner mouthed "Fuck you" to me.

"The car's real bad," said Dad. "I don't think it can
be fixed."

"The car, the car, what are you worried about the car

for?" said Vince. "You can get another one. You should be worried about your job."

"Did you hear anything?"

"Nothing, just what I read in the paper."

The prisoner gave me the finger. I decided to stare it out with him. Our eyes locked. He had a big sixties-style afro and wore an orange golf jacket and green knit pants, the sharp crease just touching the top of his white Pro-Keds. I had a good two inches and twenty pounds on him. "What the fuck you looking at?" he said.

Vince got up and kicked the cage. "You keep your mouth shut."

The kid put his face to the mesh and began a disco rap, half singing, half talking. He sounded like a cross between Barry White and Curtis Blow. "I go by the name of Johnny Flash. When I get on the floor the ladies crash. I'm so bad I wrestle whales, kick lightening's ass and put thunder in jail. I'm so bad I make medicine sick and I'm so slick . . ."

Vince flew around and cracked a night stick across the cage. "Now shut up!"

But he continued, "What's the price, twenty twice. What's the word?" Thunderbird, I thought. "It's Thunderbird," he sang. "Who drinks the most? Colored folks. When you mess with the best you mess with the rest . . ."

Vince opened the cage. The guy on the floor opened his eyes dreamily. Dad shot around his desk and grabbed the kid by the hair. He shut up fast.

"You're a big mouth!" screamed my father. He winged the kid's face into the cinder block wall. I heard the thud.

I couldn't believe what had happened. Vince relocked
the cage. The kid was quiet. He had a mouthful of blood.
He stood there looking out at me like an animal after
it's been hit by a car. Through the years I had heard
stories. There was the time Dad stuffed a gas-soaked
rag in a guy's mouth and waved a lighter under it to
make him talk, the time he lifted a rapist off the floor
by his balls, the time he put an empty gun in a guy's
ear and pulled the trigger. I looked at my father and felt
sick. He sat at his desk holding his head as if it were
going to explode.

"They're what you call smack niggers," said Vince,
his voice trying hard to sound normal. "They're bone
heads. Solid bone from ear to ear. You couldn't crack
their skulls with a sledge hammer."

Dad rubbed his eyes, then looked up as if to say, OK,
it's a new day. He put his hands on his desk and pressed
himself out of his chair.

On the way home we averaged eighty-five miles an
hour. The ride cooled us both off. The wind was cruel.
I pulled my jacket up over my face. My breath was warm
against the inside of my coat. One hand bracing the
dashboard, the other on the edge of the seat, I sat there,
my mind flashing on that kid's bloody mouth. My father
would say "That kid asked for it, and got it." But he
shouldn't have hit him so hard.

I felt the car pull off the parkway. I unzipped my coat
and yanked it down to my shoulders. The cold and wind
had streaked Dad's cheeks with tears. Even in the
shadowy streetlight I could see the redness of his eyes.
"You should get some motorcycle goggles."

He wiped his eyes with the back of his hand.

We went a couple of blocks and stopped at a red light. "Promise me one thing," he said. "Don't you ever become a cop."

"It's not one of my top ten career choices."

"Just promise me."

"OK, I promise."

"You stick with that college. You know I'm no genius, but I'm no jackass either. I can't help you too much with, what is it you're taking?"

"Business administration."

"It's out of my ballpark, but I just want you to know your tuition is in the bank waiting for you."

Each word pounded on my head like a jackhammer. I felt buried. Tomorrow was my accounting midterm, another D or F, another handful of dirt. For the rest of the ride I couldn't say anything.

My father hiked up his pants, walked into the kitchen, and received a tight-lipped stare from my mother, who was filling the steam iron with water from a Fred Flintstone jelly glass. Louise looked up from her books and papers, and I made a funny face. She twirled her finger around the side of her head and pointed at me. My mother claimed that thirteen was a bad age and that Louise was going through a stage. Dad, looking like the cat that swallowed the canary, watched my mother's face. "We waited until six o'clock," said Louise, "and then we ate without you." Louise loved icing the cake. She smiled and twirled her naturally curly hair around her index finger. She had nice blonde curls that she hated and tried desperately to straighten. The result was a wavy, I-just-got-caught-in-the-rain look. If my mother was a flamingo, Louise was a hummingbird. When she was a baby, I was afraid to touch her. I thought she would break.

Our suppers had been staying warm in the oven. Mom brought them to the table and removed the aluminum foil from each plate. Feeling like two bad boys, Dad and I washed our hands quietly in the kitchen sink. Steam rose from the roast beef, potatoes, and peas smothered in brown gravy. "Joy, you outdid yourself again," said Dad sitting down.

"You could have called," she said. "I had everything ready at five-thirty."

I wondered what kept my parents together. They were two very opposite people. Groucho Marx would have leaned between them, taken out his cigar, and said, "I've heard of opposites attracting, but this is ridiculous." When I was about eight my father packed and left. My mother had explained, very carefully, that even grown-ups fight, and all that other crap. About a month later, I got up and he was lying in bed next to her as if he'd never been gone. I remember how she had missed him; for the month she had stood in the kitchen every evening looking at the door.

"What are you writing?" I asked.

"A stupid history report," Louise sighed. "It's due tomorrow." She was already in the ninth grade. In first grade she had been put ahead because she read a third grade text fluently. The problem now was that her maturation rate didn't match her intellectual development. In short, she looked like she was eleven years old—and yet she was in high school.

"If it's history, then it's not stupid," said Dad. His

philosophy had always been, if it's hard, it's good for you.

Louise exhaled, raised her eyes, and contemplated the ceiling. She was a real actress. When she was a kid and relatives came, she'd roll around the living room floor doing cartwheels and somersaults. Once I organized a little show and hung a bed sheet in the kitchen doorway. At four years old Louise sang the theme from "The Addams Family" show. During the chorus she snapped her fingers just like on the show and brought the house down.

Dad finished his plate, setting a new world's land speed record. "Delicious," he leaned back. I hadn't even buttered my bread. "Louise, history is the foundation," he said.

"Don't listen to him," said Mom.

"Joy, I'm telling her a fact, a goddamn truth. History is the foundation." He had this blank questioning expression on his face as if he'd gone to the Ralph Kramden School of Acting. We all started laughing, even Louise.

"I don't know what we're laughing about," said Mom. "It hasn't been the best of days."

CHAPTER

3

They came for my father the next morning; sometime between night and dawn. The door bell rang. I sat up in bed. It rang again.

There were two men, both in suits, one brown, one blue. They both wore too much of the same shade. Their jackets were dark, the blue, navy, the brown, chestnut, the shirts, powder and tan, the ties, sky and dirt. One had gray hair and cheeks that looked freshly slapped with Aqua Velva. The other guy looked like a Brooklyn zipper head, a throw back to the days of *Saturday Night Fever*. He had one of those ninety-mile-an-hour haircuts, every piece blown back standing on end, and a thin black mustache that reminded me of John Belushi's eyebrow. Mr. Dance Fever couldn't have been more than thirty. Dad stood with them in his undershirt and pants that he wore around the yard. "Go back to bed," he ordered over his shoulder. I didn't move. Mom passed in her robe and slippers and stood next to Dad.

"Who are they?" she asked as if the men were in another room.

"We're from the investigative unit," said the man in the blue suit.

"Shoeflies," said Dad. It was an expression I had grown up with. It was slang for cops who hunted and arrested other cops. They had the right to arrest a policeman for a line of duty action. My father, Vince, Larry, and other cops called them rats, pigeons, and curtain hangers.

"Oh," said Mom. "Oh, my God." She had her hair pulled into a short pony tail. There were wrinkles around her eyes that looked strangely out of place.

Dad stuck his hands in his back pockets. They spoke in hushed voices. "It's a bullshit story," he said.

Louise leaned over the upstairs banister. "What's the matter?"

"Nothing, go back to bed," I said.

"No," she said.

"Yes," growled Dad.

She went back into her room.

"They tried to kill me," said Dad flatly searching the men's faces. "And they destroyed my car. I ought to go out there and shove both your heads through the windows. Maybe then you'd believe me."

"It's not a question of belief."

I positioned myself on the other side of my father. We were the Patterson wall. I could feel the two cops growing tense. They were both about my size. The older cop had a beer gut that pressed his belt buckle to a ninety-degree angle. "Well, you've got to come in with us," he said.

"It's five-thirty in the goddamn morning. You got my whole family up."

The cop shrugged his shoulders.

Dad went to the front door and glanced out as if he were checking to see if the house was surrounded. "All right I'll go," he said. "But not because you're making me. And you're going to wait until I shave and shower." He pounded up the stairs.

My right hand was in a fist. I opened it. The men and I stood there awkwardly. The darkness at the windows was turning to gray. "Do you want coffee?" said Mom.

We sat at the table while Mom waited for the water to drain through the grinds. "Nothing will come of it. I'm sure it was self-defense," said the guy with the mustache.

"Then why arrest him?"

"It's not an arrest, just a questioning." He said it too fast, as if he were saying, keep out of it, it's none of your business.

"What's your name," I asked.

"Detective Rizzoletto."

"You're Italian?"

He nodded.

"You like disco?" I wanted to bust his chops. I wanted him to remember me as the son who broke his balls.

"No."

The older cop leaned forward on his elbows, a smirk on his face.

"You look like John Travolta's little brother," I said.

Rizzoletto tipped his head to one side and stared at me.

"You like to dance?" I continued.

"I don't see how that's any of your business."

"How many years have you been a cop?" My foot started tapping the floor.

"Nine."

"My father's got twenty-one years in."

My mother faced us with the coffee pot.

"You better watch your ass," I said, pointing my finger right in the guy's face. I sat back in my seat wondering what the hell I thought I was doing.

My mother poured the coffee and apologized for not having milk. I could have strangled her. "We have whip cream in the can," she said.

Rizzoletto said nothing, the other cop said he'd try a little. As Mom squirted Reddi Whip into the cop's cup, her hand trembled.

It started to rain. Mom and I sat in the kitchen listening to the news station and the leaky overflowing gutters around the house. We heard the lost dog and cat update, the president's speech on the economy, "How much is a trillion dollars?" he asked. "If you took a stack of one-hundred dollar bills one inch thick, a trillion dollars would fill a football field ten feet deep." Another fun fact from the White House, I thought. Then, the weather watch, "Rain today, high in the low forties, turning colder toward evening, possibly dropping into the thirties." And then today's top metropolitan story, "At least one member of New York's finest is being investigated for actions taken during the storming of the 74th Precinct yesterday. Detective Bill Patterson, a twenty-one-year decorated veteran of the force, was taken from his Long Island home in the early hours.

More investigations are expected."

Mom turned white and traced a daisy on the table-cloth with her finger.

"Bill Patterson, twenty-one-year decorated veteran," I repeated.

In the living room, behind the television, hung an award called the Hero of New York, given out annually by the *Daily News* to someone who did an especially heroic or brave deed. My father had won it for acting above and beyond the call of duty. That's what the plaque said. He didn't like to talk about it.

There had been a crash at Kennedy Airport and he had been the first police officer to arrive. He had worked around the clock for three days. "Some of the bodies looked perfect, not even a scratch," he had told me. "But I'll never forget when I picked them up. They were like jelly, every bone in their bodies was broken." Some time later the press and ground crew had begun talking about a huge cop who had walked in and out of the smoldering wreck carrying body after body. The *News* had found my father, written the story, and presented the award to him.

"It's a lousy way to win anything," he had said.

"A cop," said Mom. "That's all he is, that's all he ever wanted to be, that's the sad part, and you know your father did what he had to do."

"Mom, he didn't have to."

"I'd like to believe he did what he had to. Was he just supposed to stand there and take it?"

"No, I guess not," I said. "If you want people off your car, smack their heads on the curb. That's good think-ing, don't you agree?"

"Charles, you've never gotten along well with him."

She pulled the rubber band out of her hair. The pony tail opened, and her hair fell to her shoulders.

"What? We get along fine."

"OK, you do." She tapped my hand.

"We do."

"I'm going up to get ready for Mass."

"How could you say we don't get along?"

"You do." She pushed her chair.

I felt terrible. I got my coat and got the hell out of the house. My car, a '62 Corvair ragtop, in the literal sense, was parked in front of the house. It was pouring. I ran through the rain.

Inside the car, drops fell like bombs onto my lap and head. I have to sell this piece of shit. I slammed my hand on the dashboard. It was my first car and I never had any luck with it. The guy who sold it to me was such a con artist he deserved a government grant. "This car is strictly a money-maker," he said. "The longer you hold on to it, the more it will be worth. First off, it's a convertible, they don't make convertibles any more; second, it's a Corvair, they don't make them any more, either. It's dependable, it gets twenty-five on the highway, it should get twenty around town, and look at those lines. Straight classic all the way." I had considered myself the luckiest guy in the whole wide world. I was buying a Corvair, a classic convertible.

The first week of ownership, someone hit it and bent the classic lines. I couldn't collect a cent because the book value was seventy-five dollars and it had been a hit and run. I had gone out that morning to go to school. The driver's side was scraped and the door was gone. I couldn't believe it. The police took the report claiming they had never seen anything like it.

My neighbor found the door down the block, lying in the gutter. It was one giant dent. Dad and I managed to reattach it. I spent a weekend searching junkyards for a used door and discovered the car was a collector's item.

After ten minutes of turning the key and pumping the gas while trying to find a dry spot on the seat, I felt like I was ready to climb the Empire State Building and swat planes. The motor finally hit, sputtered, and caught. I revved the engine and sent a cloud of black smoke down the street. I reached for the stick shift and saw my accounting notebook in a puddle on the floor mat. There was still time to make the midterm. I put the car in gear. I had studied Saturday night, the tuition was in the bank, and I had no place to go anyway.

Bang. I blanked out. I sat at my desk looking at the questions as if they were in Chinese code. The guy in the next row was hitting the keys of his pocket calculator as if he were playing the *William Tell* Overture. Everyone in the class was playing a song on a computer. I didn't even bring a pencil.

Forget cheating. Mr. Matts was leaning against his desk, head moving like a prison search light. He was such a little turd. Every Monday, Wednesday, and Friday he wore a different three-piece suit and never unbuttoned one button. At the end of every class he mentioned the fact that he couldn't stay late, "I'm a corporation accountant, this is what I do for fun." Fun? What did he do on Friday nights, have his prostate examined?

His surveillance landed on my face, and I gave him my best Charles Manson eyes. He resumed patrol as if

he hadn't seen me. He may have been rich and had a
gross of three-piece suits, but God had gotten back at
him. He had the curse of the uncombable hair. Whisk-
broom bristle implants would have been an improve-
ment.

I examined the test. It was simply a matter of knowing what to debit and what to credit. Debits are entered
on the left side. OK, I'm on my way.

> Omega Company applies overhead to jobs on a basis
> of direct labor cost. Job A, which was started and com-
> pleted during the current period, shows charges of $5,000
> for direct materials, $8,000 for direct labor, and $6,000
> for overhead on its job cost sheet. Job B, which is still
> in process at year end, shows charges of $2,500 for direct
> materials and $4,000 for direct labor. Should any over-
> head cost be added to Job B at year-end? Explain.

I cradled my head in my hands. I felt like I had a
fever. Too bad I couldn't ask for a pass to the nurse.

I didn't want to be the first one finished, but I couldn't
take sitting there watching Mr. Matts watching me. I
coughed and stood, collected the test and put my blank
scrap paper on top.

"Done so quickly?" he asked, examining my paper.

Everyone in the class looked up. I felt like the emperor
with no clothes. "Why don't you buy yourself a brush,"
I said loudly.

I walked out. Some other flunkie began to clap. I
passed the fountain, the bulletin board, the business
club banner that said, "We're always looking for new
executives," and headed out the door.

I ran across campus. On the lawn I kicked a No Dogs

Allowed sign twenty yards. The field goal is good, good, no it's blocked. You missed again, Patterson. In the drizzle, in the middle of the campus quad, where some of the best frisbee throwers in the Long Island area met, I dropped to one knee. I couldn't catch my breath. I started to shake. "Relax, relax, relax," I repeated. "It's OK, it's OK, it's OK."

———————

I drove to my old girl friend's apartment. We hadn't really talked since our breakup. I saw her all the time, though. Tracy was a waitress at the diner in town, and I had been eating a lot of hamburger deluxe platters lately. She refused to wait on me, though. All the waitresses had been tipped off, so when I sat at Tracy's station, one of them would saunter over and say, "Hi, Charlie, can I take your order?"

On the parkway, I passed my exit and turned off at the next town. I had only been to her apartment once when she first moved in. What I needed from her was a hug, and, in the front of my mind, I was hoping one thing would lead to another. I tried to think of something to say to her. They arrested my father this morning and I dropped out of school—that might get her attention. I started getting into a fantasy trip. Her answering the door in a towel dripping wet, Charlie, come in. I'd unwrap the . . . Sex with Tracy had been phenomenal. It had settled our arguments, made us miss a concert, a wedding reception, and dentist appointments, and gave me bags under my eyes for five months. Five months. It was my record long relationship.

We met at an outdoor pool on opening day. The place was deserted. The lifeguard sat up in his blue fiberglass seat wearing orange sweats. It was so windy the pool could have had small craft warning advisory flags. With a spring-fever-get-in-shape-summer's-on-its-way plan pumping in my veins, I stripped to my Jones Beach Guard black nylon swimsuit. What do you get when you cross an ox with a tug boat? A Jones Beach State Park lifeguard. It was my father's old suit, a bit baggy, but very prestigious.

And, then, Tracy entered. She was wearing a black Speedo racing suit with gold stripes running from her armpits to the top of her thighs. On her head was a matching rubber swim cap. Dangling from her fingers was a pair of Spitz goggles with tinted lenses. There were a million empty lounges but she put her towel on the chair next to mine. I began a series of warmup exercises, touch my toes, sidebends, I straightened up and she smiled at me. "Are you a guard?" she asked.

I nodded.

She tucked a few brown curls into her cap. "Do you know Steve Morrell?"

"No."

"Really? He's in charge of—"

"Oh, Mr. Morrell. Yeah, I know him."

She gave me a strange look and started stretching. She had a body that wouldn't quit. Long runner's legs, a firm ass and tits, less than a handful, more than a mouthful. "Not too crowded today," I said. Her eyes slanted down when she smiled. She gripped her hands behind her back and pushed her chest out. I was falling in love fast. "What's your name?"

She bent, held her knees, then popped up. "Tracy."

The suit was tight. Her nipples were standing out like two overgrown M&Ms. I waited for her to ask my name and finally volunteered, "Mine's Charlie."

"I hope the water isn't too cold," she said and snapped her suit down over the cheeks of her ass. I dove in the water like a member of the Polar Bear Club.

"How is it?" she asked standing at the edge of the pool.

It was like ice. "Nice!"

She jumped in. "It's f-r-e-e-z-i-n-g," she said. She spit into her goggles, washed them in the water, then adjusted them on her eyes. She snapped her cap over her ears and pushed off.

I took off swimming free style, legs kicking, arms flying, as if I'd just seen a man-eating shark with a bib around its neck. About halfway down the pool I looked back. Tracy was sitting in the lounge chair with a towel on her shoulders. I did the backstroke to the side and got out, adjusting my nylon suit. "Only a lifeguard would call that nice," she said.

My skin was doing the goosebump and my teeth were chattering. I saw the confessional door looming ahead. "I'm not really a lifeguard," I said.

"I didn't think so. Steve is only sixteen years old. When you called him Mr. Morrell, I almost freaked."

"Well, you know, I respect kids." I gave her my best please-love-me smile.

"You're funny," she said.

———————

I parked in front of her apartment and snail-walked through the rain to the building. The wetter the better. How could she turn away a soaking-wet old boyfriend. The place was called the Heritage House and had plastic flower beds flanking the walk. The lawn was dotted with piles of dried dog shit. In the lobby two couches covered with clear plastic faced a broken fountain that held a cemetery of soggy cigarette butts.

During the dating days, she had lived at home. The house was a Cape Cod and her room was the entire second floor. There was a sandalwood-colored beam running the peak of the ceiling that had a dozen potted plants hanging from it. The walls were pitched to the floor. Her bed was in the center of the room. At night she had snuck me past her parents' room saying, "Step where I step. Shhh."

Tracy once told me, "I never had parents, only two extra grandparents." Her mother was forty-four when Tracy was born. Supposedly, Mrs. Horowitz couldn't have children because of a cyst on her ovaries. A classic case of blocked tubes, and a child that was conceived by accident. This was a popular story with Mrs. Horowitz. "Tracy is a miracle," she said.

When Tracy was two years old, she was sent to nursery school, then on to day-care, pre-kindergarten, and so on. It was an organized life she led. There was always summer camp waiting at the end of June and boarding school in September. If I mentioned my childhood backyard clubs, lemonade stands in the summer on the front lawn, she listened as if I were telling the secret of eternal youth. "Gosh, I don't remember anything like that except the day my father brought me to a matinee on a Saturday afternoon. He got hit with a candy bar and it got stuck in his hair."

On weekends her father had walked around the house in boxer shorts singing Yiddish songs. He called Tracy "Angelface" and shook my hand whenever he could grab it. In the five months I knew him, I never said anything more to him than "How you doing?" Tracy's mother resembled a Florida sea cow with legs, too much makeup, and a red wig. Mrs. Horowitz ate chocolates, chain smoked, and kept the TV on twenty-four hours a day. Even at 5 A.M., when I was sneaking down their stairs from Tracy's bedroom, I heard the set humming with static.

At her apartment, I rang the bell and looked in the spy hole in the door. I couldn't see a damn thing. It was about 9:30, maybe 10 A.M. Tracy worked the four-to-midnight shift at the diner. I imagined her in bed sleeping, curled up with the covers over her head. I rang again. The carpeted hall was dead quiet.

I put my forehead against her door. The metal was cold. Where the hell could she be? I slid down the wall and sat.

In the summer I had worked for a landscaper. I was in charge of two lawn mowers. One was always broken because my boss thought a few good kicks would fix anything. In the hot sun I had pushed the mower just waiting for two o'clock. I spent afternoons with Tracy. We went to the beach, rode bicycles, played racketball, swam at the pool, and ate lunch at a new health food store with an outdoor counter. Tracy always ordered a tuna salad and insisted that we split it. On cloudy or rainy afternoons we went to her house. In her hot bedroom we made love until the sheets were soaked and we were sliding off each other. She was the first girl I had ever really made love to. With others it had been in the backseat of cars or rushed attempts, pants at your ankles, on a couch with one eye out the window watching for the parents.

Then what happened? I began college, the pool closed, the health food store went out of business, Tracy began working nights at the diner and moved out of her house.

She broke up with me over the phone. It was a Friday, my last day pushing the lawn mower. I had just finished cutting lawns and was about to take a shower when the phone rang.

"Listen, I can't see you today," she had said.

"What's the matter?"

"I just can't see you. It's not fair to you."

"What's not fair to me?"

"I'm getting serious with someone else." Her voice had been so soft I could hardly hear her.

"What?"

"I'm seeing someone. We started playing golf together and he bought me a glove and wristbands. He's been treating me really nice."

I had begun to panic. "You've got to see me tonight."

"I can't," she had said desperately "And I've got to go. I'm in a no parking zone . . . My car's going to get a ticket."

"You just can't tell me it's over."

"Charlie, I've got to tell you something, I've been sleeping with him." I held the phone, everything draining out of me. "And I don't want to hurt you."

"Hurt me?" I wanted to kill her. "Hurt me?"

"You were strangling me."

"Tracy."

"Bye."

I had punched the refrigerator door. There were tears in my eyes. I hadn't known what to do. "That fucking little whore," I screamed.

It was six weeks later and I still didn't know what to do about Tracy. I pressed my forehead against the wall, wondering where the hell she could be. I thought about slipping a note under her door but didn't have any paper.

And, then I almost had a heart attack. Tracy came out of the elevator shaking the rain off a black oriental jacket, the hall lights reflecting off her purple stretch pants. I wanted to run.

"Tracy," I said as if we were meeting on the street and this was an incredible coincidence.

Her jaw dropped two inches and her brown eyes hung open. "What are you doing here?"

"I have the apartment next door," I said.

She dropped her keys. I thought she was going to faint.

"Just kidding." I picked up her key ring and held them by an attached miniature koala bear. She snatched them from my hand.

"I just wanted to talk."

"You're checking up on me."

"I'm not." It was very obvious she had been out all night, probably dancing, then getting laid. Her curls were piled on the left side of her head and, besides, who wears electric-purple pants at ten in the morning?

"You're soaking wet," she said.

I let out a deep breath. It was the first civil thing she'd said since our phone conversation. I knew the old stand-out-in-the-rain trick would get to her. Under her hardness, she had a heart the size of Saint Louis. "Can we talk?"

She tilted her head. "I guess."

Maybe she was in worse shape than I was. I sure hoped so.

The apartment was super clean and had Tracy written all over it. It looked like she had furnished it from the Roosevelt Race Track Flea Market. On Sundays they closed down the track and sold everything from plastic coat hangers to ostrich feathers. Ninety-nine percent of the college dorms on Long Island had been adorned with the market's merchandise. Tracy was into natural wicker and similar shades. The windows had bamboo curtains and were surrounded by a half dozen palm and rubber plants.

On the walls there were sunset posters in metal frames. Standing on the sand colored rug, I set a cane rocking chair in motion with my foot and walked over to Tracy's pride and joy: a floor-to-ceiling display case filled with Norman Rockwell plates. "Your collection has grown," I said in my Orson Welles' voice.

"I just bought the 'Ship Builder'," she said.

I had given her the "Toy Maker." It was on the bottom shelf. Tracy handed me a towel swimming with an odor of musk oil. It was Tracy's scent.

"You didn't just come by to say hello," she said. "You can never just say hello."

"Did you listen to the news today?"

She kicked off a pair of silver high heels and was a lot shorter.

Of course she hadn't heard the news. "What happened?"

"My father was—"

"Wait a minute, let me get out of these clothes." She went into the bedroom and shut the door.

I felt like yelling, "Do you want me to take out your diaphragm?" All the time we went together she had used one. I called it the "Midnight Trampoline." I considered myself an expert inserter, a regular amateur gynecologist. Tracy even let me put in her tampons. I'd give the little string that extra tug for a safe, secure fit.

The kitchen was just a big cabinet with a built-in

sink, a two-burner stove, oven beneath, and a twelve-inch counter top. I sat at a small, round formica table. The chairs were unfinished natural wood. I remembered seeing them in her mother's basement.

Tracy reappeared barefoot in a black cloth house-dress. It gripped her bosom, then flared like a maternity dress. Her curls were freshly brushed.

So did you get laid last night? "How's the Diner?" I asked.

"You know, kind of fun, kind of tough, the money's still good." She filled the kettle with water and put it on the front burner.

"How's your love life?" It was a risky question, a real finger crosser.

"Good, how's yours?"

"Getting better. I'm going to be on "The Dating Game" next week. Meet Bachelor number three, he enjoys White Castle hamburgers by the sack. Bachelor number three, say hello."

She laughed; I could always get her laughing. "You haven't changed."

It sounded a bit like an insult. "You haven't changed either," I said flatly. "So your love life is just good, not spectacular," I was fishing around for an I-miss-you.

"Charlie, I know I hurt you, and I don't want to hurt you any more."

I had to break through the shell and reach the sensitive Tracy. There were times she had cried over the littlest things: a girl friend not returning a call, her parents letting her plants die when she went away for a vacation. She had to have missed me. It's me, good old lovable Charlie, I wanted to yell. I couldn't have become just an old boyfriend that fast, just another two or three pages in her photo album. "You're looking good," I said.

"I've gained five pounds since the pool closed."

The kettle began to whistle. She took down a small jar of Maxwell House coffee. "Remember this?"

No one in her house drank coffee and she had bought it for me. "Let's give it another try," I said.

She gave me a tired look. I wanted to reel the words back in. "Charlie, that's your problem, you don't listen. You show up here uninvited, putting me on the spot, I'm tired and to tell you the truth, I'm sorry you're here."

I wanted to ask, why are you so tired, but it was strike two, bottom of the ninth and I was holding the bat by the wrong end. "Are you playing hard to get?" I smiled.

"You're thick in the head, you always were and always will be." She sat. "You're a nut."

Now, I hit her with the story. I twirled the spoon in the coffee and told her everything from the time Dad came home to the end of my brilliant accounting career. "Next semester I'm going to switch to psychology," I lied. No one likes a loser. "That way I can work with people, not numbers. You could come and tell me all your problems. Open up to me," I cocked an eyebrow. "Any problems at all."

"You really quit? Tomorrow you're not going to change your mind?"

"I'm finished."

"Have you seen your father yet?"

"No." We sat there for a while not saying anything. The herbal tea she sipped smelled like peppermint. I took her hand off her cup and held it.

"I'm really confused." She got up and went to the couch. I went and sat next to her. "You always screw me up," she said. Slowly, I put my arm around her, first on the couch back, then, gently, gently, to her shoulders. I waited for her to flinch. Nothing. I felt as if my chute had just opened.

She lifted a foot and crossed it on her leg. She had ugly feet. The callouses were as thick as leather. In the summer I had rubbed them with a pumice stone about once a week. "You want me to do your feet?"

"Would you?"

"Sure."

She lay on her stomach and I sanded away the dead yellow skin. It was instant intimacy. How could you be mad at someone who was sanding your feet? She put her face on a silk pillow. I lifted her foot into my lap and her dress rose on her thigh.

"I was out dancing last night, and my feet are killing me."

She had the most beautiful legs.

"Remember when I tried to get you dancing," she laughed. "We went shopping and bought those knit pants with the one back pocket. You kept complaining that you had no place to put your wallet."

"They're still hanging in my closet."

"And we bought a silk shirt with a horse on the back. You never liked dancing, did you?"

"No." I had about as much fluid motion as Dr. Frankenstein's creation. I was standing on the dance floor with my new clothes on, lights twirling, music pounding, Tracy rocking to the beat, yelling "Get down, get funky," and my only thought was, when is this song going to end?

I put the stone on the coffee table and lay next to her. She sat up. I pulled myself back to the couch. The dress fell between her legs and she lifted it. "This is definitely wrong," she said.

I had pushed today to its limit. I was on first base and the game was over. "Let's go out tomorrow night."

"I can't."

"Any night you want." I hated groveling, but I wanted her back. I wanted her badly.

"All right, Friday. Let's go bowling. I'm on a team and doing terribly."

On the way to my car I remembered an old Black-byrds' song. I crossed the wet street and sang, "It's been so long since I seen her. I'm tired and so all alone. I've traveled so very far. I've got to get back home, got to get back home . . ." I swung the door open and started the engine? "Walking in rhythm," I sang, "moving in sound. Humming to the music, trying to move on." I took off and a puddle of water came through the roof like Niagara Falls. I started laughing.

CHAPTER

4

The rain had stopped. The afternoon remained dark.
I climbed out of the car. The leaves were falling from
the trees. Flat and slick, they covered the black asphalt
driveway like a colorful quilt. The storm had left the
neighborhood in dream-like quiet. Up the block, kids
played kickball in the street on my old bases. About
ten years ago, in the middle of a hot summer night, I
painted that infield. The next day there were yellow
tire tracks from one end of the block to the other. After
breakfast, my father brought me out to the garage and
gave me a rag and a half gallon of turpentine. "Get that
paint off your hands," he said. "And don't you ever pull
a stupid stunt like that again."

I had been the terror of Mill Street, the organizer of

giant snowball fights, football games, and Ring-a-Levio games. At ten, I was a regular derelict and pulled my craziest feat. My best friend, Ralph Josephs, and I made a newspaper-stuffed dummy. It had a masking-tape head, no face, and a black wig. We decided to have a hanging. Out in the street we threw a rope around a tree limb and wound up tying the other end to the dummy's waist, because the head kept coming off. We hoisted the dummy up and dangled him ten feet off the road. There was a car coming, and Ralph decided to let the dummy fly into the street. The car went into a skid and stopped. I raised the dummy back into the branches. The guy looked back, then took off. The second car almost crashed into the tree I was hiding behind. Before I could get my legs moving, Mr. Peeples, my neighbor, picked me up like a loaf of bread and started smacking me in the head. "You like to play," smack. "You see what you did," smack. No one had been hurt, except the dummy. Jimmy got away and I wound up with a Juvenile Delinquent Card. I had to stay in the house for two months. Whenever my father saw me he'd squeeze my neck and push me into a wall. Every time he had a friend over he'd tell the story and go into hysterics. "You should have seen this dummy," he'd laugh. "My shoes, my pants, my shirt, and a goddamn black lace bra." The bra had been smuggled out of Ralph's sister's room. "The driver was so upset she was picking up pieces of the dummy and laying them in a pile."

I watched the kids for about five minutes. I wanted to run over there, take a kick, and boot the ball to kingdom come. I imagined them sticking their hands in their pockets whispering, big show-off.

"Bill?" called Mom as I came in.

"No, it's me." I threw my jacket on a chair in the corner of the pantry. "Dad home yet?'

"No, and he hasn't called." She clutched her blue bathrobe tightly around her, wiped her nose with a tissue, then stuffed it in her sleeve. Dinner was on the stove, it smelled terrible. "Where were you?"

"College, accounting midterm. Remember?"

She sat down, and I wanted to tell her how badly I had done. She put her hands in her lap and examined them.

"Where's Louise?"

"Upstairs. She cut school again today. Where she goes I'll never know. Just thank God your father wasn't home when the principal called. He would have had a fit. I want you to talk to her. I can't. I asked her where she was and she told me on a class trip. She must think I'm a fool."

"I'll talk to her." The blind leading the blind. I opened the pot on the stove, the steam burnt my nose. "Smells like baked dog farts."

"That's your father's favorite. Kidney stew." Mom twirled her wedding ring around her finger.

"He's probably out with the boys from his office or down at Kelly's." Kelly's was Dad's in-town hang out, a bar about a mile away, near the railroad tracks.

"Do you know what Louise said when I told her about your father? 'Goody gumdrops,' and stomped up the stairs."

"You're kidding?" I almost laughed.

Louise came down and pulled me by the hand into the den. "I know what you're going to say." She sat. I stared at her sneakers. The rubber was worn through on one shoe from a pigeon-toe walk that the doctors

said would correct itself. I wondered when. Her blue
eyes, large and without makeup, waited for me to say
something.

"Goody gumdrops?" I said.

"They can't put him in jail and I was only kidding
anyway. They don't send cops to jail." There was writing on her faded jeans. On her right thigh there was a
picture of a dog, a heart with a bleeding arrow, and her
initials, L.P., in three dimensions. On the left it said,
"Death before disco." "Even if the guy dies, they
couldn't send him to jail. The criminals would kill him."

"How was school?"

"It's still there," she sighed. "You ask me that almost
every day." The next moment she was up, pacing the
room. There was an oversized brush in her back pocket
that looked terribly uncomfortable. She froze and stared
out the window. "I don't know. I didn't go today. I hate
school. I hate gym and lunch more than anything and
I had gym and lunch today."

"Gym and lunch. They were my favorites. Those are
the only two subjects I passed."

"I'd explain it but, all right, I won't explain gym, but
at lunch I have no one to sit with." She blushed and
put a strand of hair in her mouth. There was no doubt
that she would be a beautiful woman.

"What about Dee?"

"She has lunch sixth period. I have lunch seventh."
She sat next to me.

"How about if I eat lunch with you tomorrow?" I put
my arm around her and felt like the knowledgeable older
brother. She smelled like the autumn air.

"You have to go to college."

The words felt like a medicine ball to the stomach. "What time do you eat?"

"Eleven forty-five."

"I'll be there."

"That's tomorrow, but what about the rest of the days."

"Just meet me in front of the school tomorrow. OK?" She stood and I punched her in the butt. "Be there or be square." I held up my fist. "And you better start going to gym."

"No. I'm not going to gym anymore." The serious look was back.

"If you don't go, you can't graduate no matter how many A plusses you get." She was in honor courses and I had never seen a test grade under ninety.

"I'm not going. I hate the girls, I hate them." She was gritting her teeth.

"Why?"

"They make fun of me, that's why. First they made fun of me because I wore my gym uniform under my clothes. So, I brought my uniform and they still made fun of me. They're all so immature."

"Did you tell your teacher?"

"Are you kidding me? I'd never hear the end of it." There were tears in her eyes. "I should see a doctor, that's what I should do." She scrunched up her face trying to hold everything in.

"There's nothing wrong with you. They're just older. Tomorrow I'll meet you for lunch. We'll straighten things out."

"OK," she swallowed. "Do you want me to bring money?"

Dad didn't come home and no one else liked kidney
stew. On everyone's plate was a bacon-and-cheese
omelet; Louise's specialty. Mom sat on the edge of her
chair and covered her omelet with ketchup. She still
hadn't dressed. I ate my eggs while reading the paper.
There was a story about a Mr. John Showers who wres-
tled alligators in the South. He had his license taken
away because he choked one to death. He continued
wrestling alligators, and when the police arrested him,
he killed an officer with his bare hands. I was about to
read the article to Mom, when the phone rang. I dove
across the kitchen beating Louise by a tenth of a second and grabbed it. "Hello." Mom and Louise's eyes
were on me.

"Is your father home?"

"Vince?"

"Charlie?"

"Yeah, what happened? He's not home yet."

"They're blowing it all out of proportion. They called
for a hearing before the civilian complaint review
board."

"That's bad?"

"Christ, it's not good."

"They aren't holding him?"

"No, they let him out at ten this morning. You tell
your mother not to worry. I got to go." He hung up.

"There's going to be a hearing."

Mom went white, she shut her eyes.

"And you know whatever they say he did, he probably did," said Louise.

"Don't say that," I snapped. "You don't know what
you're talking about." Yell at Louise and she didn't talk
to you for a month. She banged the pan in the sink.

"We got to stick together," I felt like I was walking through a mine field.

———————

At six o'clock we sat in the den. Louise flipped through the TV stations looking for something about the storming. I lay on the floor, Mom perched on the couch. She never leaned back in any seat. Instead, she leaned forward, like a football player stuck on the bench. It was the second story on channel seven.

"Mayor Koch came to the now-quiet Borough Park section of Brooklyn, the scene of yesterday's violence," said the newscaster. They cut to a film clip. The mayor stood at a podium crowded with microphones. He was on the steps of the precinct house and had a nervous look on his face.

"We cannot have a repeat of yesterday's confrontation," he said. "The police are not the enemy, they are here to serve and protect you." The crowd booed. The microphone began to hum. The camera panned the street filled with Hasidic Jews. There must have been over a thousand of them. "I am also a Jew," said the mayor. The crowd roared. "I know what you are going through, but I cannot condone your actions. So, please go home. Let us do our job."

They cut back to the studio. "A thirty-year-old Brooklyn man and two youths were charged in the shooting of Norman Coleman, whose murder led to the violent confrontation at the 74th Precinct. There does not appear to be an anti-Hasidic attitude by the assailants."

"Good they got 'em," said Louise.

"Sidney Cantor," said the newscaster, "charged at a news conference that a policeman had clubbed him on the head and exclaimed, 'I'll kill you if ya come any closer.' Cantor received ten stitches to close a gash incurred in the brawl. Civilian complaints by Cantor have been filed against Detective William Patterson, who was questioned today." They cut to a clip and there was Dad getting out of a car walking up steps, surrounded by other detectives and cops. He looked straight ahead. "The police commissioner has not released a statement at this time."

A beer commercial flashed on, and we watched it as if we were hypnotized. "He's in big trouble," said Louise.

My mother stood and walked back and forth, "He could have assaulted anyone in the world, but your father picked Sidney Cantor," she laughed, then stopped and started taking deep breaths.

At 1 A.M. Dad still hadn't come home. After the first half hour of the David Letterman show, we went to bed.

I heard the chairs move on the linoleum floor in the kitchen. I slipped out of bed and into a pair of pants.

Downstairs was dark. I poked my head in the kitchen and flicked on the light.

"Dad?"

"Shut it off." I hit the switch. He was sitting in the corner of the room. On the table I had seen his nightstick and gun.

"Vince called."

"What did he want?"

"He just wanted to talk to you."

"Did you watch the news?"

"Yeah."

"Was I on?"

"Yeah." He was a dark figure against the wall. The outline of the gun was black against the tablecloth. I thought about him shooting himself. Cops shoot themselves. "What are you doing with the gun?" I began to cross the room.

"I'm going to blow my brains out."

I jumped, but he grabbed the gun.

"Don't be an ass." He spun the chamber. "It's not even loaded."

I pulled out a chair and sat. "You think that's funny, don't you?"

"Nothing's funny anymore."

I heard the drunkenness in his voice. The curtains were closed, the darkness thick. "How long have you been sitting down here?"

"I've been down here about forty-nine years." He threw a beer bottle at the garbage. It missed.

"Vince said they were going to have a hearing."

"Correct."

"You should have called. Mom was worried out of her mind."

"I should have done a lot of things." He threw a beer cap and missed.

"You're 0 for 2."

"That's for damn sure. That's the smartest statement I've heard all day. Do you know the crap they asked me? They asked me if I had any Jewish friends. I said, 'Yeah, Jesus Christ and they crucified him!'" He laughed. "Can you believe that? Do I have any Jewish friends? My partner over in the 13th was Ben Goldstein and I saved his goddamned kike ass so many times it isn't funny. And he was the most Jewish looking son of a bitch in Rego Park. He had the nose, the hair, everything. When his wife died I brought over that stew, you remember, that stew I made and they were all in the living room doing their shivering and moaning, but one by one they came in for a plate of Irish stew and they were damn glad to have it."

"Why didn't you tell them that?"

"Because I'm not telling them shit. I did my job the way I thought it should be done and if they think I hate Jews that's their problem." His breath came slowly. He was so stubborn that he was stupid. He was going to hang himself.

"And you know the son of a bitch smiled when I told him that I wanted the car fixed. He looked it up in the books and said it was worth three hundred dollars. I told him to shove the money up his ass. I bought that car for your mother and you kids. He doesn't make enough money in a year to buy that car."

"If he saw the condition that it had been in."

"Charlie," he sounded like he was pleading, "they don't care. Book value, everything's done by the book, that's what he said. I told him to shove the book up his ass." His fingers touched the dark scab on his forehead. "They asked if I had gone to the hospital. Which means, there's no record and there's no witnesses except the Jews." He leaned across the table and folded his hands. "I'm guilty because I'm a cop."

Fight, fight it, I wanted to scream. "But, you've got to fight it."

"It's a kangaroo court, everything's stacked against me." Even in the darkness I could see him smiling. "Nobody's taking my job from me." He picked up his .38. The blue metal gleamed. "Nobody." He pulled the trigger.

CHAPTER 5

*I*t was a cold, cloudless afternoon. I parked in front of the school and waited for Louise. The building was ugly, prison-like. Students stood like criminals at the corners and in the baseball field. In the car across the street, four girls were passing a joint around. Nothing had changed except the faces and the graffiti on the handball wall. I was surprised to see Guy Paulino and three of his biker friends coming toward my car. Two years ago Guy had sat behind me in my homeroom class. It's funny how some people just can't leave a place.

Guy hadn't changed. It looked like he was still wearing the same clothes: jeans, boots, and a leather motorcycle jacket. He had been the biggest guy in our graduating class, and some considered him the roughest. He lumbered closer like a prehistoric monster.

"Yo, Patterson," he said planting his heels.

I got out of the car with the list of the homeroom names racing through my mind; Pagnotta, Palk, Patterson, Paulino.

Under his black leather, Guy pulled his shoulders back and we shook hands.

"Where you been?" he asked.

"Around," I said wondering what the hell was going on. Besides belching at the back of my head in homeroom, Guy had never paid me any attention.

"I've been in my skin, drinking gin, committing sin," smiled Guy. Beneath an inch of black hanging mustache, I could see his crooked teeth. I scanned the sidewalk for Louise wishing she would hurry. "You still driving this piece of shit," said Guy pounding the canvas roof of the Corvair.

"No, I'm using it as a planter," I said.

"A what?"

"Forget it," I said. "It was supposed to be a joke."

"How'd you like to do me a favor," he said. All of Guy's boys came over as if on cue. Two leaned on the car, and one stood behind Guy. I wondered if they were as tough as their biker duds made them look. I hoped not. "We need a ride over to the Motor Vehicle Department."

"Where's your bikes?"

"Gone," he said. "Police impounded them, and we've got to pick up some forms to get them back."

They were bikers without a bike. I almost laughed. It reminded me of a comedy take-off on the Carol Burnett Show. I could see Tim Conway sitting on his b⸃ .t in the middle of the street holding imaginary handle-bars.

"I can't. I'm meeting my sister," I turned and saw Louise standing on the sidewalk. "They're bikers without a bike," I said to her. She didn't laugh.

"Well, you just met her," said Guy. "Now how about a ride," he smiled. I hated guys that smiled when they wanted to scare you.

"Where are your bikes?" asked Louise. No one answered her.

I tried to open my door but Guy put his foot on it.

"Listen, I'm sorry but . . ."

"I'm sorry, too," said Guy.

I remembered my father saying, "Bring your right hand back, fake, and hit him in the breadbasket with your left." I made two fists. The advice seemed ridiculous. The guy didn't have a breadbasket. He had a Harley Davidson belt buckle that would surely rip my knuckles to shreads and a leather jacket with half a dozen nasty zippers.

"Why are you giving me a hard time?" I said.

"Just give us a ride."

I had to think fast. One of them was heading toward Louise.

"Do you know who I am? Do you?" I asked as if everyone else in North America knew. I took out my wallet and waved the miniature gold detective's badge that my father had given me. I stuck the wallet back in my pocket. OK, I thought, I played my card, there's no backing out.

"What was that?" Guy demanded.

"A badge."

"You're a cop? You're kidding me?" Guy took a step back.

"He's not a cop, but my father is," yelled Louise. "And he'd punch you right in the nose."

I almost passed out.

"And if you don't leave my brother alone," yelled Louise, *"he'll* punch you in the nose." She got into the car and slammed the door.

Everyone was grinning.

I swung my door open. Guy grabbed my coat and said, "I ought to break your face."

I shoved him and slammed the door on his fingers. He let out a hell of a noise. I locked the door and started the engine. A fist came through the roof just missing me. The hand reached for my head and I ducked under it. Louise jabbed her pen into the palm. It stuck there and dangled. The hand shot back through the hole.

The engine turned over, caught, and we tore away, grinding gears. Before I caught my breath I screamed, "Louise, are you crazy or are you just totally out of your mind."

She was looking over the seat at them. "He's still holding his hand," she said excitedly.

"I get them believing I'm a cop and you tell them I'm not," I shouted.

"They didn't believe you," she said. "And did you know that's a crime? Impersonating an officer is a crime. You could have gotten arrested for that."

"A crime! They were going to kill me."

"Oh, you could have taken him," said Louise. "That big lunk head would fall for any one of Dad's sucker punches."

"That guy would have cut me into little pieces and

worn me on his jacket. I swear to God you're not very street smart."

"You could have beaten him," she said.

"Who do you think I am, anyway?"

"OK, you couldn't have taken him. OK, does that make you feel any better?"

I thought about it and it didn't make me feel any better. "You know, maybe I would have taken him. I'm afraid to use my moves."

"That's right," said Louise.

I felt pretty good about that. I gave the car the gas and the engine sounded like machine-gun fire. The convertible top started flapping from the wind. I stuck my hand through the new hole in the roof. "Now I can wave to everyone," I said.

Louise laughed. "Did you see the way I stabbed him?"

"Yeah, where did you learn that?"

"I don't know." She was almost hysterical. She picked the pen off the floor and checked it for blood. "I can't believe I did it," she said.

"Let's go get something to eat," I took the pen from her hand and threw it out the window.

"I wore this dress in case we go someplace nice," she said.

I can't tell you how good that made me feel. It was a sky-blue jumper with a high waist line. Under it she wore a white turtleneck sweater. All that for me.

"Of course we'll go someplace nice." I had planned on pizza or a hamburger at a fast-food joint, but now they were out of the question.

"I heard you and Daddy last night," she said, acting busy by arranging her notes, folding them, then refolding them.

I went through the gears on the old Corvair. "I always knew he would get in trouble some day." She stared at the dash. "Remember what he did to that Rastafarian? I'm surprised that he didn't get into trouble for that." Louise never forgot anything.

A couple of years ago, Dad was questioning a Rastafarian about a cop-killing. I'm not sure what happened, but Dad lost his temper and set a guy's dreadlocks on fire. The burning hair stunk the office out and the cops had to drag the poor guy to the bathroom and stick his head in the toilet. Dad used to tell this story all the time and get a good laugh from the other cops.

"He'll get out of it," I said. "He always does."

We went into the Emerald, the Greek diner in the next town where Tracy worked. It was a fancy, prefabricated building with a fake stone front and red velvet curtains.

I followed an old chicken-legged waitress to a corner booth and slid in. As soon as we sat Louise sunk fifty cents into the connecting jukebox at our table.

When she was younger, I had taken her out all the time. We went to the movies, the beach, to the city a couple of times, and then, all of a sudden, we stopped going out together. I don't know when or exactly why it happened. "How come we don't go out together any more?" I asked.

"I don't know." She opened the menu and began to sing along with a song. It was slow and sweet.

I had never heard it. "I like that song," I said.

We talked about Guy and his boys. She still insisted that I could beat him. The waitress came over and Louise asked for a tuna fish sandwich on white and a glass of milk. "That's what you bring to school everyday." I said.

She smiled, "If I had my way, I'd have tuna fish for lunch and macaroni and cheese for supper everyday."

Another song came on. It was the same guy.

"Who's singing this?" I asked.

She told me a name I had never heard of. "You must really like him," I said.

She nodded.

Wow, I didn't know everything about her. I leaned back, grinning at her as if I just learned she was married and had three kids.

I ordered breakfast: eggs and coffee. "How did classes go today?"

"OK, I guess. Dee wasn't in school so there was no one to talk to in study hall. We had a fire drill and half my science class never came back in."

"Where'd they go?"

"Cutting, I don't know. Oh, and this crazy guy, George, locked Mr. Newton out of the classroom and wouldn't let anyone open the door. He carries a knife. I've never seen it but Dee has."

"What happened?"

"A janitor opened the door and the hall guards took George away." The guards were town policemen on overtime.

It was a rough school. Too many different types thrown together. In one class there might be a doctor's kid and a kid who couldn't afford the hot lunch line.

Our food came, my eggs were watery. Louise cut her pickle in half and ate it with a fork. She ate pizza and watermelon the same way. The rest of the family were basically slobs. We ate ice cream from the container, sucked water from the faucet, and stirred chocolate milk with the wrong end of a fork.

Louise looked cute. She had clips over her ears and somehow had managed to straighten some curls into bangs. Why didn't she have any friends to lunch with?

"Didn't you make any friends at school?" I asked.

"A couple."

"Couldn't you eat with them?"

"I guess," she shook her head. "You don't have to meet me for lunch any more. I'll go to the library."

"That's not the point."

"The kids are stupid." She took a chipmunk-size bite of her sandwich and twirled the selection handle of the jukebox.

"Need a quarter?"

She played the same two songs. "I never get to hear these songs," she explained.

I wrote down the titles on a napkin and stuck it in my shirt pocket. Louise smiled.

I watched her eat. Her face was slender, sparrow-like, yet she had full lips and large eyes. Sometimes I couldn't believe she was my little sister.

"Doesn't Tracy work here?" she asked.

"Nights."

"Why don't you see her anymore?"

I was going to tell her about the date but I figured it would be better to wait and see how things turned out. "I can't go out with her when she's seeing other guys."

"Maybe you can."

"I can't," I said flatly.

"Sometimes you're childish."

"Childish!" I couldn't believe it.

"I'm sorry." Again she played with the jukebox dial. "It's just that, no, forget it."

"Say it. I want to hear it."

"Well, you love her, right?" It took me a second but I nodded. "Then you should see her anyway. Remember that time she was late for dinner at our house. While we were doing the dishes she started to cry."

"She cried?"

"Yes," answered Louise.

My mother had spent the afternoon cooking and Tracy had come an hour late for dinner. Dad wanted the family to eat without her, but I insisted that we wait, claiming that she must have gotten run over or something. When Tracy arrived, she bit her lip and said, "I fell asleep at the beach."

The jukebox played, "I'm drunk now baby, but I've got to be, or I never could tell you what you mean to me," and Louise said, "Didn't you see her yesterday? I thought I smelled her perfume on you."

I sat there blushing like a big jerk. "Yeah, I saw her. I have a date with her Friday night."

My father read the Thursday morning paper over and over. Inside it there were three stories about the storming: Borough Park was getting extra police protection, the Jewish Community Relations Council met with Mayor Koch, and, the big news that made my father wave his fist in the air, Sidney Cantor had been arrested with four other men.

"One misdemeanor charge," read Dad, "against Mr. Cantor was that he pushed, shoved, and kicked Detective William Patterson—the Detective he had accused in front of a Civilian Complaint Review Board of clubbing him and bloodying his head while he was trying to calm the situation." Dad laughed.

"Did you club him?" asked my mother.

"I could have. I clubbed a lot of people." Dad closed the paper. "But, I'll tell you, if I did club him, he had asked for it."

"Then arresting him is a good sign," said Mom.

"A good sign?" said Dad. "This is the best thing since canned beans. It doesn't mean I'm out of the woods, but at least both sides are feeling the heat."

I was sitting at the kitchen table waiting for them to ask me what I was doing home. I was ready to admit that I was a dope and a dropout.

Dad went to the window and stared out at the backyard. "I've got that whole yard and garage to clean," he said. "You know this isn't a vacation. Who knows, maybe they'll make me retire, maybe they'll take my job. This could be it." He turned and faced us.

I swirled the bottom of my coffee around. For the past two days he'd been wearing out the carpet and station tuner on the TV set. He'd walk around the house for a half hour, then turn the TV on and spin the knob. He watched three soap operas in three seconds. We had a big argument about a handprint on the wall next to the stairs. "See that, that's your handprint," he yelled. "See that, that's a banister. Why don't you try using it."

"That's not my handprint."

"Give me your hand."

"No."

"I'll prove it to you."

"That's been there for ten years."

"I painted last year, wise guy."

He made Louise and my mother match their hands to it. It was definitely mine, but I refused to verify the evidence. "Stop playing house detective," I had said. His face had dropped like the Times Square ball on New Year's Eve. Anytime someone mentioned his job he shut up for a half hour and sulked.

"Do you know what *it* is?" he asked looking at me. "This is it. This house, that yard, and that garage filled with my son's crap."

"My crap?"

"All right, our crap. Does that make you any happier?"

"Bill, why don't you and Charlie go over to the boat show." My mother held up a full-page newspaper ad, "The Tenth Annual Coliseum Boat Show."

I gave her a look that could peel chrome. Dad waited for me to say something, I knew he wanted to go. "Those things are always the same," I said.

"A day out would get your father's mind off things."

"Well, I don't have anything on my mind." It was a rotten thing to say but I didn't want to go. I could just see us standing on the top of a cabin cruiser with our hands at each other's throats.

Dad left, slamming the back door. From the window I watched him throw open the garage doors and ghost ride my bicycle into the dead vegetable garden. It crashed into a tomato stalk and tumbled over.

"I paid two hundred and fifty for that bike!"

"Why didn't you go?" asked Mom. "I'm trying to get him interested in something. He'll drive us all crazy, he picks and picks and picks at the littlest things. My heart jumps everytime he opens the refrigerator. Who knows, he might find a bad pear or a moldy yogurt."

"Why didn't *you* go?" I asked.

"Charlie, he wouldn't go with me. You know how he is."

I groaned and went out to help him.

The garage was either a barn that was made into a garage or a garage that looked like a barn. We painted it red every couple of years. It had big square doors with X-supports, and above them, a window that might have been used as a hay loft.

It was cold. I picked my bicycle up and stood it in the driveway. "Charlie, you want to keep this?" My basketball hoop clanked into the doorway. "You never used the damn thing."

Dad had bought it for me on my twelfth birthday. It had never been put up. "Yeah, I want it, maybe my son can get as much enjoyment out of it as I did."

"I would have put it up. All you had to do was ask me," he yelled.

Every wall in the garage was covered with some hanging object; there were rakes, shovels, gas cans, hoses, barbeque utensils, lanterns, old coats, everything and anything. Along the walls were chests and cabinets packed with tools, knives, dishes, locks without keys, keys without locks, Barbie dolls, you name it. And in this pile was an empty space that the car fit snugly into. Dad was bent over, pulling apart a corner of the clutter that was reserved for my sporting equipment. "Remember these?" He threw a pair of black puffy boxing gloves at me. The leather was cracked and worn, stuffing pushed out. I put them on.

In the summer between seventh and eighth grades, Dad had bought me the gloves. We stood in the yard circling each other, him yelling, "Keep your jab up."

His punches came a sixteenth of an inch from my nose. "Hit me," he said. "Hit me." I'd tap him on the arm. "Harder. That's it, now hit me in the face," Left jabs bounced off my forehead and I let him have it, right smack in the face. "Good," he yelled and then blood came streaming out of his nose.

Nights later, and years later, my father spoke of that day. "He's a wildcat," he'd say. "I never saw a kid with a left hook like his."

I touched the dusty gloves to my face. "They're shot," I said.

"You know what I paid for them?" Dad put the other pair on. "Ten dollars. That used to be a lot of money." He threw a punch at me. "Well, we'll keep these, maybe we can use the leather for something."

He cleared a spot on the workbench and rubbed each pair with linseed oil. "That should stop them from cracking," he said.

There were a million things that needed to be put away but Dad tugged out my minibike. It had taken me two weeks to build, with him helping every minute. The motor, a three-and-a-half horse, was mounted on a steel grey Schwinn Sting Ray. The padded leather banana seat was covered with grease and dirt, the chrome U-shaped handle bars were breaking out with rust bubbles. It had been fast as hell.

When I had ridden it, I felt like Steve McQueen in *The Great Escape*. My father made me promise not to ride in the streets, so I'd leave on foot, pushing the bike by handle bars to a hilly meadow at the end of town that had a track. But two blocks away from the house I'd start the engine and zoom down the street, the frame shaking, wheels ready to explode. To me that mini bike felt like a 1200 cc Harley Electra Glide.

I recalled once doing about forty miles an hour, past the deli where my friends hung out and hearing "Pull over and shut your engine off." There was a patrol car three feet behind me. Kids were running out to the road screaming, "Go, go!" I slowed and eased to the curb. I remembered my promises to my father and figured either way I'm dead, so I gunned the gas. I flew up a driveway and roared down the sidewalk. I hit a garbage can and was airborne.

They brought me to the hospital bleeding from the head. I pleaded, "Don't tell my parents. P-l-e-a-s-e don't tell them." I received forty-seven stitches. My parents came, and my father refused to talk to me. I was on one of those rubber-wheeled tables yelling, "I'm sorry, I'm sorry." My mother came over and held my hand then my father came over and said, "All right, shut up, it's OK."

In the driveway, Dad dusted the bike. It hadn't been ridden since the accident. "I never told you, but this thing could have gone faster. I put a governor on the carburetor," said Dad.

"It's a good thing it didn't go any faster." It was amazing that the bike hadn't suffered a scratch. "You think it will start?"

We laid the bike on its side on a drop cloth in the garage. It was a Briggs & Stratton engine, one of the best made. I disconnected the carburetor and Dad pulled the head off. Everything I knew about mechanics, he had taught me. My father had a knack for mechanics. Don't be afraid to take something apart, he once told me. The worst thing that could happen is you'll have to ask me to put it back together.

Dad cut new gaskets for the carburetor and I cleaned

all the parts in diesel fuel. We didn't say much to each other, just nodded and pointed. "How's the float?" he asked.

I nodded.

About an hour and-a-half later, he filled the tank with gas, pumped the tires up with air and wheeled it into the driveway. "I used to think I was the wild one," I said.

"Wild one? You were wilder than fifteen kids." He punched my shoulder.

If nothing else, he could brag about that.

"Well," he said.

"You do the honors."

The motor started on about the fourteenth pull and shook like a paint mixer. Dad sat on it looking like a circus bear on a miniature bicycle. He let the clutch out and gave it gas, and slowly took off down the driveway. "I'm gonna take it for a spin," he yelled.

About two minutes later he came roaring up the driveway. He came closer and closer, not slowing down. With his right hand he was trying to pull the wire off the spark plug. He was still trying as he sped into the garage. Boom, he flew into the wall, a shower of gardening tools rained down on him. There was a rake across his lap and a shovel on his shoulder. The bike lay next to him, the motor had ripped off the mounts, and the front spokes were snapped and sticking out like uncooked spaghetti.

"The damn gas was stuck," he said. I pulled him up. "And the brakes aren't worth a shit."

"Are you OK?"

"Fine." He picked up the bike. The back tire was egg-shaped.

"Can you fix it? I might want to give it to my son."

"I'll fix it," he snorted. "It will give me something to do."

After lunch we went to the boat show. Dad had talked me into it. "Come on, it'll be a day out together and who knows, maybe we'll buy ourselves a boat." It was the look on his face that made me go. I sat in the back of the car so that the wind didn't hit me in the face. He had both hands on the wheel and could see me only through the rearview mirror. It seemed like a good time to tell him about college. "I'm not doing too good in college," I said resting my elbows on the back of the front seat.

"That's because you never study. I know you're smart, you just have a . . . what the hell did they call it?"

When I was in about the fourth grade, my teacher told Dad that I had an application problem. The term had stuck with him like day-old oatmeal. "I don't know."

"You know," he thought. "An application problem. You don't apply yourself."

I fell into the seat. Wasn't that the truth. "Well, I'm doing real bad." He didn't hear me. "I'm failing everything." He hadn't heard that, either.

Admission at the show was four-fifty. "Christ, for that price they should give everyone a boat." I paid while Dad tried to shove a ten-dollar bill into my pocket.

"My treat," I said, dancing away from the ten.

"Take the damn thing," he grabbed my coat. If I hadn't taken it, he would have continued pushing the bill down my shirt, or into my coat. Then, if he ever did give up, he'd leave it on my dresser the next day.

We both had on jeans, flannel shirts, and dungaree jackets. About the only difference was my clothes were brand names and his were J. C. Penney's and Sears. I don't know if he dressed like me or I dressed like him.

It was the last day of the show and there was a huge crowd in the lobby of the Coliseum. Dad pushed through and we got on the beer line. He bought six plastic cups of beer and the girl put them in a cardboard holder. "We'll finish some of these," he explained balancing the beer. "And then we'll go take a look." He winked at me.

Between a popcorn stand and a cotton candy machine, we leaned against the wall. I polished off my first beer, Dad did overtime on his second. "You know something," he said. "I never did anything with my old man. I don't think we ever had a real conversation about anything." He lifted his eyes to the iron beams high above. "You probably call me the old man, don't you."

"Nah."

"Oh, you do so," he said in a chummy voice. "But just remember, I'm not so old. I could still knock you on your ass."

"Don't start that shit. Who cares? You don't have to prove anything to me."

"I'm just stating a fact."

"There you go with the facts again. Why bother saying shit like that?"

"I don't know, it's just a fact." He downed his beer. "You want popcorn?"

I punched him in the arm. People streamed by like the Chinese in a Godzilla movie. "There you go, I started it, go ahead, knock me on my ass."

"I just might one of these days," he bent and handed me another beer. "You want popcorn?"

He seemed to love getting me annoyed. "No."

"How about some of that cotton candy?"

"No."

"Boy, you'd swear the flood was coming." He was watching the crowd.

I felt like putting down the beer and walking home.

"Boats are like a hole in the water. You just keep throwing money in and the hole never fills up." He put his hand on my face and tapped it lightly. "Come on, Chuck, cheer up." He clicked his plastic cup to mine and I drank the whole cup in one gulp. "Friends?"

"Well, relatives anyway."

Inside the show I had a nice buzz going. We stood dwarfed by giant fiberglass yachts. Over our heads smaller boats hung from the rafters. Next to the carpeted steps that led to the decks, people waited to board. Wall space was crowded with tables selling or demonstrating nautical equipment. Dad and I stopped by a girl in a red one-piece bathing suit holding a microphone. She had a pouting lower lip, blonde hair, and black spiked heels that sent her posture slightly off center. She compensated by pushing out her stomach. She was centerfold-seductive. Dad and I probably looked like we were just shot with a stun-gun.

Smiling shyly, as if she had butterflies in her stomach on opening night, she took a few carefully placed steps forward. "Universal heads are self-contained, no smelly odors and very flushable. Would you like me to demonstrate?"

"You're going to what?" said Dad, eyeing the toilet.

"Demonstrate." She pressed a button on the toilet. Woosh. "One press is all it takes."

"You mean you don't need a courtesy flush?" I asked. She couldn't have been older than twenty-one. I wanted to have a meaningful discussion, then bring her home and screw her to death.

"No, it's as easy as one, two, three," she said and flushed it again.

"You'd need a courtesy flush if he used it," I said, pointing to my father. Dad gave me the ho, ho, ho very funny routine, but didn't take his eyes off her.

"I guess you get an ass for every seat," he said.

We stood there ogling for ten minutes, saying every dumb thing that came to our minds.

"Will you guys cut it out," she said, holding her hand over the mike. "I want to keep this job."

We went and bought more beer and hot dogs covered with the mustard that you can't get at home. On the outskirts of the show, I climbed aboard a speed boat with candy-cane striped seats and a padded steering wheel. Dad handed me the dogs and the beer and hopped up. We sat in the cockpit, trying to look as inconspicuous as possible. Dad put his beer in the drink holder between the bucket seats, and I kept my franks on my lap. I gripped the steering wheel and stared through the tinted windshield at fifteen feet of sparkling metal flake red.

"How would you like to have this baby?" said Dad.

I pretended that I was choking on the hot dog. "I'd give my left nut for it."

"How much?" A guy poked his head into the boat, the light reflected off his bald head and glasses.

"It's sold," said Dad. The guy backed away, pulled an instamatic from his breast pocket, and snapped a picture. "Well, good luck with it," he called.

Dad ran his hand along the dashboard, then felt the carpeting. "How much could they want for it?" he said.

"A lot."

"About?"

"Twenty thousand."

A salesman appeared out of the horizon wearing a black-and-white captain's hat, a dark tan, and a name tag. It said, 'Larson Speed Boats. Hi, I'm Bob Field.' He said, "Come on fellas, you can't have lunch here."

"We're thinking about buying this boat."

"Well, you'll have to think about it from the other side of the ropes like everyone else."

"I'm serious."

The guy raised an eyebrow and stuck his tongue in his cheek. He was young, probably never sold a boat in his life. "OK," he clapped his hands, dollar signs popping in his eyes.

First stop, the cabin. The three of us stepped in and were surrounded by a ten-foot crushed velvet V-bunk. Mounted to the wall was a tape deck, and a pull-down bar. The low ceiling over the bed was covered with mirrored reflective tape. It was designed for serious fucking. "The perfect overnighter," I said. We all laughed nervously, like some little boys who had broken into their sister's underwear drawer.

"Maybe I'll buy it for myself," said Dad.

The salesman explained how the top popped up so that you could have more headroom. He lifted a cushion. Under it was a Universal Head.

"Does it have a self-contained storage tank?" I asked.

"Yes, sir."

"We've been doing a little research," laughed Dad.

On deck, he lifted the engine cover and revealed a mass of chrome, carburetors, and hoses.

And then Dad popped the question. "What are you asking for it?"

"One hundred and twenty-five, but that's a package show deal, everything you see here, plus a trailer." The salesman stuck his hands in his pockets. I thought he was going to apologize.

"You're kidding!" said Dad.

"Well, take this anyway," the salesman stuck his card in Dad's hand.

Not giving up the ship, we boarded a forty-foot cruiser, a thirty-three foot sail boat, then a twenty-six foot fishing boat. The cheapest was forty-four thousand.

"We couldn't afford one if we sold the house." I said.

"I'm just looking," he snapped. "Can't I even look?"

I leaned into a wooden boat with a small diesel engine that pull started like a lawn mower. "We could afford this."

"It's a life boat. What are we gonna do, ride around waiting to be saved?" He stared at a big cruiser. "Do you realize that they want over a thousand a foot for that thing."

"Let's go."

"I've always been saving my money for a rainy day, that's one of your mother's favorites. 'Save it for a rainy day.' It'll be raining at my funeral."

"I'm glad you're having a good time."

He took my arm and squeezed it. "Hey, I had a great time."

"Let's get out of here."

Dad took a couple of last looks then followed me through the crowds.

CHAPTER
6

On Friday at about five I began getting ready for the date with Tracy. It had been a long, dragged-out day. A registered letter had come. Dad had been put on suspension and had to appear on Monday 11 A.M. for his hearing. He began drinking beer and booze, a shot of whiskey, a slug of beer. My mother and I sat watching like spectators at an operation. I told him that he'd had enough, my mother told him. "You mind your own business. Do me that one favor," he said.

I was afraid to touch the bottles. It would have been like taking meat from a starving bear. The scary part was he didn't say anything, he just reread the letter to himself at a low mumble.

After three hours, he went into the living room, lay

down on the floor, and fell asleep.

I took a long hot shower and shaved in the steamy mirror. I felt like it was my first date with Tracy. It felt great. I blow-dried my hair, wet it, and dried it again. I did fifty pushups, then fifty sit-ups with my feet tucked under my dresser. I stood in front of the mirror flexing. I wasn't big but I was tight.

The house was real quiet. My mother and Louise had gone out for dinner and then planned on seeing a movie. I strutted across the room and did a quick Mick Jagger imitation into the mirror. "Let's spend the night together, now I need you more than ever."

I slipped on a pair of freshly washed Levi's, nice and tight, slightly faded, a grey V-neck sweater, and a pair of white high-top Nike's. It was my casual jock look.

Back at the mirror I stuck my hands in my pockets, lifted my chin. "Joey, I could have been somebody but what did I get?" I pointed just like Marlon Brando in *On the Waterfront*. "A one way ticket to Palukaville." It was about my best imitation. I turned, looked over my shoulder, and checked out my ass. I had read in *Cosmopolitan* that girls loved a nice ass even more than guys did. Mine was a little lean, but my pants were snug.

I crept down the stairs. The kitchen light was on. Shit. Dad stood in front of the door. "How you feeling?" I asked. He looked like death. The color had even drained from his eyes. In one hand he held a glass of beer, in the other a spatula dripping with hot-dog grease.

"Where are you going?" His pants were falling below his waist and one sock was almost off his foot.

"Out."

"I know damn well you're going out."

I didn't want to mention Tracy's name. I remembered when they met at a family barbeque. It had not gone smoothly. She had been wearing patched cut-off jeans and a tube top. Dad never took his eyes off her. "She's all right," he had whispered in my ear.

After dinner he stared at Tracy's chest and said, "Looks like it's getting cold out." Tracy excused herself, thanked my mother, said goodbye to my sister, and left. I chased her down the driveway.

"He's a dirty old man."

"He didn't mean anything by it." She got in her car and pulled away. "I'll call you," I yelled.

For the rest of that night Dad acted as if we were high school buddies and one of us had just been caught making passes at the teacher. He kept poking me in the ribs and pouring me drinks.

The only other thing Dad knew about Tracy was that she had hurt me. I had spilled my guts to him on the night she had broken up with me over the phone. Seeing something was wrong, Dad had asked me if I wanted to take a ride with him in the Buick. It was his way of saying, "Let's talk." Taking deep breaths, I climbed into the car and we eased out of the driveway. Dad asked me what was bothering me. "You look like you just lost your best friend," he had said.

At first I didn't want to tell him. I was afraid he'd say something like, "There's other fish in the ocean." We crossed into the next town and waited at a light. I wiped my eyes and couldn't hold it in. I told him that I had just lost Tracy, and that she was sleeping with a guy who had given her a bunch of presents.

Dad pulled into a Carvel. He bought two cones and we leaned on the car in the parking lot, "Stay away from her," he said. "I knew she was no good the minute I saw her. She's what we used to call a floozie, a hussy."

Today, in the kitchen I looked into my father's drunken eyes and looked away. I had to lie to him. "I'm going to meet some of the guys," I said.

"In those tight pants? They'll think you're a queer," he laughed.

I tried to get past but he stuck his arm out.

"Sit down," he said. "I made you a hot dog." He waved his hand and grease flew onto my sweater. I sat staring at the dark spot while he slid the frank out of the frying pan. I was furious. I could have boiled water with a stare. I picked up the frank, wanting to throw it in the garbage. "Wait, I have rolls," he said.

I dropped it like a dead fish and pulled my sweater over my head. I rolled it in a ball and threw it in the pantry.

"If you had to buy your clothes you wouldn't treat them like that."

I got up and dropped the frank in the garbage pail.

Dad's eyes pushed out of their sockets and he threw the roll at me. "Don't eat anymore, don't! Get skinnier, I don't care."

I picked my sweater off the floor and walked out.

———————

Tracy came out of the lobby of her apartment lugging a bowling bag. It was a misty night and her curly hair, held by two clips above each ear, was becoming an afro. I slid to the passenger side and opened the door. The seat was damp. "How you doing?"

"I'm getting a cold," she smiled, swung the bag into the back, and climbed in. Her bottom touched the seat and she sprang up as if it were hot coals. "When are you going to get that roof fixed?" she whined. Wham! She slammed the door so hard I imagined the glass cracking.

"The roof can't be fixed, it has to be replaced."

"I can't believe this car is still running."

"Never say die." I started the engine, one turn of the key, "See what I mean."

"You should put it out of its misery and buy something nice." Grind, I put the car in gear, it lurched and she fell into her seat. I banged into second, then third.

"You know, I love this car, it's a collector's item. You just don't know how to appreciate it."

"Just like old times. The same old car, the same old arguments."

"You forgot to give me a kiss," I said.

She rummaged through her purse and found a piece of gum. She unwrapped it. I opened my mouth and she popped it in her mouth. "Come on, give me a kiss." She turned the radio on. It didn't work. It wasn't hooked up. "And now the news," I said. "Charlie Patterson strangles Tracy Horowitz over a kiss. More after this message. Winston tastes good like a cigarette should— no filter, no taste, just a forty-cent waste."

She gave me a peck on the cheek. I slipped my hand on her leg and squeezed. "One thing, I can always find my car in a parking lot."

"The least you could do is get a new air freshener. It smells musty in here." She removed my hand and held it. I had to smile. I loved the games.

The car did smell musty. The pine tree-scented cowboy hat dangling from the cigarette lighter had turned yellow. I opened my fly window and stepped on the gas. Tracy stepped on an imaginary brake and gripped the arm rest.

"A car is a reflection of a person's personality. You drive a Datsun compact. That means you're a sensible, trendy consumer."

"Slow down." A few blocks ahead there was a green light that I always missed. I was doing fifty.

"Me, I drive a sixty-two Corvair convertible, which means?"

"Come on, slow down." She braced herself on the dash.

We zoomed through the intersection at sixty, the car shuddering like the 7th Avenue Express.

"Charlie, I swear to God."

"Which means that I'm an individual."

"Don't you ever fucking do that again." At the next light I tried to kiss her and she pushed me away, threatening to get out and walk. It felt good to scare the shit out of her. She was too sure of herself. My friends said she acted as if she had a broom handle shoved up her ass.

The bowling alley smelled like wet rosin and was as quiet as a closed library. No one was bowling, the pro-shop was dark, the bar was lit but had no bartender or customers. "Alone at last," I pinched Tracy's ass and she swatted my hand. At the desk I tapped a bell and an old man came out of a shoe-lined room. "Are you open?"

"Yup." He had a wandering eye and seemed to be looking at Tracy and me at the same time. I goosed Tracy again, and she shot me a look that could evaporate milk.

"Why don't you grow up," she whispered.

I figured I had better cool down, and at the same time I wanted to tell Tracy to fuck off. I hadn't realized how mad I was about the breakup.

"It's league night and you'll have to be out by nine," said the old man.

At lane one, we put on our bowling shoes and I wrote our names on the score sheet. I hadn't bowled in years. When I was ten or eleven, I had been on a team and won a trophy for most improved bowler. My average had gone from a thirty-three to a ninety-seven in two months.

Tracy opened her bag and pulled out a cherry-swirl ball that had a finish like a new Caddy. I was beginning to feel a little better and circled our names with a heart. "Aren't you going to get any practice shots in?" she asked.

"I'm going to try it cold turkey," I said.

A few inches left on the starting mark, she stood solemnly facing the yellow wooden lane and the white pins. The quiet seemed louder than fifty rolling bowling balls. Through her sand colored corduroys, her panty line showed. A nice, strong ass. She began her approach, one, two, three, swing, slide, she was a work of art. The guys on the Saturday afternoon probowlers tour would have been proud of her. Strike! She raced back to the table. "I'm not taking any practice shots, either," she said. I marked an X.

I screwed my fingers into the ball holes. A lane ball that fits your fingers is about as rare as a Burger King with golden arches. The holes are either beer-can-size or as tight as a dead cat's ass. I placed my feet where Tracy's had been and bowled. I knew I was taking too many steps, and when I tried to release, I was sure I was going down the alley behind the ball. The damn thing wouldn't come off. My arm swung over my head like the Muhammad Ali sucker punch. On the second time around my fingers popped out and the ball zipped into the gutter.

Tracy was cracking up. "I'm sorry," she laughed. "But you looked so funny."

"I could have broken my arm." I sat in the score chair.

She rubbed my shoulder, still laughing, then apologizing.

There was a lot of silence during the game. In the fifth frame she had a ninety-six and I had a thirty-one. "Do we have to finish?" she asked.

"Yes." I was a sore loser and I was trying to hide it. I was doing a terrible job. Tracy sat next to me. "I'm sorry," I said. "I'm such a lousy sport."

"Now you know how I felt when you beat me at chess." I was a vicious chess player and never gave mercy. I kissed her. "You're up again," she said.

"You bowl for me."

"No, how do you expect to get better?"

At eight forty-five a herd of ball-toting bowlers flooded in. They wore nylon bowling shirts complete with underarm sweat absorbers. On the backs written in script thread were the team names, the Lucky Strikers and the Alley Bobbers. A ladies' team, named the Ivory Girls, plopped in chairs behind our lane. A woman wearing Danskin stretch pants, her hair in a beehive hairstyle, waved at me.

I smiled back.

Soon, balls were thundering down the lanes, kids were chasing each other, hiding under their parents' coats, which were piled in a giant heap on a vinyl couch. A bald man with a round, hard beer gut and bowling-ball-size biceps asked, "You two finishing up?"

"Yes." Thank God.

"You got an eighty-seven," said Tracy.

She had rolled a one eighty-nine. I was a little proud of her and hoped the fat guy would notice her score. I pulled her face to mine and we kissed. "Maybe we can make it," I said.

"Don't try. Let's just see what happens."

"I know it can work."

"You can't make something work." My hand tightened around her fingers and I searched her face for some sign that she cared about me, about us.

The fat man's team came onto the lane. They were called the King Pins. One old grey-haired guy with droopy pants looked liked my father. I grabbed Tracy and headed for the door.

The parking lot was lined with cars. Mine was at the end of a long row with its lights on. Shit!

"You left your lights on," said Tracy.

We jogged to the car and climbed in. "Say a prayer." I turned the key. Nothing. "Damn it."

"You can't leave the lights on in my car. It has a buzzer." I swallowed, tried to ignore her, and tried it again. Nothing.

"I'm going to call my mother, she'll give us a jump."

Ten minutes later, the Buick pulled into the lot so fast it spun in a circle, just missing my car. Tracy almost leaped onto my lap. My father waved, and I sunk lower in the seat. "My God," said Tracy. "They really wrecked the car."

We got out of the Corvair. Tracy bit her lip and smiled at the same time. "Hello, Mr. Patterson."

"Hello there, Tracy." He was weaving drunk. It was cold and he had no coat. His tab collar shirt was open at the neck. He was standing in a puddle, and his Indian moccasins absorbed the water like sponges.

"C. B., leave your lights on again?" A pair of jumper cables hung around his neck like red-and-black spider crab claws.

I nodded.

"What does C. B. stand for?" asked Tracy.

"Charlie Brown," he laughed. "Right, Charlie Brown?" He grabbed me and put his arm around my neck.

I hooked up the cables, and the Corvair started like a champ. "Next time you need help, you ask for me, not your mother," said Dad. I raced the motor, recharging the battery. Tracy got in, Dad closed her door and leaned on the window. "So where you two headed?" I shrugged. "I'll buy you two a drink."

"Well, we got to meet somebody," I said.

His face collapsed, "One drink."

Tracy didn't say a word and I couldn't say no.

"I'll meet you at the Shamrock." He smiled as if it were the happiest day of his life.

————————

There was a parking spot a block away from the Shamrock Pub. I squeezed the Corvair in, touching the car behind. I should have told Dad that we had other plans. If he started with Tracy, I'd have to take sides. "Don't listen to half the things my father says. He's been drinking."

"Don't worry."

"He'll say things that he doesn't mean just to get a rise out of you." Tracy adjusted my rearview mirror to face her and brushed on eye shadow. "If he starts, we'll leave."

A few spaces away, Dad emerged from his car, running a comb through his hair. Traffic whizzed by. He stepped into the lane and stood on the white line like a tightrope walker. Tracy's eyes lit like electric lights. Two cars sped around him. I tried to yell. He stepped into the oncoming traffic. Dad froze, the headlights flashing in his eyes. "He's going to get hit," screamed Tracy.

"Dad!" I yelled. The car began to skid, then somehow spun around him on the wet street. Tracy and I jumped out of the Corvair and ran to him. He stood dazed in the center of the road. I took his arm and walked him to the sidewalk.

A tall man wearing a parka came running toward us. "Don't you even fuckin' look?" It was the driver. He had left his car parked in the middle of the street at an odd angle. Tracy stood at my side holding her pocketbook with both arms. Dad raised his eyes from the pavement and stared at him. "Are you drunk?" screamed the man.

Dad's eyes steadied.

"Is he drunk?" boomed the driver.

"Why don't you just forget it. Nothing happened," I said.

"Nothing happened?" His eyes were wild with rage. "I've got my wife in the car and she's got a bloody nose."

"Shut up," said Dad. "You shut up."

"Don't tell me to shut up." He was taller than Dad, taller and broader, but Dad was thicker and now stood steady.

"I said, shut up."

I tried to step between them. "Why don't you just get out of here?" I said.

The guy pushed me, "Where do you come off . . ."

He never finished the sentence. Dad hit him, followed
through with his right, and hit him again.

The driver fell like a long pole, his head smacked the
cement. Tracy was backing up. I grabbed her coat and
she twisted away. The man rolled over and got to his
knees. He held the parking meter.

Tracy stumbled backward, looking at Dad, the man,
and me as if she had just come across a horrible accident.

"You meet me at Pete's," said Dad. He crossed the
street quickly and got in his car.

I ran after Tracy and took her hand. We raced across
the wet, black street. I was numb; tried to think, to
feel, but couldn't. Dad is dangerous. Dangerous. The
man's front tooth was hanging by threads.

"He's crazy," said Tracy.

Why didn't I stop him? I knew it was coming. "I'll
take you home," I said. Pete's. I had to go to Pete's.

———————

The white stucco bar was a few blocks from my house.
In the morning, guys lined up at the door waiting for it
to open, and by noon the bar was lined with shaky,
unshaven men.

In front, the Buick was parked, one wheel on the curb.
It was a full moon and the tide was coming up from
the sewer. Dark water with floating street litter came
to the front steps. I hopped around the flood and jumped
to an island of garbage. My foot sunk and the water
seeped into my sneaker. I hopped to the steps and listened to the voices and the music. The red door flew
open and someone fell against me. I was so spooked
that I shoved him away. He tripped into the water. It
was an old man. There wasn't a hair on his head. "I got

two jaw-heads," he laughed. "Two jaw-headed sons in the Marines." He came up the steps. "The stubborn one's still a private and never writes me. But the Sarge," he stepped out of the water, "he writes me every week, but that damn little one." He tried to grab me. "I love him. He's the crazy one."

We went in together. "Here's Charlie," yelled my father. Every head turned.

"This young man saved me from the puddle," said the old man.

A cigar-smoking man said, "You should have left him out there." Behind the smoke, his eyes swam and he smiled. No teeth, a black hole.

Dad had my shoulder and pulled me through the men. They were as thick as smoke. He found his spot at the bar. "Where's Tracy?"

"I dropped her off."

"She's some piece of ass." He punched my arm, his eyes were wild. He grabbed an old man's face and squeezed it. "Meet my son."

"Name's Scotty," the old guy shook my hand and tried to crush it. I squeezed. He let go and smiled. His face was cut with a hundred creases. On his head he wore a fisherman's cap. "You look like yer old man. You can thank Satan for that."

Dad took the ice out of his drink and held it. His fingers had swelled, the knuckles had disappeared. "I can't move 'em," he said. He tried to open his fingers, concentrating as if it were magic. "I ruined your date." He laid his hand gently on the bar. "You invite Tracy over for dinner."

"You know you knocked the man's teeth out?"

"I had to hit him. He asked for it."

"You didn't have to. I didn't have to hit him, so don't tell me you had to."

Over Dad's shoulder Scotty watched me.

"You really don't know why I hit him," said Dad. "You really don't know, do you? I hit him for you."

"For me?" He was out of his mind. "For me?"

"I did it for you, goddamn it."

Scotty stuck his face inches from mine. "Walk softly and carry a big stick," he said.

"You're damn right." Dad slapped Scotty's back. "He's a philosopher. He never went to school in his life and I bet he knows ten times more than any college teacher. Just wish you're half as smart as him when you're seventy-four years old."

Scotty nodded and they raised glasses, "Wishes won't wash dishes."

"Wishes won't wash dishes," repeated Dad. "You see what I mean?"

"He that will conquer, must fight," said Scotty. They touched glasses again. Dad downed his drink and flagged the bartender. The jukebox whined out Hank Williams. More people pushed through the doorway.

"You ever been in here before?" asked Dad.

"No."

"Good, stay the hell out of here."

The bartender spit into a napkin and stuck it in his pocket. "So you hit him for me?"

"You wouldn't have. Somebody had to."

"Let's go home."

"Too early." He bought another drink. "Here's a toast. To your girl friend's ass."

"You're sick. I swear to God you're crazy."

He cocked an eyebrow and a little blood colored his

face. "You don't ever call your father sick."

I pulled away from him and pushed my way to the door. Outside, the tide was lapping against the doorstep. In the water, propped against the building sat the old bald man. He was asleep or passed out.

The door flew open. "Where the hell are you going?" yelled Dad.

I started running straight down the road.

At the dock, I sat on a wooden piling along the bulkhead and dangled my sneakers inches above the smooth canal. Lights burned inside the cabins of the commercial fishing boats. The odor of fish and the sea came from the nets that hung drying above the decks. It was a high full moon tide. *The Explorer*, a black, iron-hulled clam boat, was straining its securing lines. The taut ropes squeaked as the water rose.

I thought about my father, the kid in the cage, and the tooth hanging in the man's mouth. He hit him for me, for me. "Why the hell is he doing it for me," I said. I tried to put the pieces together. I was sweaty from the run and the dampness was giving me the chills. He had to get his job back and I had to do something. "I'll go to Tracy's in the morning." I stood and walked back to Pete's.

Outside the bar, the water had risen to the hubcaps of the cars. The Buick was still there, Dad slumped behind the wheel. I opened the door and shook him.

"All right," he said sleepily. His chin rested on his chest and his mouth sagged. I pushed him over, his body tipped and he rested his head on the passenger door. I climbed in and lifted his legs one at a time, so that I could get to the gas and brake. The car keys were in his hand. I uncurled his fingers and removed them. I drove slowly through the streets, shivering as the wind rushed through the windshield.

He wouldn't wake, so I left him in the car, and went into the house. In the living room, I ran my hand over an orange afghan folded over the back of the rocking chair. I stood there a moment, then climbed the stairs and went to bed.

CHAPTER

7

The next morning I woke with the realization that I had lost Tracy. Last night, I had practically thrown her out of the car, explaining a mile a minute that she had to understand that when he's in a mood like that he doesn't even know what he's doing, if I didn't meet him at Pete's he might start more trouble.

"I can't take you there because all these sick old men hang out there."

Tracy had lifted her bowling bag, "You're sicker than he is. You know that." I grabbed her and she pulled free.

"Tracy!" I yelled. "Let me just get this fixed up."

She slammed the door. "You got a lot of fixing to do," she said. As the words left her mouth, I was already jamming into first gear.

I dressed quickly. In the kitchen, I went right by my mother and out the back door. "Hey Chuck, where's the fire?" Dad popped his head out from under the hood of the Buick.

I stopped, fighting with the zipper on my ski coat. The catch was made out of plastic and never fit together correctly. "You ought to be committed," I said. The zipper catch came off in my hand. I threw it at the dead tomato stalks in our garden.

"You just broke your zipper," he said. He came over and began looking through the plants for the piece. "I can fix that zipper," he said.

"You blew it for me. And last night is the last time it's going to happen."

He was bent at the waist fishing around in the dirt. Taped over his knuckles was a grease-covered gauze. "I don't need the goddamn zipper, for Christ's sake."

He straightened, his face was red. "What happened? I mean . . ." he raised his bandaged hand.

"You don't remember? You're kidding." I spun around. "You almost killed someone. You almost killed yourself."

He lifted his right shoulder and dropped it. "I remember getting your car running, right?"

"You better think about it, 'cause I can't talk now." I walked down the driveway.

"I'm going to get the windows fixed," he yelled. "You want to go?"

I walked to Pete's to get my car. Lines of dirt and garbage were the only signs of the flood. Through the window I saw men at the bar.

On Main Street I parked and went into a florist shop.

A girl wearing jeans and a cowboy shirt was sticking flowers in a styrofoam base. I leaned over the counter. "A bouquet," I said. "Can you make something nice for five dollars!"

"What kind of flowers do you want?"

"Mixed, whatever looks good."

"You got it," she smiled.

I crossed the street and went into Roma's Italian Deli. It smelled like provolone cheese and smoked white fish. I stood on line sniffing it in, pushing around the sawdust on the floor with the tip of my sneaker. If the flowers didn't work, stuffed bread would. Inside a loaf of the steamy hot bread were cheese, sausage, pepperoni, onions, and peppers. In the summer, I had turned Tracy on to stuffed bread and it had become our after-sex snack. I spun a hanging salami and was beginning to feel better.

"Two, no, better make it three loaves of stuffed bread." I said. An old, big-busted Italian woman wrapped them in white wax paper. I paid and dashed back to the florist.

The flowers weren't ready. I stood looking out the front window. The display was the typical Halloween scene. There was a scarecrow propped on a pole, hay sticking out of his cuffs and collar. At his feet, cardboard black cats leaped over pumpkins. From a wooden crate in the corner of the store I selected a pumpkin, a small one with a long goofy stem, and put it on the counter.

Next to the cash register there was a display case of round glass balls with red roses inside. The flowers were anchored in a bubbleless liquid that magnified them to three times their size. I picked one up. On the bottom it said, "Eternal Rose. The Flower That Lasts a Lifetime."

I called into the back room, "Hold it, I changed my mind."

The girl came out with a bouquet of small dainty, white flowers on a bed of ferns. "I couldn't do much for five dollars," she said. "I'm used to having more free rein."

I left the store with twenty-two cents change, three loaves of stuffed bread, an Eternal Rose, a pumpkin, and the worst bouquet I had ever seen. I had better get a job soon because my lawn mowing money wouldn't last until spring.

Tracy opened the apartment door a couple of inches and stuck her face out. I had my arms filled with gifts like a door-to-door Santa. "Sorry about last night. I brought you some presents and . . ."

"No," she said. "It's over."

"Stuffed bread." I opened the bag and smelled inside. I could feel myself getting choked up.

"You're insulting me right now. It's not going to work, Charlie. I'm sorry. For a second last night I thought it might, but, no, it's over."

I felt dizzy. I had just run up six flights of stairs. "The elevator's out," I said.

"Well, I'm sorry about that, too."

Her face was going in and out of focus, my eyes were filling. "Just take this stuff, then. I bought it for you, so you might as well take it."

"I don't want it."

"I'll put it right here in front of the door and you can get it when I leave. I got you this thing that you'll really like." I put the packages down and began walking to the elevator. The floor rocked under my feet. I took some deep breaths and counted to ten. The floor steadied. A sauna-size sweat broke out on my forehead. I was going to lose her. I pressed the elevator button, praying she'd call me.

"Charlie, you just told me the elevator's not working, and will you come back here and take this stuff. Charlie!"

"Keep it." I started for the stairs.

"All right, come in for a second." My heart jumped. I had just pulled a blank in a Russian roulette game.

Tracy was dressed in a red sweat shirt and blue flannel pajama bottoms. I hugged her. She barely put her arms around me. "I got that cold," she sniffed. "And I got my period today, so I probably look terrible." I touched her face. There was a deep familiarity between us. We had once been inseparable. We had once been lovers. Tracy pulled away.

"Are you hungry?"

"That's the only reason I let you in," she smiled.

"Watch it, I'll take my bread and go home."

Before we did anything else, I made her open the box with the rose in it. She carefully undid the tape on the flower-patterned wrapping paper. She was compulsively neat. "It's beautiful." She gazed into the glass ball as if looking for the future.

"They call it the Eternal Rose."

She shook it, probably expecting fake snow to whirl in the water. "Thank you."

"And here's a pumpkin."

She examined the little thing, it was no bigger than a softball. "It's so cute."

"I'll cut it up for you."

"No, I'll paint on a face on it."

The bouquet was inside sheets of brown paper. She peeled back the scotch tape and unwound the cover. "Charlie, I'm going to kill you, they're gorgeous." She made a big fuss about finding the right vase and finally decided on an old Borden's milk bottle.

The kiss she gave me was a quickie but she had put her mouth on mine. "You're about the sweetest guy," she said. Disappointment hung on the words as if I were already dead. Tracy was great at giving me compliments that made me feel terrible.

At a small kitchen table, we shared a loaf of bread. Whenever I came upon a piece of sausage, I pulled it out of the dough and put it in her mouth. She loved sausage. In the living room sat the flowers, the pumpkin, and the Eternal Rose. I knew I had been deceitful and felt a little hollow. But, whatever Tracy and I had had in the summer, I wanted back.

"How's your father?" asked Tracy, putting a string of mozzarella cheese into her mouth.

"Fine, he doesn't remember a thing."

"Doesn't remember?"

"No, nothing. That's the way he gets when he drinks. You'd swear he's sober but he's walking around in a blackout." I don't think she believed me.

"What happened at Pete's?"

"Nothing. We had a few drinks and I took him home."

"The only time I've seen a fight like that was in the movies."

"I told you my father had been a boxer."

She got up, went into the bathroom, and came back with a tube of nose spray. She squirted it up each nostril and popped her eyes open. "I'm going back to bed," she said. "I've got to work today, and I barely slept last night." She headed into the bedroom. I'm sure she expected me to leave.

"I'll make you some tea," I called.

Waiting for the water to boil, I opened her telephone directory and flipped to P: Charlie Patterson

22 Mill St.

878-4391

"Charlie, put honey in my tea. It's in the refrigerator," she called. I found a pen and put four stars next to my name.

———

The bedroom shades were shut and in the dim light I could see that almost nothing had changed. The plastic statue that I had given her in August was still on the ledge above the bed. It was a little man in a night shirt holding his arms apart. On the pedestal it said, "I love you this much." Tracy was under the blankets. I balanced the teacup in one hand and put the milk on the dresser. The top drawer was open and in the corner, half covered by underwear, was a tube of contraceptive cream and a white diaphragm case. It was a new tube. "Come under here with me," said Tracy.

I took my sneakers off and slid under the covers. The bed was warm. She leaned against the headboard and sipped her tea. "I was going to call you today. I was worried about you, but I was afraid your father would answer."

"He can't bite you over the phone."

"I bet he could."

I propped my head on a pillow. On the far wall she had three ballet posters. There was a photograph of a tattered pair of pink ballet slippers, another of a woman bending at the waist while being supported by two strong hands, and one of a young girl in a tutu kicking her leg, her face twisted in concentration. I had seen these posters in a dozen stores and at the raceway flea market.

I should have been overjoyed, a half hour ago I had been fighting my way in the door like a vacuum salesman, but I was staring at these posters and thinking about her new supply of cream. During the summer, she had told me to buy it, that she was too embarrassed to ask for it. In five months we had gone through one tube. In September, I had left her with half a tube. It didn't take too much math to know she'd been screwing her brains out. I hadn't even had a date.

I laid my head on her stomach. Through the sweat shirt I could hear it gurgle. "I want to make love to you," I said.

"I want to," she said. She put her cup on the nightstand and shimmied under the covers.

"We've got to stick together," I said. "From now on, Tracy, because I've missed you so much."

She closed her eyes. "Don't say anything. Let's just make love."

I slipped my hand into her pajamas then under the elastic on her panties. She lifted her hips and I pulled them off. From an orange box she pulled a tissue and wrapped her sanitary pad in it. I could smell her. "I've got to put something down or I'll leak all over," she said. Wearing only the red shirt, she hopped out of bed.

A line of blood ran down the inside of her thigh.

We made violent love and then we snuggled together. It had been the same as in the summer, but I felt sad.

When I woke up she was watching me from the crook of my arm. Dim daylight shone through the shades. Her leg, warm and soft, lay across mine. "You've been sleeping." Her voice sounded far away. I kissed her and moved on top of her. "Let's just lie here," she said.

In ten minutes she was either asleep or pretended to be. I slipped out of her arms and went into the bathroom. My stomach, pubic hair, and legs were red with drying blood.

There was some sort of attachment on her shower nozzle that made the water pound on my head like gravel. I worked up a lather with a bar of blue soap. The shower floor was crowded with shampoos and conditioners. I tried them one by one: strawberry, beer, herbal garden, lemon, and wheat-germ-honey. The shower was making a racket. Tracy had to be awake. "Tracy," I called. "Tracy." She didn't answer. I shut the water off, my hair still full of suds. "Tracy?"

"Boo!" She leaped into the shower and scared the hell out of me. "I scared you," she laughed.

We soaped each other. I concentrated on her breasts. "Tracy, we should go away together. To the islands or something." She turned around and I lathered her thighs and ass. "Maybe if we save, we could go away in January." I wanted to be in the sun and to swim in the ocean. "I'm going to have to get a job now that I'm not in college. Maybe we could even rent a yacht for a week and just cruise."

She just smiled at me. We washed the soap off each other. "I can't believe you're saying this because I'm going away next month with Bonnie."

"Where?"

"Saint Thomas."

"With Bonnie?" I remembered a Jewish girl who had gone to the beach with us and got sun poisoning on the top of her tits. She had covered herself with so much oil that when the sand blew she looked like breaded veal. I stepped from the shower, imagining them on some island beach getting third-degree burns and sipping piña coladas.

"You're mad, right?" Tracy stood naked, a towel around her shoulders.

"No."

In the bedroom Tracy blew me. It took too long a time for me to come, and when I did she spit the sperm into a tissue. "It was a lot," she said, wiping her lips. I was just glad it was over.

Before we dressed, Tracy danced around doing splits, jumps, and shuffles to a disco song. I ate it up. She shook her hair in my face and darted away, bent over and danced looking at me between her legs. Instant turn on. I tried to forget about the trip, about everything.

———————

Supper was already in Tupperware containers in the refrigerator when I came home. An open beer stood on top of the toaster. The garbage pail was littered with empties. My father's snore was coming in loud and clear. It sounded like a cartoon snore, a regular log-sawer. I went into the living room. He was in the Lazy-Boy recliner, the chair tilted back, his boots sticking in the air.

On Saturday nights my mother dragged Louise to the teenage coffee house in the church basement. My sister was a little too young to mingle, so she helped my mother cut coffee cake and give out sodas. I refused to go. "They are such a nice bunch of young people," my mother had said. They probably were, but I couldn't imagine myself drinking coffee on a Saturday night and rapping about Jesus while a folk group sang, "The Answer is Blowing in the Wind."

I backed up and went out, closing the door silently.

I swung around the corner in the musty Corvair and slowed in front of my best friend's house. Ralph went to Princeton and every blue moon drove home on a weekend. A year ago the idea had been that we were both supposed to go to any State University in Nowhereville, New York, but he was accepted into the Ivy League, and I had settled for the community college after listening to my father's good solid practical reasoning. "What are you going to do with your car? Why move to a little room, pay board, when you can have the whole house rent-free? How do you know you're going to like it up there? Since when do you like snow? I'm not paying for a party . . .," and on and on. Ralph had everything going for him. He was a Samuel Johnson freak, was majoring in engineering, came in number 14,701 in the city marathon and in his last letter wrote, "I'm shacking up with an American Indian chick who looks like the girl on the Mazola Margarine box." So, here I was dropping out of Rinky-Dink College. I felt like getting out of the car and kicking myself in the ass.

I drove to the firehouse where my other friends hung out.

Most guys lose their buddies when they get married or join the service; I lost Paul and Kevin to the Volunteer Fire Department. We used to be closer than Siamese triplets. When they joined the fire department I said, "You got to be kidding. Those guys are a bunch of townie dicks. I suppose you're going to parade down Main Street behind the fat baton-twirler." And, that's exactly what they did. Last summer, I sat on my tenspeed bike watching them parade by, and I'll tell you what really scared the shit out of me, they looked exactly like the other volunteers.

Every night it was another function. Monday: truck wash; Tuesday: meeting night; Wednesday: poker game; Thursday: tournament team practice; and weekends they hung out behind the truck garage in headquarters drinking at the bar, shooting pool, and watching X-rated cable TV while waiting for a fire.

In the summer, Saturdays were parade days. The company traveled all over Long Island to march. After the parade, the tournament team competed against departments in other towns. Their team was called the Hydrant Tappers and they specialized in running a ladder fifty yards, throwing it against a twenty foot arch, then racing to the top. They held the New York State record.

For about two months they tried to get me to join. "You get a place to hang out, we're always having a party, and you're doing the community a service," said Paul one afternoon.

"I've got too many obligations already. You wouldn't believe the homework I get."

"Charlie, man, the company," his face screwed up with sincerity. "They get like family."

I had too much family already. Their camaraderie gave me the willies. When a bunch of good old regular guys do a lot of hand slapping, back patting, drinking, and yelling I get this lonely feeling. Instead of joining in, I'm suspicious of their wholehearted enthusiasm. No one can be best buddies with thirty guys.

Most of the members, including Paul and Kevin, worked for the town for shit pay and bragged about the benefits, vacation, and days off. Paul was in the highway department. I'd see him around town leaning on a rake or shoveling asphalt into a pothole in the street. There was always a styrofoam container of steamy coffee in someone's hand, with a small corner ripped out of the plastic top so that it didn't spill. "Fuck, we don't do shit," Paul boasted. "On rainy days we get to fuck off and read fuck magazines."

In a little green-and-white Chevy Chevette Kevin buzzed around town, serving summonses for anything from long grass to renting a room without a permit. "It's a living," he'd say as if he were forty-nine with two mortgages, two kids, and a wife who went to the beauty parlor every Tuesday. He was twenty-one, for Christ's sake, and already had two life insurance policies. "Charlie, what are you busting my chops for? I just want some security."

I parked behind the red brick firehouse knowing I'd catch a rash of shit from them because I never called or came around, and a "Hey, when are you going to put your application in, anyway?"

I sat at a ten-stool bar in a wood-paneled room, flanked by Kevin and Paul doing shots of Jack Daniels. There were six married men at the bar making a lot of noise, making sure they were having a good time because it was their night out, their drinking night. Behind the bar, low-budget porno played on a twenty-six inch color TV. A metal plaque attached to the side read, "Donated by the Holy Name Society to Our Brave Fire Fighters." In the darkness behind, the light on the soda machine flickered, advertising its five selections: Budweiser, Miller, Schaeffer, Black Label, and Piels.

A shiny-headed bald man with glasses, nicknamed T-bone, played bartender and told a fire story. "I saw those fuckin' flames crawl right down the stairs." He paused and lit a cigarette. "And I'm standing there holding a dead hose wondering when the fuckin' clowns from Hose Company would hook into a hydrant. And then the water starts shooting like a dick in a whorehouse and I'm getting lifted right off my feet." There was a round of laughter as T-bone had a fake struggle with a broom handle.

Paul had gained a lot of weight. His T-shirt reached only to the middle of his belly button. A soft roll of fat hung over his belt. He was growing a goatee, just the chin hairs. It was scraggly and uneven. Kevin didn't have a belly, but his face looked as soft as an old woman's. He was double chinned, and his eyelids were puffy. His steady brown eyes watched every move I made. "I heard about your father," he said quietly. Paul leaned to listen. "I was going to call ya, but, shit, I figured you'd be coming up."

"I saw it in the paper," said Paul. "Yer old man is in a heap of shit, isn't he."

"Yeah."

"Well, at least he never took any shit," said Paul.

"Tracy told me about it," said Kevin. "I saw her at The Acts Thursday night. It must have been five in the morning."

"Was she with anyone?"

"A big fuckin' dude. I never saw him before."

I did another shot of Jack. My head felt like it was glowing. Tracy had worked all night and then went to an after-hours club? I thought about the afternoon and again wondered about the new tube of cream.

"Tracy told me what happened Friday."

"I think it's about time the cops started kicking Jewish ass," said Paul. "We should give all the Jews a tree to plant in Israel and then burn the place down."

"You don't know what the fuck you're talking about," I said. I wanted to pull his billy goat beard to the floor.

"Hey, don't come down on me because you're pissed off."

"Don't talk about things you don't understand."

"OK man, cool out." He poured me a shot. I knew he'd back down. Paul always backed down. "Come on, we're buddies."

The porno played on. A young girl with small tits was dancing to Mozart, having cloudy flashbacks of two women kissing and touching like blind lovers. "So, how is yer old man?" asked Paul.

"Pretty bent out of shape." I downed another shot. "He's taking it out on the world, on himself. I don't know, I'd just like to get away for a while."

Phil, the Chief, turned and looked over. "How you doing, Charlie boy?" He was a short wedge-shape guy with no neck. He was in his fifties and owned a gas station in town. One summer I pumped gas for him and on my last day he put a fifty in my hand and said, "You buy yourself something with that."

"You watching that porno garbage with those two horny toads? When I was their age I was out every Saturday night dancing."

"You ain't done any dancing since your wife kicked

you out," said Paul. "And you ain't never had nothing like that." He pointed at the TV. Everyone looked at the Chief, then at the screen.

The Chief stared into a bowl of peanuts.

"Paul, you're a schmuck," I said. "An asshole."

"None of that, Charlie," said the Chief.

I felt so bad I wanted to go over and hug the old guy. I got five dollars of change from T-bone and bought everyone a Budweiser. "When the hell you coming in?" asked Mr. Beck. He was two hundred pounds of twitching muscles and fading tatoos. He was the captain of the Hydrant Tappers, the guy who climbed the ladder.

"Probably wait till I get out of college."

"College?"

"Yeah, I'm going to put two years in at the community college and then try to get into Princeton."

"You get the college done first," he agreed. "There's plenty of time for everything else."

Beers began popping. "I want to make a toast," said Paul. An instant hush spread down the bar. "Here's to Charlie, our future member, our future brother." He put his arms around me, then Kevin squeezed me. Their soft bodies smelled like liquor and sweat.

I didn't stay to finish the beer. I told them I had to go home and study.

CHAPTER

8

On the morning of the hearing, Dad swallowed two glasses of whiskey, put his foot on the kitchen chair, and laced up his ankle holster. The handle of the .38 Special was worn where it rubbed his leg. He fixed his pant cuff and poured himself another drink. His white shirt was tight around his shoulders and neck. It was the old tab-collar type, which held his thin maroon tie neatly in place, My mother, Louise, and I were going with him. "Afterward we'll head over to Little Italy and eat in the same restaurant that Joe Columbo was gunned down in." He patted his pants checking for his wallet. "I'm personal friends with the owner. Then on the way home we'll stop over at the new movie theater in the mall and see that funny one about the kids in college."

"*Animal House,*" I said.

"Yeah, that's it."

My mother untied her apron and hung it on the cellar door knob. She wore a high-necked blouse and a checkered skirt. Her hair was up in a bun, knotted in a mysterious way that showed no bobby pins or clips. Feathery blonde bangs fell to her eyebrows. Dad poured another drink and went into the living room. "Put the bottle away," she mouthed to me.

I screwed the cap on and slipped it into the cabinet. She emptied his shot in the sink, wiped the glass, dried it, and put it back with the others. "Those people will think he's crazy if he shows up there ossified."

Dad came in carrying his black suit jacket. "That's hot shit," he said looking for his drink.

"You don't want to make a fool out of yourself," said Mom.

"You're hot shit." He hooked his handcuffs over his belt. "If I want to drink, I'll drink."

"You're breaking your own rule; it's three hours before noon," I said.

"Hot shit," he repeated pushing past.

Louise came down the stairs dressed in jeans and a T-shirt that said "Nuke the Nukes." She had protested against nuclear power and bought the shirt at an outdoor demonstration in Central Park. Louise was into issues and causes. She belonged to the Society for the Prevention of Cruelty to Senior Citizens and had another shirt that said "Think Grey."

"Do you know what a dress is?" asked Dad. "Do you even own any? Joy, come in here and show your daughter the difference between blue jeans and a dress."

"I don't want to go. I'd rather go to school."

"Oh, you're going."

"I'm not," she called, heading back to her room.

"Oh, yes you are," he singsonged.

Mom went up after her.

"Why are you making her go if she doesn't want to?" I asked.

"It will be good for her, she might learn something and besides, it can't hurt to have my family there."

"Dad, what do you think this is, bowling for dollars?"

Dad and I sat in front of the Buick, Mom and Louise in the back. The car was still a wreck but it had new glass in every window. On the windshield in the corner it said, Electra-Front in yellow crayon. Dad had paid out of his own pocket and now was talking about being reimbursed. The bill had come to four hundred and sixty dollars. We inched into the city in bumper-to-bumper traffic, listening to the up-to-date highway report. A thick cigar was stuck in Dad's mouth, so we kept the windows cracked. The parkway's shoulder was littered with banged-up, burnt-out cars stripped to the skeleton. Seagulls circled the sky over the rising garbage dump that stretched for mile upon mile. And, towering above it all, still a great distance away, were the buildings of Manhattan.

Dad gripped the steering wheel as if he were trying to pull it off. The cigar, clamped in his teeth, was going out. I pressed the dash lighter and waited for it to pop. Dad took the lighter, held it over the cigar, puffed, and said, "God darn, if it isn't going to rain."

It poured. The wipers streaked the windshield. Dad had to tilt his head to see the road. The rain splashed in and hit my face. "Look at this rain," said Mom.

"I could be in my history class learning about foundations," said Louise. "Right now we're studying the concrete era, next week is the foundationless era of the mobile home."

"Don't be smart," said Dad.

"You're the one who told me history is the foundation."

"Don't be smart." Dad began to swerve out of the lane.

"Will you watch where you're going?" I yelled.

"Joy, if she's smart, smack her."

Mom looked at Louise and put her finger to her lip. Louise made a face and Dad caught it in the rearview mirror.

"Smack her."

"I will."

I sunk in the seat. Whenever we went anywhere, it was the same crap. "Why doesn't everyone just shut up?"

"Don't say you will, Joy, if you won't. That's what the hell is wrong with this family. You kids get away with—" The truck ahead stopped, Dad hit his brakes, and everyone was thrown forward. Dad's cigar cracked on the steering wheel and bent. It looked like a plumbing fixture. Louise and I began to laugh. "You think that was funny." He threw the cigar out the window. "I almost hit a goddamn truck and you laugh. You're sick."

"I wasn't laughing about that." I said. The rain pounded on the roof.

"I'll tell you this, Joy," said Dad. "From now on you sit in the front."

"Louise, can you believe this?" I said. She made an

ape-lip face and I cracked up. "I'm sorry," I laughed.

"You're supposed to be twenty?" asked Dad. "When I was twenty, I was in the Army, fighting the Korean War. So go ahead, sit there laugh, laugh, laugh, it's funny right? The college boy thinks his father is a dope. That's funny."

"I'm only nineteen."

"At nineteen I was in boot camp."

"Well, if there was a war you know I'd go R.O.T.C."

I pointed at Louise. "Right Over To Canada," she said.

"Joy, do you think that's funny?"

"No."

"I think it's funny," said Louise.

"You see that, Charlie. Your thirteen-year-old sister thinks it's funny. That's who thinks it's funny."

I stared out the window at the rain. There were already black puddles on the side of the road. Mom touched my shoulder, "Your father is a little upset."

"That's the understatement of the century," I said. He was scared of losing his job, scared of being front page news, scared of losing his pension, scared because he probably beat that guy a little more than necessary.

The traffic was breaking up. Dad swerved into the third lane and eased the Buick up to fifty.

We sped through the Midtown Tunnel. The white-tiled walls flashed by. Dad's face grew tense. He watched the road as if he were driving through a thick fog. On his knuckles were three small cuts. Teeth marks from the storming. On his forehead, the slash was dry and hard.

At East 20th Street, we turned off Second Avenue. Large iron letters on a light brick building said, "Police

Academy." Everywhere there were policemen coming
and going. Across the street was the emergency entrance
for a hospital. Someone on a stretcher was rolled out
of an ambulance and rushed inside. At a parking ramp,
Dad flashed his badge and we zoomed underground into
the belly of the building.

———————

Mom, Louise, and I waited on a wooden bench in a
ninth floor hallway. We watched the cops go by. A young
cop wearing a new uniform and shined shoes hurried
after an old grey-haired cop with creaseless pants, a
cracked leather coat, and a battered nightstick that
bumped his leg. A jacketless detective who carried a
.357 magnum in a shoulder holster, and a sergeant with
a pot belly and watery eyes passed and nodded at my
mother. "Here a cop, there a cop, everywhere a cop,
cop," said Louise.

It was noisy. Typewriters clicked, a guy holding a
coffee cup yelled, "Who made this mud, anyway?" A
retarded kid who could have passed for eighteen or
thirty-nine ran the elevator and every time he stopped
at our floor, he waved at Louise and she waved back.
He was getting a tremendous kick out of it. He smiled
blinking, tiny eyes behind thick glasses. Each time
someone got on the elevator he'd ask, "Floor?" and press
the button.

Three doors down the hall, Dad was being investigated. I had expected a court, a jury, and a gavel-pound-
ing judge demanding order in the court. Instead, the
hearing was being held in a small room with a hanging
light and two tables. Three men sat behind one table,
Dad behind the other. An hour had passed. Louise went
for another drink at the water fountain. Holding her

hair, she leaned and took a drink. She wasn't wearing
a dress but she looked adorable. She wore rust colored
corduroy pants and a black, green, and red striped shirt
with a plaid tie. Her pants were tucked into tan hiking
boots. She looked like a Swiss school girl. Louise would
never admit it, but my mother picked out all of her
clothes.

"It couldn't be good it it's taking this long," I said.

My mother sat on the edge of the bench, back straight
as if she were waiting for her name to be called. The
elevator doors opened. The retarded kid popped his head
out and waved. "He's having a good time," said Mom.
As the doors floated shut, he stuck his tongue out. The
fingers of my mother's right hand moved a rosary from
bead to bead. She kept the crucifix in her palm. Every
other minute she nodded her head slightly.

She had prayed through the good times and bad times.
She had mumbled rosaries during the Johnny Carson
monologue, smiling over the jokes and nodding at the
Amens. Sometimes especially in the past couple of
years, her religion scared me. The Catholic Church
seemed to be growing on her like ivy. I was afraid it
was going to cover her.

"I'm hungry," said Louise.

While Mom and Louise went to find a deli, I waited
in case Dad came out. The kid on the elevator jumped
up and down when Louise got in. "What floor, what
floor, what floor?" he asked.

I paced the hall. Each time I passed the room my
father was in, I stopped. The door was metal and the
room, I imagined, soundproof. On my third trip past, I
put my ear to the door.

"Hey, what's going on?"

I whirled around.

"Could you hear anything?" said Vince with a smile.

"Oh God, you just scared the hell out of me." We shook hands.

"Your old man has them climbing the walls. Come on, I'll show you something."

I followed him down the hall (through a small lunchroom with three vending machines that sold coffee, candy, and soda), then down another corridor. Vince was a plump Italian, who looked more like a butcher than a cop. He wasn't wearing a jacket and his gun bumped a roll of fat around his hip.

The hall grew empty and quiet. Our footsteps echoed against the walls. Vince knocked three times on a door, waited, then knocked twice. I could hear it being unbolted. The door opened into a dark room. A strong smell of detergent hung in the air. Mops, buckets, a low utility sink, and black cans with spouted tops came into view as my eyes adjusted to the darkness. There was a man standing on a chair peering into a slatted air vent that ran along the wall a few feet from the ceiling. The door closed silently and was rebolted by a uniformed policeman.

"Bill's son," whispered Vince. I was led around the cleaning equipment to a chair. Light came through the vent and shone eerily on the man's face next to me. There was a tiny flashlight attached to his suit pocket. He was taking notes. I looked through the vent.

Three men sat facing Dad, their backs to me. The table was covered with papers. The middle investigator was bald, and light reflected off his head. A tape recorder was set up on a metal typing stand. I was afraid to breathe, afraid to move, fearing the chair would tip.

Dad read some papers, then tossed them across the desk.
"It's bullshit and you know it," he said.

"I have instructed you on two occasions to respect
this hearing. I will not conduct this testimony in a dis-
orderly manner."

Dad began to laugh. "Respect? Why don't you respect
me?"

"I will not have you laughing at me."

"I'm not laughing at you."

"And we will not have a debate about it, or anymore
volunteered statements of any kind. Is that understood?"

"Understood, and when I answer a question don't you
twist it around."

"Did you identify yourself as a policeman?"

"Yes. When the demonstrators moved inside the station house, I told them to back up, and then about six
of them surrounded me and I was kicked from behind.
I pulled my nightstick out and gave a loudmouthed guy
a poke."

"Do you usually carry a nightstick?"

"No, I had a feeling there was going to be trouble so
I got one from the desk sergeant."

I pressed my face into the vent and my foot started
tapping the chair. "They're bastards."

"Easy does it," whispered Vince.

"Then they grabbed me, lifted me up, and dumped
me on the ground," said Dad. "I got up and fought my
way outside." He took out his handkerchief and wiped
his forehead. "And they were standing on my car."

"Who?"

"The Jews, the demonstrators. I told them to get off
and they started shouting, 'Nazi, Nazi,' and one of 'em

snaps off my aerial and," he pointed to the cut, "whips me in the head with it."

"What medical treatment was required?"

"Well, you can see I needed five or six stitches."

"No medical treatment, then?"

"No."

"Go on."

"So I pulled the guy off the car and we start fighting; someone jumps on my back and chokes me around the neck and then I," he hesitated, "got mad. I started fighting for my life."

"That's quite a story," said the black-haired investigator. It was the first thing he had said.

"It's the truth."

"You admit to using a nightstick?" the bald guy pressed.

"Shit, yes, I used it. Any cop would have. They were on my back."

"Were any of the protesters armed?"

"That was not a protest," said Dad. "It was a riot!"

I shifted from foot to foot trying not to make a sound. It was like being at ringside. "Does he know we're watching?"

"He knows I'm watching," said Vince.

"Were they armed?" repeated the bald investigator.

"They threw rocks at the station house. Rocks and bottles."

"Please answer the question. Were the protesters who entered the station house carrying weapons?"

"Entered? They broke the door down." Dad's face was tomato-red. Above his eye, next to the cut, a vein pushed out.

"So it is correct to say they were not armed?"

"What the hell are you guys trying to do to me?" He took a deep breath. "No, they weren't armed, but they were kicking the shit out of me!"

Sweat dripped down my face. I wanted to pat Dad on the back and say, hang in there, you got 'em.

"Let me tell you something, Detective Patterson. If we find your actions not justifiable then you could do time. Cooperation is half the battle, do you understand what I'm saying?"

Dad lowered his face and nodded.

"Sidney Cantor suffered a concussion and a broken arm. In his complaint he stated that you took your gun out and hit him with the weapon."

"I never took it out of the holster."

"In six complaints they claim—"

"I never took the gun out if its holster."

"In six reports—"

"Do you fuckin' understand English?" Dad stood up. "I never touched it."

"Please sit down."

"Mr. Patterson, please relax. Right now you are not being charged. We only want to get to the truth."

"Don't tell me what you're trying to do. You're trying to make an example out of me. You're trying to screw me so that those goddamn Jews don't start shooting their mouths off for more justice." Dad sat heavily. "The truth is I thought they were trying to kill me, but I didn't pull my gun because I never met a goddamn Jew who could take a good shot in the mouth."

I'm not sure if he could see me but our eyes seemed to meet.

Minutes passed. The investigators went through their folders. "We have twenty witnesses to the beating of Sidney Cantor."

"Is that so?"

"You admit to the beating?"

"What about the prick who did this?" Again he pointed to his forehead.

"We have no record of your injury."

"Don't give me that shit, no record. Of course you have no record. Those Jews are sticking together like glue."

"But you admit to the beating?"

"Yes, we fought."

"Would you sign this statement?" They handed him an affidavit of some kind.

In the dark room I could feel the tension.

Dad picked the pen up then put it down. "No."

"It just states that you admit the incident happened."

"I don't sign shit."

Vince tugged my elbow and the cops slid a long cardboard strip over the vent. The light went on. I rubbed my eyes.

"He's something," said Vince quietly.

"Yeah." I hopped off the chair and leaned against the wall. I was wet with sweat. A young uniformed cop twirled his hat in his hand. He had short blonde hair and light blue eyes.

"Sean O'Donnell." He held out his hand.

"Charlie Patterson." His grip was firm.

"Your father talks about you all the time. You're going to college, majoring in business, right?"

"Sort of."

"I was working the night of the storming; your father's innocent."

"Do you have any complaints against you?"

"No," he smiled. "See, your father's from the old school and he gave them what they asked for. Maybe a little more."

"He's the only one being investigated," said Vince. "But that doesn't mean a damn thing."

The young cop put on his cap and looked even younger. Vince threw his cigarette on the floor, then hit the lights. The man who had been taking notes climbed up on a chair.

There were about fifteen more minutes of questioning that went nowhere. Dad was getting angrier and angrier. The bald investigator asked him again and again to sign the statement. "We'll make trouble for you if you don't cooperate."

"You just try."

"You sign and you'll save your job and stay out of the courts."

Dad looked up, his eyes fierce. He had taken his suit jacket off and was slowly presssing one hand into the other. Each pump made the veins on his neck more noticeable. "You're making me sick," he said thickly.

"The next step is the grand jury."

"Sick." He began to open and close his hands. "I walked a beat for eight years, was a detective for thirteen. So don't try to pull a con on me." He banged the table so hard pencils flew in the air and landed on the floor. "Nobody cons me."

The bald man stood. "All right then, we'll let you go to court."

Dad shut his eyes and lowered his head. He mumbled something and tried to loosen his tie. The investigators put their papers into their briefcases.

Dad began to breathe deeply, heaving his body up and down. I thought he was going to hit them. He stood, held the back of the chair, and then he was falling to the floor.

Vince jumped off the chair and raced out of the room. Sean said something and sped after him.

With my face pressing the vent, I watched. I couldn't move. I was afraid to take my eyes away. Afraid to lose contact with him.

An investigator kneeled and pulled open his shirt. "He's having a heart attack."

I hated those men. I hated them so bad. I stuck my fingers into the vent trying to rip it out and I screamed. "You get your fuckin' hands off him. You hear me? You hear me?"

And then I was charging out of the room, running through the hallways.

CHAPTER 9

On a grey box anchored to the wall above the bed a green flash beeped out my father's heartbeat. Wired suction cups stuck to his chest. His skin was chalk white. There was no place to sit, so Mom and I stood next to the bed. A bottle dripped slowly into a clear intravenous tube. The needle was taped to the back of his hand, and a purple bruise had formed around the insertion. "I thought I was going to lose you," said Mom.

Dad didn't stir.

The intensive care unit had no solid walls. The beds were separated by green curtains that ran along ceiling tracks. Light shone from plastic panels above. The air was thick with the smell of alcohol and new equipment. It was hard to breathe. I wanted to put my ear to

Dad's mouth so that he could tell me it was all a gag. The muscles in his arms were too big for a sick man, his heavy legs were too wide under the sheets.

My mother held his left hand. She bent his fingers around hers and she prayed. "Hail Mary full of Grace, the Lord is with thee. Blessed art thou—"

Dad's head tipped to his shoulder. Still praying, she touched his face. "You've got to stop killing yourself," I said and started to pray along with her.

———————

From the kitchen window I watched the sun slip behind the trees. Almost all the leaves had fallen. A pile had blown against the garage and back fence. On the stove Mom cooked hamburgers in a black frying pan. She opened a can of beans with the electric can opener and poured them in a pot. Louise, still dressed like a little Swiss girl, went to the refrigerator and brought a loaf of bread to the table. "He shouldn't have been drinking so much," she said. "And he was always smoking those cigars. Everyone thinks they're not as bad as cigarettes but Mr. Newton, my science teacher, says they can be just as bad. It depends if you inhale or not and I know he inhaled because he used to blow the smoke out his nose."

Smoke rose from the frying meat and floated around the ceiling.

Mom washed her hands.

"And do you remember the way he ate eggs?" asked Louise. "He ate about ten eggs a week. That's the worst thing you can do. It builds up your cholesterol level and clogs up the veins and arteries. Then, the heart has to pump harder to get the blood circulating." She sat down. "Did he say anything?"

"No."

The phone rang, my mother picked up. "Hello, yes."
She smiled. "He is," she nodded to us. "OK, at seven.
Thanks so much for calling."

"What is it?" asked Louise.

"It was the doctor. Your father was asking about us."

I drove the big Buick back to the hospital on the same
road we had driven that morning. It had stopped raining but the roads were still wet. The car smelled like
my father. It was a mix of after-shave and stale cigar.
Louise was in the backseat trying to think of a poem
for a get-well card she had made out of construction
paper. She kept mumbling, "Roses are red and violets
are blue." Mom looked into her compact mirror that
lit up and put on lipstick. "When I was dating your
father," she said, snapping the case closed, "we drove
on this road to Long Island for picnics. Compared to
the Bronx it was like the country. Could you imagine
him and me on a motorcycle?"

Louise leaned over the seat, "You rode on his motorcycle?"

"My parents didn't know. He parked it at the gas
station around the corner and walked to my house. He
loved that motorcycle and was always explaining how
the motor worked and that it had special tires, but I
couldn't tell one bike from another. One time we were
on the parkway and guess who was riding next to us?
My father on the way home from work. I tugged on
Bill's jacket and we pulled over. My father made me
drive home with him. He was so strict with me, and
Bill was so mad. He took off like a maniac. Oh, that
bike was noisy."

"I never heard that story," I said.

"You've got to understand that your father used to make me the happiest woman in the country, the happiest woman in the world. Anything," she turned and faced Louise, "he ever tried to do, he did for us."

"What happened to the motorcycle?" asked Louise.

"He sold it when we were married to keep the peace. It went toward a down payment on the house. Things used to be simpler. No one divorced, or separated, you just kept going, figuring things out as they came up. When Charlie was born, we didn't even have a crib. You spent your first week in a blanket-lined fruit crate. We lived day to day but it was a better life, there were more laughs, more good times."

"We have good times," said Louise.

Mom wiped her eyes. "Your father and I are old now and it's a whole different world."

"No, it's not," she said, putting her hand on Mom's shoulder.

Outside, the oncoming traffic flashed by. I entered the Midtown Tunnel and gave the big car the gas. It responded with power, gripping the road as no small car could. Dents, broken windows, not even a beating had killed the Buick. It didn't feel as though we were going sixty miles an hour. There wasn't a shudder in the steering wheel, no rattles anywhere. During the gas crisis Dad had stored five-gallon gas cans in the garage and drove at sixty-five, whizzing by cars with a satisfied grin. But, now it was a whole different world.

"I thought you weren't coming," said Dad, trying to lift himself off the flat mattress. The green dot above his head registered a steady heartbeat. He coughed and the dot jumped. The color had returned to his face. He pulled himself higher in the bed and the suction cups were almost popping off his chest.

Louise looked as though she was going to faint. Her eyes were open wide and she was pulling her lips into her mouth. She handed him the card. "I made it," she said.

"Thank you," he opened the envelope clumsily with his free hand. "Roses are red, life is a riot. You better get better, and watch your diet." He put his hand on the back of her neck and kissed her cheek.

"How do you feel?" Mom sat on the side of the bed. Louise moved back against the curtain and stood like a soldier.

"Tired. Everytime I fall asleep they wake me up to take my blood pressure or give me a pill." I couldn't help smiling. Same old Dad. "And my stupid son stands there with a grin on his face."

"Well, I'm glad to see your back to your old rotten self."

"Charlie, why don't you smuggle me in a slice of pizza. I'm starving."

"Honey, you're on an I.V.," said Mom.

"They call this food," he said, lifting his hand. The bruise had gotten larger and had turned almost black.

"I'm sure the doctors know what they're doing."

"I'm not," Dad shot back. "I'm not even sure I want to spend the night here. I keep on thinking about everything going on out there and it's going so damn fast. I don't know what's going to happen." He looked at our faces. The doctors must have had him on some kind of drug. His eyes looked far away. "I keep thinking, if I stay here tonight maybe I won't wake up in the morning." It sounded like the confession of a child.

"You have to stay to get better," said Mom.

"Don't you understand? I might not get out of here, not today, not tomorrow, not the next day. Do you want them to cart me out the back door?" He tried to get out of bed. The I.V. tottered and Louise caught it. I pushed him down. "Charlie, they're trying to take my job."

A nurse rushed in with two orderlies and grabbed his wrists. The green dot was in a frenzy. "Mr. Patterson, relax, you have to relax."

"Bill, please," said my mother sternly. She pulled Louise's face toward her. "For your daughter's sake."

A security guard in a blue uniform came in. "I'm a cop, too," moaned Dad. "I just wanted to go home." He fell back into bed.

Canvas straps were fastened to his arms and legs. "Sometimes you got to show 'em that you're not fooling around," said Dad closing his eyes. "I don't let nobody push me or my family around." The straps were tightened and he strained his arms upward, fingers reaching. There was no fear on his face, only confusion.

———————

"Charlie," said my mother, opening my bedroom door. "Tracy's on the phone. Should I tell her you're sleeping?"

"No, no." In the dark room my digital clock-radio flashed 11:47. It felt like the middle of the night. I put my pants on and tripped over my construction boots. "Shit."

"She shouldn't call at this hour."

———————

I waited for her in front of the diner, my head filled with sleep. I kept the Buick running so that the car would be warm. The glass door opened, and out came Tracy wearing a short rabbit fur coat over her black uniform. She was holding a blue suitcase. She came down the five steps unsteadily, leaning so heavily to one side that it seemed her arm would pop out of its socket. I hopped out and took the suitcase from her hand. It was unusually heavy. "Hi, Charlie, thanks for coming up." There was a tiredness in her voice as if she just walked miles and miles.

"That's OK, is your car broken?"

"No, I got dropped off."

I placed the suitcase on the backseat and opened her door. She slid in, her nylon stockings caught the diner light and shimmered.

I eased the Buick into traffic. Tracy slipped off a white rubber-soled shoe and rubbed her foot. She looked as if she were ready to cry. "What's going on?" I asked. "What's with the suitcase?"

"Everything is a mess, my whole life is a mess."

"Did you get fired?"

"No, but I'm quitting as soon as I find something else. Anything else." She sighed and took off her other shoe. Her hair was layer upon layer of blonde ringlets. It made her face look small.

"You did something to your hair."

"I hate it." She took an afro pick from her purse and gave each side a couple of pokes. "I had it done today for forty-five dollars. It usually costs one hundred. I don't know if you can see it," she leaned toward me. "But, it's lighter, too. It's so curly I feel like I'm wearing a hat."

"What's in the suitcase?"

"I'll tell you everything, Charlie," she put her head

on my shoulder. I smelled hair spray. "Let me just relax for a second."

"Well, I've had a humdinger of a day. My father's in the hospital, he had a heart attack."

"Oh, I'm sorry." She sat up. "Charlie, is he going to be all right?"

"Yeah, I think so. He's taking it really bad. He's so afraid of everything—doctors, the nurses." I didn't say dying, but that's what I was thinking. "They had to strap him down, Tracy. They did it right in front of Louise. She just turned thirteen in September. All this shit has got to have some kind of effect on her. She thinks there's something wrong with her physically, because she's not developing. Some girls don't get their periods until they're fifteen but how am I supposed to tell that to her?"

"I got mine when I was ten," said Tracy dreamily.

"That figures," I squeezed her leg. "And my mother tells me to talk to her. I don't know what to say. Louise likes you, did you know that? She told me that I should get back together with you. She's so fuckin' smart it's unbelievable. Do you know what she did last week? She took the back off the TV and fixed it. My father kept saying, 'Well, I'm dumbfounded.' Louise said, 'I just followed the schematic.' "

Tracy stuck her hand between my legs. It was cold. I watched the road. I was happy that she had called me.

I was starved, so Tracy made me a ham sandwich and heated some tomato soup. On the table the newspaper was opened to the comics. I glanced at them for a second, then back at her. She wore a sheer blue nightgown. I could see the outline of her yellow bikini underwear, and the curve of her breast. She stirred the soup quietly. The open can lay on top of the garbage, red soup dripping out. I closed the paper and took a bite of my sandwich. The unbuttered toast was getting dry and hard. I was still waiting for her to tell me what happened. She looked into the pot as if the words would appear from it. I unfolded a paper napkin, blew my nose, and waited.

She poured the steamy tomato soup in my bowl and sat. She lifted her tea bag up and down. The tea grew darker and darker. "Do you know what I hate?" She played with the knife in the mustard.

"What?"

"I hate it when someone gets mayonnaise in the mustard, or peanut butter in the jelly jar."

"I know, I hate that, too." I watched her intensely. "Are you going to tell me?"

"I've been living with someone. Well, not really with him. He's paying the rent here. That's why I had to break up with you."

I dropped my spoon. It splashed in the red soup. "Wait a minute, do you mean to tell me you're a mistress?"

"I don't know, yes, I guess I am."

"Who the hell is this guy?"

"You don't know him."

"Who, who is it?"

"Al."

"Al? Al Taylor?"

She nodded and pressed her knuckles into her eyes. Al? His father owned Taylor Construction. Al drove a Corvette, was about twenty-eight. He had a boat named the *Cocaine Cutter* that he drove full throttle in four-mile-an-hour canals. He was a schmuck, a rich schmuck. I picked up my plate and slid the sandwich into the garbage. I thought about pouring my soup over her head.

"So what happened?" I was trying not to lose my temper. I wanted to hear the story. Of all of the people she could have called, she had called me. "What?"

"I'm trying to get out of this whole mess. I just can't take it anymore."

I held on to the arms of the chair.

"He started living with someone," she dried her eyes with her fingers. "Don't make me tell you this. I'd just like to get out of it."

I walked into the living room. In front of the plants, I looked out the window at the deserted street corner. I wasn't sure how I was supposed to feel. Mostly I felt sick. My head was numb and my stomach was twisting. Tracy came and put her arms around my waist. All the pieces of our breakup started coming together. Her moving out and refusing to see me, the nice apartment, and all the fuckin' Rockwell Plates. "Are You OK?" she asked.

I couldn't say anything. After a minute she walked to the couch and sat with a pillow on her lap. I watched her from the reflection in the dark window. "What was in the suitcase?"

"I had some clothes at his apartment."

"What type of clothes does a mistress wear?" I imagined the suitcase was filled with garter belts, crotchless underwear, and purple negligees. "Did he give you money?"

"Sometimes."

"How much?"

"It doesn't matter."

"How much did he give you?"

"A lot, about two thousand."

The figure stunned me. I swallowed. "And it's over?"

"Well, he doesn't know yet."

———————

It was after two in the morning. I was lying on the carpet, staring at the swirls in the sand-painted ceiling. The low hum of a TV could be heard and, through the wall, came the sound of a couple making love. They had been at it for about a half hour. Tracy, propped on one elbow, watched my face and listened. The bed was banging the wall harder and harder. Someone shut the TV off. It was very quiet.

Tracy's curls fell around her face. The new blonde highlights caught the light when she moved. We had not touched since the trip from the diner. "How could you do it?" I asked. "I mean even if you didn't know me, how could you do it?"

"I just let it happen. I guess I knew what was happening all along but I didn't think about it. He made things so easy. I said I couldn't make my car payments, so he wrote a check. I didn't even ask him. And you know how much I wanted to move out? Well, he found the apartment, put up the security and the first month's rent."

"You were seeing him and me at the same time?"

"Only for about two weeks. I shouldn't have broken up with you the way I did, but he was taking me to Florida on a fishing trip. He asked me to go with him on our first date. I knew it was wrong but I couldn't say no after he'd paid for my car and apartment." She took my hand and said, "I'm sorry."

"Did you catch anything?" I felt like I was getting

eaten alive from the inside out.

"Charlie, you wouldn't believe the fish. We trolled on a private boat just like the guys on TV. I hooked a barracuda. It jumped all over the deck and the mate had to club it."

"I can't believe you did it, or would do it. God, I was such an asshole. Here I was thinking he bought you golfing equipment. That's what you told me. Remember that?"

"I didn't know what to say." She got up and sat on the couch. "Suppose you met some beautiful woman who wanted to take you away to those islands you're always talking about, what would you say?"

"Back then, when I was seeing you? I'd say no. Right now I'd go to Coney Island with a shopping-bag lady."

"You're just trying to fuck my head up. You wouldn't go anywhere ever, you're too into your family. That's one of the reasons I went on that trip, you'd never take me, you just like to dream."

"Shut up."

"You haven't hit the real world yet. I used to think that I was going to be some kind of success story, that someone would come along and dump something in my lap. I used to be a dreamer, too."

"Maybe I am a dreamer." My voice was almost breaking. I stood, "But at least I don't use people."

She pulled her knees up to her chest and wrapped her arms around them. "I'm tired," she said. "And I'll be on me feet all day tomorrow."

"I should go home, I've got to think about everything."

"Will you call me?"

My mind said, yes, but I said, "Maybe."

CHAPTER
10

It was breakfast hour at the Emerald Diner and the counter stools were full. I went down the aisle and nodded to an Electrolux vacuum cleaner salesman who had hit our house last month. "How's your mother's machine? Does she need bags?" He had been eating eggs and there was yolk on the corners of his mouth.

"Fine, I don't think she needs bags." I took a card from his hand.

"Let me see," he gazed up like a mystic. The black toupee on his head looked so much like a cheap rug I wondered why he bothered. "Patterson, right?"

"Yup." He either had an amazing memory or sold only one vacuum cleaner a year.

"Tell your mother I'll be stopping by. Did she get the new drape attachment?"

"I don't know." I tried to give him the brush.

"That's everyone's favorite." He smiled and nodded his head as if to say, listen, you little wise guy I'm just trying to make a living. "Yeah, I'll be by sometime next week," he said.

"I'll tell her."

Down the counter, I passed a guy with a jogging suit. Supposedly, he ran to the diner every day, ate, and walked back. Further down was the highway crew. Paul, dressed like the others in dark green pants and a light green shirt, was hunched over a bowl of hot cereal and had his finger hooked through his coffee cup. I gave him a poke in the ribs. He spun around and spilled his coffee across the counter. "Sorry about that," I said.

"You're lucky refills are on the house." We shook hands using the old locking thumb grip. "What's up with you?"

"Not too much. What have you been doing?"

"Just hanging out. We had a hooker at the firehouse last night. Did ten guys for thirty bucks. She was some fucking sled-puller, though."

"When you gonna shave this thing? You look like you ought to be eating cans." I gave his goatee a tug. The other men laughed.

I slipped into a booth, and Maria, a heavy-thighed Puerto Rican girl, came to take my order. Occasionally she had worked nights with Tracy, "Hey, Charlie, what are you doing here so early?" she said taking out her order pad from an apron pocket.

"Let's cut the small talk," I said like a gangster. "And give me the usual." I didn't feel like gabbing or explaining. I had left the house with my mother thinking I was off to college. I didn't want to lie twice in fifteen minutes.

"What's the usual?"

"Two clucks wrecked, a stack of shingles, and a cup of black Joe."

"What?" she laughed.

"Two scrambled eggs, pancakes, and coffee, some toast, too." She swished away, laughing, pantyhose rubbing, her uniform riding up her ass.

Yesterday they had taken Dad out of intensive care and moved him by ambulance, against doctor's orders, to our town hospital. Last night he had been in good spirits and was talking about coming home, "I feel fine, like a million dollars. Hospitals are for sick people. Do I look sick?"

I went to the cashier and bought a newspaper. I figured I had better start looking for a job. My summer savings were down to four-hundred dollars, and I would have felt a lot better if I were an employed dropout.

In the classified section I was overwhelmed with ads.

> Have Legacy?
> Why wait! Funds to heirs
> Legacy Funding Corporation

> Buy a Job
> Auto-loan Offices
> Earn a Min. $40,000 a year
> Lending our Money.

I turned the pages looking for the want ads and found Offers to Buyers, Buyers Wanted, Career Training and

four pages of Employment Agencies. Paul passed by with
the men in green and leaned on my table. "You're not
looking for a job?" I gave him a dumb look. "Shit, we
got a guy retiring. Come in with us."

"I appreciate the offer but, I don't know, I think I'd
like to work in the city." I surprised myself with that
one.

"Doing what?"

"Something in sales," I said, looking at the Electrolux man.

"I thought you were in college."

"I quit."

Paul nodded his head as if it were what he had
expected. "Well," he said, "You're not going to find
any sales jobs in that paper. Look in Sunday's *New York
Times*." He stroked his chin hairs. "I'll tell you though,
there's not much around. I've been doing a little looking myself."

"Really?"

"Sure have." He waddled toward the door. Joey was
trying to find another job? I was astonished.

Maria came, balancing a plate of eggs on her forearm,
a cup of coffee in her hand. "You see Tracy anymore?"
she asked sliding the food to the table.

"Yeah, we see each other."

"Really?" She made a face as if she had smelled
something sour.

"Why, what's the matter?"

"Nothing," she said, lumbering away.

"You forgot my pancakes and toast," I called. Maria
gave me a look, and I knew she knew about Al and the
arrangements with Tracy.

When Maria came back I wanted to explain that Tracy

didn't want to see Al anymore, and that it was all a big
mistake that she let happen. She's not like that really,
I wanted to say. Instead, I salted my eggs, rolled up a
piece of soggy, over-buttered toast, and started shoveling everything down.

———————

Our town hospital was a small three-story building
in the middle of an exclusive neighborhood. The two-
lane street that wound to the entrance was wider than
Fifth Avenue in Manhattan and had center islands with
grass and trees. Every other house had a shingle on a
white post that said D.D.S., M.D., or some similar
combination. On a stroll down the block one could get
braces, a flu shot, knee surgery, or an abortion. I pulled
the Buick into a tight spot in the lot between a Mercedes
Benz and a Porsche. The sign said, Official Parking Only,
but my father had enough P.B.A. and D.E.A. cards on
his dash to get into a presidential motorcade.

I walked down the indoor-outdoor carpeted hospital
halls, peaking into the rooms from the corner of my
eyes. There was an old man in a wheelchair watching
a nurse change the sheets, a black man twisted on his
side with his face in a pillow, a girl with black eyes and
a big nose-bandage sat watching TV. I passed a room
where a kid was gluing a plastic airplane model together.
I went back. He had his leg in a cast. It was lifted off
the bed by a nylon rope that ran over a pulley and was
attached to a dangling weight. Carefully, with his tongue
darting around his bottom lip, he lined the edge of a
wing with cement. He glanced up. He was a real rough-
tumble type looking kid. "What happened?" I asked.

"I broke my leg playing football. I used to be a quart-
erback for the Randle Rams."

"That's a tough break," I said.

"Very funny." He had red hair, pink skin, orange freckles, and squinty blue eyes. "You want to do me a big favor," he said.

"Sure."

"Turn on the TV. My mother told the nurses I could watch it only two hours a day. She expects me to do homework all day."

The control was lying six feet away on the window sill. That was torture. I handed it to him and he flipped stations and found some cartoons. "Fan mail from some flounder?" asked Bullwinkle in his dumb moose voice. Rocky, the flying squirrel, zipped around the sky and landed on a snowcapped mountain. "No, this is what I really called a message," he squeaked.

"I'd let you sign my cast but no one's allowed to." He pressed the wing to the fuselage and glue oozed around the seal. "This is my first plane," he explained. "I usually do cars."

"You've got to use less glue." I wanted to sit down and help him but I felt a little weird. I have that adult phobia about fooling around with kids when you're not their uncle or something. "My father's sick, so I guess I'll be seeing you," I said.

"I guess so." He knocked on his cast.

At the elevator, I pressed floor three and thought of the retarded kid at the Police Academy. Vince had pushed him out of the way and everyone had crowded into the elevator around the stretcher. Dad was moaning and the kid started yelling, "No, no," as the doors shut. I hadn't been any help at all. I just stood near the buttons as if *I* were retarded. I had run across the street with them and was left standing in the emergency room entrance.

On the outside of Dad's door, a sign said, "B. Patterson," and under that "G. Williams." I stepped in.

Dad was sitting in bed eating a bowl of something white, maybe oatmeal. He looked up. "Charlie," he whispered. "Is there a fat, redheaded nurse in the hall?"

"No."

"Good. Dump this in the toilet." He handed me the bowl. I swirled the soggy kernels around. "That goddamn redheaded nurse has orders to drug me."

"Oh, come on."

"You eat that crap and you'll not only shit your brains out but you'll be too tired to wipe yourself."

"They wouldn't put it in your food."

"Yes, they would. I refused my horse tranquilizer today. They're trying to keep me in bed."

I poured it in the toilet bowl and flushed it away.

"These are the things I need," he handed me a list written on the back of a get-well card.

    A jar of Instant Coffee
    Peanuts
    3 boxes of Candy
    TV Guide
    Cigars
    2 bottles of Rye

He moved his feet, and I sat on the end of the bed. "And tell your mother to bring me whatever she makes for supper."

I read the list aloud. "Are you kidding me?"

"The candy is for the nurses."

"Well, that makes a big difference."

He leaned into his pillows. "You know I didn't show your mother that list because I knew she wouldn't bring me a damn thing."

"Neither will I."

"Just see what you can do."

"I'll bring you the food."

"No balls," he smiled. "You piss sitting down, too?"

"Dad, don't pull that shit." I ripped the card and threw it in the trash. "It's not going to work," I leaned around the curtain and in the next bed was the skinniest man I have ever seen. He wore only a hospital gown, his knees were the size of baseballs. His head was on a pillow and he stared steadily from sunken sockets.

"How do you do?" he said formally.

"Good, how are you?"

"I've had more exciting days."

I pulled my head out of the curtain.

"He's paralyzed," said Dad quietly. "From a stroke. Can't move a goddamn finger. He used to be a teacher. Last night he recited the Bible for an hour. 'Mine eyes fill with tears, my bowels are troubled, my liver is poured upon the earth because children are running in the streets,' or something like that. It was nice to hear. Your mother is gonna love him."

"Do you want me to bring you a Bible?"

"A Bible?" He made a face and put another pillow behind his back. "Did anyone tell you I'm going to die?"

"No."

"Well my bowels are going on and off like a city fire hydrant and my liver must be shot," he laughed. From the nightstand drawer he took out a cigar and unwrapped it. "Connections," he said. "I had it smuggled in."

"You shouldn't be smoking."

"No smoking, no drinking, no solid foods. I bet you'd like me to be a vegetable." He pointed to the next bed. "He doesn't even shit." He licked the end of it and lit up. "Don't tell your mother." He puffed and the smoke curled around the white room.

"It's your life. If you want to kill yourself, be my guest." I thought reverse psychology would work.

"Thank you," he said.

"Is that a cigar I smell?" asked Williams in his clear voice.

We both froze.

"Do you have an extra?"

Dad got out of bed and whisked the curtain aside. The muscles on the sides of his spine showed through the back of his hospital gown.

"I've smoked quite a few of those in my day," winked the old man.

"You really want to smoke this?" asked Dad.

"Please."

Dad put the cigar in Williams' mouth.

The old man moved it around in his teeth and puffed.

"Well, you enjoy it," said Dad. He wheeled the breakfast tray to Williams' chin so that the ashes fell on the formica table. "When you're finished, just holler."

"It's got a beautiful aroma," he said.

"They're DeNobli. I've been smoking them since I was twenty." Dad swung his hairy legs back into bed.

"Boy, if a nurse comes in, you two have had it."

"I believe she would have a coronary," said Williams.

Dad and I watched the old man puff the cigar. There was nothing left of him except a voice and two alert eyes. The skin on his head was stretched around his skull and his thin lips were white from the tightness. "Do you know, this cigar is the first enjoyment I've suffered since my arrival six months ago? It will be six months tomorrow. Six months of severe disappointment. Would you believe I walked in here on two almost sturdy legs." Dad's face went white. "No, I'm no advertisement for modern medicine."

A short time later, when the cigar was about half smoked, it tumbled out of his mouth and rolled on the breakfast tray.

———————

Dad and I watched TV for the rest of the afternoon, marking off the half hours by using the shows as a clock. During "Gilligan's Island" the redheaded nurse came in. "Mr. P., it's pill and temperature time."

"This is the one I was telling you about," said Dad. "Miss Marlboro Country."

She was a big woman whose uniform stretched around her rear like the skin of a drum. With the flick of her wrist the curtain raced around the ceiling track enclosing them.

From behind the curtain Dad said, "No kinky stuff. In the mouth."

"Roll over, honey, or else I'll have to roll you over." Her head popped out of the curtain. "He's our biggest baby."

Dad hummed the Marlboro cigarette song and said, "Come to where the freshness is."

"You said the same thing this morning and it's not very funny."

"I thought it was humorous," said Williams from behind his curtain.

"You're next," she called.

When everything was finished she kissed Dad on the forehead, looked at me, and pointed to the hallway. "Give him the treatment," said Dad.

In the hallway she said, "Try to keep him in bed and calm. He's not as well as he wants you to think."

"He things you're drugging him."

"We are," she laughed and touched my arm. "Tranquilizers to keep his blood pressure down." She gave my cheek a squeeze and went buffaloing up the hall.

In the middle of "Wonder Woman" (Linda Carter had three bank robbers locked in a safe), my mother came in carrying a brown paper bag. A second later, Louise popped in with her school books in her arms and a wrapped present on top. "How are you today?" asked Mom. "Did you have any pain?" She unbuttoned a collarless wool jacket.

"Pain in the ass."

"Well, he hasn't had any pain since I've been here," I said.

Louise kissed him on the cheek. "I made you a cake, but it was so burnt I threw it out," she said. "I set the oven at three-twenty-five but I forgot to turn it to bake."

"She broiled it," said Mom. "But she made a meatloaf for tonight's dinner."

"I had mush for lunch," said Dad.

Louise gave him the present. Dad's eyes lit as he tore away the paper. "I didn't know what to get you."

It was a Rubic's Cube puzzle, the type of puzzle that drives you out of your mind. In four turns Dad had lost the one solution out of a million combinations. He tried

to get the colors matched again, and Louise said, "That's
it, mess it up real good and I'll bet you I can solve it in
less than a minute." Dad continued turning, and Louise
took her off her coat. Her shirt said, "The Grey Panthers" and had two canes crossed behind a snarling cat.
"They gave these out at the last meeting," she said,
showing it off. "They're going to have a march on
Washington next month."

She solved the puzzle in fifty-two seconds. We all
took turns trying. My mother managed to get two sides,
Dad and I had trouble with one side.

"You didn't hear anything," asked Dad, turning the
puzzle. "No mail from the department?"

"Nothing."

"I might have to get myself a lawyer."

"I think you should retire." Mom took a plastic container from the bag and opened it. "I brought you a
salad. I checked with the doctor. You're going back to
solid food in a couple of days."

Louise looked behind the curtain. "Let him sleep," I
said.

"There's only one problem: I don't want to retire.
What the hell will I do, sit home with Charlie all day?"
While he ate, Mom held the dish so that it didn't slide
around the tray. "Charlie over there will have to support us," he laughed. "When he gets out of college he
can administer a business. What kind of business are
you going to administrate?"

"If I open a zoo, you could be the main attraction and
I'd just have to supply the bananas."

"Joy, did you know he was learning to run a zoo?"

"Yes."

"You did?" He stuffed a piece of lettuce in his mouth and took a slice of white bread from the nightstand. The little drawer looked like a condiment table at Nathan's. It was filled with mustard, ketchup, salt, pepper, and tea bags.

"What are you opening? A restaurant?" I asked.

"Joy, put them in the bag and take them home."

"We have enough at the house," said Mom.

"Oh, all of a sudden we have everything?"

"We're not a welfare case," I said.

"You don't use ketchup?"

"We have a full bottle at home."

"You don't use ketchup?"

"You know I use it."

"OK, then keep your mouth shut. When you don't use ketchup, then you can talk."

"You make me sick."

"Charlie, please." Mom sat there filling the bag with the little containers of sugar and relish. I wanted to fling it across the room.

"No, he makes me sick."

"Then call a nurse." He pushed the salad away and turned the cube not even watching the colors.

Louise was behind the curtain talking to Williams. I slipped through the opening.

"You two are just like little boys," I heard Mom say.

"It's an organization for the protection of senior citizens." explained Louise. "We have a slogan from a song by the Hollies. It's, 'She's not heavy, she's your mother,' or if it's a man, 'He's not heavy, he's your father.' " Williams smiled and Louise sat on the corner of the bed. "We have our meetings at the Senior Center. The oldest member is a hundred and two. He's the honorary president," she giggled. "He's not exactly all there, and he's very funny."

"You're an extraordinary girl," said Williams.

"I'm the youngest member," said Louise proudly.

"I had a daughter," said Williams. "She died in an automobile collision. She was an accomplished violinist and cellist at the age of sixteen." He breathed heavily. "Are you musical?"

"No."

"Nor I," said Williams.

"Well I'm sure you can play the radio," said Louise smiling.

———————

I drove Louise home. Mom stayed behind doing the night shift. On the way out of the hospital, I stopped by the redheaded kid's room. "How did you make out?" I called from the doorway.

"Not too good." The model sat on the window sill. One wing was off and the other had drooped. I went in, followed by Louise. "This is my mother," the kid said.

The TV was off and school books were open on the bed tray. "I was helping him with the plane," I said.

"Thank you," she said.

"This is my sister."

"Hi," said Louise.

It was awkward. "I'll see you tomorrow." I backed out of the room. The unfinished model made me feel sad. What he needed were a couple of rubber bands to hold the wings in place while the glue hardened. My father had always helped me with my models.

———————

On the way home we pulled up to Sal's Pizza. Louise said she had to get something from Dee and was meeting her inside. The place was in a mini mall. The line of ten stores had put most of the mom-and-pop businesses out of business. On Long Island one-stop shopping is the be all, end all. In front of the steamy glass window, there were six teenagers on bull-handled ten-speed bikes. They were expensive racers with alloy frames and aluminum rims. Louise weaved through them and went in.

Years ago, I had sat in Sal's sucking ice from a Coke cup, my friends passing cigarettes around like joints, steaming them down to the filters. The pizza had tasted like cardboard. Sal used only the cheapest ingredients. The kids on the bikes whizzed out of the parking lot, gears clicking faintly. Their red reflectors flashed in the headlights of the passing traffic. Louise came out and got in the car. "Let's go," she said.

The pizza joint's door banged open and Dee came running out. She was an overdeveloped fourteen year old with braces and too much makeup over her eyes. I liked her; she could never sit still and was always over reacting to everything. "Don't be so sensitive all the time," she said through the window. "Micky's just a big jerk." Louise didn't look up. Dee rolled her eyes. "I'll get you an invitation."

"I wouldn't go now if you paid me."

"God, Louueese," she whined. "I'll come over tonight, OK?"

"I might not be home."

"Where are you going?"

"To Hollywood. I don't know."

I started the engine. "Then I'll call you," said Dee.

We pulled out of the parking lot. I wanted to put my arm around Louise, but I kept my distance. An older brother's arm at a time like this wouldn't do much good. "Don't let it get to you," I said, punching her in the leg.

"Why not?" She gave me a shot as hard as she could and folded her arms. "I guess I'll look back and laugh at this, right?"

"No," I said. She was too smart to believe that.

I stopped at the record store. She didn't ask where I was going or what I was doing. A couple of minutes later, I came out with an album. On the cover was a blurry photograph of a fat guy wearing dark sunglasses and a blonde in a V-neck sweater. It looked like a photo from my parents' high school yearbook.

Out in the car I handed the record to Louise. "Thanks," she said, giving me a shot in the arm. "I can't believe you remembered."

———————

If I could describe Louise's meat loaf in one word, it would have to be "burp." I didn't know anyone could mess up a meatloaf. At supper I had called it "spicy."

"You don't like it?" asked Louise.

"It's good and spicy," I said.

Dee came over. Louise scraped her plate into the garbage, and then the two of them went up to her room. I did the dishes and left them in the rack to dry. I had just finished paging through the paper, reading only headlines. I looked at the phone, hoping Tracy would call. Slim chance. She worked until midnight on Wednesdays and the Greeks gave her only two fifteen-minute breaks.

Everytime I thought about her and Al, that sick feeling crept into my stomach. "It's over," I said. "He's history." I called Tracy's apartment just to make sure she wasn't home. I counted twenty rings and hung up.

I went into the living room and lay on the rug. It was thick and smelled like a new car. My mother didn't let anyone in the room unless company came. I closed my eyes and tried to picture Tracy waiting on tables in her black-and-white uniform, bending to clean a spill, the dark tops of her pantyhose showing. Tracy once told me that any woman who wore stockings instead of pantyhose probably had a yeast infection. Tracy was kind of crazy. She claimed the reason imported cars were better was that they were made by smaller people. She told me that if you didn't fart once a day you'd die. She liked to analyze questions like, If a tree fell in the forest, and no one was there to hear it, would it make a noise?, or, How do you know that everything isn't an exact duplicate? I decided to go to the diner.

The sky was black and clear. My breath hung in the air for a second and then disappeared. The diner was a good two miles away. I figured I'd kill some time and walk. She could give me a ride home. The upstairs shade was open at my neighbor's house. My childhood sweetheart, Maryanne, was hanging clothes in the closet. We had gone through grammar and high school together. I stepped into the curb for a better view. I thought she was away at fancy-smancy Skidmore College. She pulled her T-shirt over her head. Cupping my hands, I yelled, "Hey Maryanne, put some clothes on."

She dove for the shade and I began laughing. She was so prim and proper, so refined and cultured, she'd probably dress in the closet for the rest of her life.

A half hour later, still smiling over Maryanne's little tits, I hopped up the steps of the Emerald. The night crowd sat in the booths and left the counter empty. I walked past the stools, giving each one a spin, and took a spot in front of the dessert case. A four-layer vanilla cake with a piece missing revolved on a glass stand. Below, lemon meringue, apple, peach, Boston cream, and blueberry pie, their insides spilling onto the plates, glistened under the fluorescent lights. My mouth started watering.

"Charlie."

"Hey, Tracy." Above her lip was a bead of perspiration. "It's busy tonight."

"Not too bad." She spun a chair around and sat. "Your face is all red."

"I walked."

"In that coat?" She shook my windbreaker. "You're going to catch pneumonia." She examined her order pad. "I'm so tired that I'm messing up orders. I'm going to quit, my ankles are starting to swell. Next thing you know, I'll have varicose veins." She shoved the pad into an apron pocket stuffed with receipts.

"You look tired."

"I am. I met this guy tonight and he told me he'd give me a job as a barmaid out at the Beehive. I could make my week's salary in one weekend."

"But that's such a shitty job."

"I know." She stretched her left leg into the aisle. It was long and muscular. "I'm off in an hour. Do you want to come back to my place and give me a massage?"

"OK."

Tracy had the grillman make me a special double-decker bacon cheeseburger with tomato and lettuce. It took two hands to pick that monster up and I could barely get my mouth around it.

———————————

Tracy stood on the off-white rug, arms at her side, head leaning on her shoulder. "Did you do anything about Al?" I asked unzipping the back of her uniform.

"No." She pulled her arm through, wiggled, and the dress fell to her ankles. "That job's going to make me old." She turned and put her arms around my neck.

"You didn't see him today?"

"No." She kissed me and I unhooked her bra. She slipped it off and threw it on the couch. She wore only pantyhose over black bikini underwear.

"Did he call you?"

"Charlie, stop it," she whined.

She lay on her stomach. I knelt over her and rubbed the muscles near her neck. "It's going to take time," she said. "I've got to figure it out for myself."

"You will stop seeing him?"

"Yes, I told you that." I wondered when. "He's not the easiest person in the world to talk to and I'm pretty far into this thing. To tell the truth, he's a spoiled brat."

I pressed my thumbs in small circles and the red impressions from her bra strap faded. I rubbed her back until the muscles in my hands ached.

I peeled the pantyhose off her. She rolled over and I kissed her breasts. When I began to take off my shirt, she pushed my hand away. "Let me do it," she said.

The phone rang. We both froze. "Don't answer it." I counted the rings: three, four, five.

Tracy crawled over to the phone and picked up the receiver. "Hello." She sat and faced the wall. "No , I was up," she said. "Really, did you play today? Yesterday, my ball wouldn't stay on the fairway."

Golf. Definitely Al. Fuck.

"I can't. I'm too tired tonight," she said.

"Tell him it's fuckin' two o'clock in the morning," I said.

She put her hand over the receiver and shook her head at me, then continued talking. "No, I'm really beat tonight."

I pulled the phone out of her hand and hung it up. "You're not going to chat with Al while I'm sitting here," I yelled.

"That was really stupid," she said.

The phone began to ring. "Tracy, don't answer that phone. I swear to God I'll walk right out of here if you do."

She eyed me for a second, picked up the ringing phone, and walked into her bedroom. Bam! She slammed the door, jamming the wire.

"Tracy!" I screamed. "Tracy!" She didn't answer, I raced into the kitchen and got a knife. "I'll cut the damn cord," I said, pointing a wooden-handled steak knife. "Tracy, did you hear me?" My lips were almost touching the door. "I'm gonna cut the fuckin' cord."

I held the white wire and waited for her to say something. Nothing. I threw the knife across the room. It bounced off the wall and stuck in the seat on the cane rocking chair. I tried the knob, it was locked. The crack under the door went dark. "Tracy, what are you doing?" I said trying to sound calm.

"Right now I'm sleeping."

"Open the door!"

"I'm sleeping."

Shit. I marched around the room and considered wrecking the place. Throwing every goddamn Rockwell collector plate out the fuckin' window. "You know I'm not wrong." I yelled. "I'm not. What do you want me to do, crawl around here like a dog? Well, I can't do it, Tracy. I'm sorry but I can't do it." I went over to the door again. "Will you open this thing?"

"You were wrong," she said. "And I'm trying to sleep."

I threw a magazine on the floor, stood there raging for a moment, then grabbed my coat and left. The apartment door locked behind me.

───────────

I stood in the street looking up at her window, waiting for the light to go on. She knew I had gone. The door had slammed so hard that something crashed to the floor. A group of cars sped by. It was cold. My unlined windbreaker wasn't much good. "Tracy," I said, hopping up and down. "Please. Don't do this." After five minutes I began to walk, not home, but to the hospital.

A sliver of moon hid behind the clouds. As I passed the street lights, my shadow grew small and then large. The houses were dark. Cars were parked in the driveways, bicycles and children's toys lay on the porches. I went to the center of the road and looked back. There were no headlights in sight. At the corner, I stepped on the remains of a black dog. It was flat and hard as leather. Tire marks creased the matted fur. A row of crushed white teeth was implanted in the asphalt.

I began to run. Along the curb, brown plastic leaf bags waited for the morning collection. I kicked one, it tore easily. The leaves spilled into the street. I zig-zagged back and forth, kicking the bags. It was either Al or me. I wasn't going to crawl.

———————

At the hospital an old woman at the switchboard told me it was too late to visit any of the patients. She adjusted her earphones over her thin blue hair. "I'm sorry, I don't make the rules."

"You don't understand. This is my father and it's an emergency."

"Do you know what time it is:" Her washed-out eyes fixed on my face.

"Yes. It's three-thirty in the morning and I just walked three miles to get here."

"Well, then you know it is too late for visiting."

Up the hall a security guard sat in a wheelchair reading the paper. I gave up.

I collapsed in the lobby on a vinyl couch. I put my feet on a windowbox full of shriveled plants with leaves like brown tissue paper. The soil was so hard it had cracked. The air smelled like cafeteria food. I considered calling Tracy but she could use that phone like a deadly weapon. She might hang up or let it ring and ring. I wondered if she was out looking for me. I opened an old *Smithsonian* magazine and read an article about hurricanes and typhoons. Mostly, I looked at the pictures of flattened houses, bent palm trees, and boats sitting in the middle of the street.

———————

I woke up with my face pressing the couch, my hands gripping the armrest. I had dreamed that I was at a party. Everyone kept telling me to leave and I couldn't find my way out. I just kept bumping into guests saying I'm sorry, excuse me.

The sun was rising. The grey light of the new day was dim. The overhead fluorescent lights overpowered the sun and shone on the spotless marble floor. I got up. My back hurt. I walked right past the switchboard operator and hurried to the elevator.

Dad's bed was empty. It was too early for lab tests and I remembered what the nurse had said about keeping him in bed. The great escape. I didn't put it past him. I backed through the curtain and shook Williams' shoulder. He woke instantly, opening his eyes as if spring-controlled. I asked him if he knew where my father was. The old man turned white. He stared with frightened eyes, not moving a muscle.

The toilet flushed. I pushed the curtain back and Dad came out of the bathroom wearing a hospital bib, the *Daily News* tucked under his arm and a cigar in the corner of his mouth. "Damn thing is so high it makes your legs fall asleep." he said.

"I thought you might have escaped."

"What time is it?" He studied me. "What are you doing here so early?"

"I figured I'd drop over before school."

"You look like hell. What's the matter?"

"Nothing." I sat in a chair and he lay on the bed. "I woke Williams up and I must have scared him to death."

"He's had another stroke," said Dad. "He can't talk. Now he's completely paralyzed. Can't even move his lips. They're going to transfer him someplace."

A gurgle came from the mouth of the old man. Dad pulled the curtain to the wall. "You trying to say something?" asked Dad.

"Can't they do anything?" I watched Williams' face. His eyes were straining to look at me.

"They took him somewhere last night. A couple of
nurses brought him back twenty minutes ago. I'll tell
you, I don't think I've slept an uninterrupted hour since
I've been here."

Williams gurgled again.

Dad climbed out of bed. He went to Williams' side
and held his hand. "You trying to say something?" His
voice was gentle, like a young father talking to his
infant. He leaned over, his flower-print boxer shorts
showed through the back of his gown. He put his ear
to Williams' mouth. "What?"

The old man gurgled. It sounded like a noise from a
dentist's office.

"I don't know." said Dad, straightening up. "Maybe
he wants some of this cigar."

"It wouldn't be too good for him."

"Who the hell cares if it's good for him?"

We sat on the sides of the bed taking turns holding
the cigar in his mouth. Williams took up almost no
room at all. The smoke went in his mouth and out his
nose. Although there was no real expression on his face,
I thought he was enjoying the cigar. He was breathing
harder and faster. His yellow-rimmed eyes stared at us.
"I wish it were a real Cuban Cigar," said Dad. "Those
Cubans know how to roll a cigar."

Williams blinked twice.

"It might be Morse code," I said.

"I used to know it when I was in the Army." Dad
flicked the ash on the floor. Williams blinked three
times, and Dad put the cigar back in his mouth. "Wish
I had a book on Morse code." Williams blinked once.
"But who the hell knows, he might just be getting
smoke in his eyes." He looked at Williams, "Right?"

He blinked.

"Blink twice if you can hear me," I said.

He didn't blink.

"Blink once."

He blinked.

"I don't know," said Dad.

Dad and I kept this up for about five minutes. Sometimes Williams blinked, sometimes he didn't. The cigar grew too small to hold. Dad threw it in the toilet. "I hope the nurse sees it. I'll tell her Williams smoked it."

I pulled the sheet to the old man's chest. He shut his eyes. "Tommorow I'll rake the leaves," I said, thinking about the damage I had done to those bags.

"If I hadn't had this goddamn heart attack, they would already be carted away."

"Well, I'll do it tomorrow."

"Maybe you should take it easy, you don't look so hot. You feel all right?"

"Not that good," I said, getting choked up. I could feel it in my eyes.

"Hey, what's the matter."

"Nothing."

"We can leave those leaves for the spring. It's no big deal. You shouldn't be here this early. What time is it, anyway."

"About six."

"Six. Jesus, I thought it was about nine. You lose all your senses in the hospital. You don't know whether you're coming or going."

"I guess it makes going a little easier." I said.

There was a gurgle from the next bed.

"Sorry, pal, I'm out of cigars," said Dad. When I didn't

smile he said, "Hey, that's a joke."

A nurse came in carrying a tray, looked at me, at
Dad, then at Williams. "Hello, honey," said Dad. She
was young and cute. Her black hair was tucked under
her cap. "This is my son, Charlie. Charlie, this is Miss
U.S.A."

"It's nice to meet you, but visiting hours haven't
started yet."

"Really? I didn't know that," I said, hoping she'd let
me stay.

"Well, now you do." She picked up Williams' wrist
and looked at her watch. He started blinking. Maybe
he was in pain. "Was anyone smoking in here?" she
asked, sniffing the air.

"Williams is a chain smoker," I said.

"He's old enough to smoke," said Dad smiling.

"Mr. Patterson, smoking is against hospital policy
and your doctor's orders."

"Ask my son."

"Your son has to leave." She put the old man's arm
under the sheet.

"Who voted you Miss U.S.A.?" I asked. We locked
eyes, and she walked out of the room.

I stalled for a couple of minutes saying goodbye to
Dad. I really didn't want to leave. "Get some rest," he
said, grabbing me around the neck. "And see if you can
smuggle me in a bottle of something nice."

That day a letter came from the police department. I
opened it. Mom and I were opening all his mail.

Detective Williams Charles Patterson,
    John Canon, the New York City Police Depart-
ment's Chief of Operations, and the Board of Investi-

gation have ruled, after careful review of police station claims and your duty conduct on October 17, 1979, suspension of pay upon recovery from the cardio-infarction suffered on October 27, 1979. The police medical examiner will determine this date.

A hearing will then be scheduled by the Manhattan Supreme Court Justice Michael Chimera. If you are found guilty of misconduct or abuse of authority the City of New York will not be responsible for compensatory or punitive damages sustained in civil suits heard before State or Federal Courts.

Police Commissioner

I read it over three times, then brought it into the den to show my mother. She was watching a talk show. A woman and three men in swivel chairs were discussing the benefits of vitamins. "Check this out," I said.

She crossed her long legs and held the letter to the morning sun that came through the window. "Lysine is now being used as a cure for herpes," said the woman on TV. "One thousand units a day is the usual dosage."

I shut it off.

"If he loses his case then he's on his own," I said. "They'll sue us for every cent we have."

My mother rubbed her forehead. "They couldn't send him to jail, could they?"

No one was supposed to tell my father about the letter. The doctors did not want him excited, but that night his room looked like a misplaced Detective Endowment Association meeting. There were eight men in the room. Vince was there; Peter Gorman, president of the Patrolman's Benevolent Association; Mr. Smith, the D.E.A. lawyer who was representing my father; John Haggerty, the D.E.A. president; Larry; and Sean O'Donnell, the cop I had met at the hearing. The other two men had been introduced, but I couldn't remember their names.

Dad conducted business from the cranked-up hospital bed in an undershirt, jeans, and bare feet. He puffed his cigar and waved it around when he spoke. My mother sat next to him with a worried look on her face. At one point she stood and said, "There's no smoking in here."

"Joy, this is business," Dad had said. "I've got to smoke."

Louise and I sat on Williams' bed. He had been moved downstairs to intensive care. Sean had been sent out for coffee a couple of times. Empty and half-empty containers were scattered on the floor and furniture. Almost everyone was smoking, using the paper cups as ashtrays.

Peter Gorman, a buck-toothed, thin man with a lined face, leaned over papers on the nightstand. "They can do it," he said, flipping through a book, "but, it's unlikely. Section 50 K has never been denied before. I think it's a bluff. They want you to hand your retirement papers in."

Section 50 K was a state law enacted in 1976 that made cops immune from paying civil judgments out of their own pockets for actions taken in the line of duty. Protection did not apply if a cop had abused his authority and was found guilty. This had been explained by John Haggerty. He was fat and had jowls like a bulldog. He leaned forward on the chair, his round belly bulging under his suit. "We got to be careful," he said. "They're after you, Bill. The city is being sued for two million ten thousand. If you lose your case then it's on your shoulders." The numbers, two, million, and ten seemed to float in the air.

"Well, I'm innocent," said Dad.

A chorus of "Hey, we know that, I know that" sounded around the room.

Mr. Smith paced in front of the bed. "The protection

isn't what it used to be. The court garnished a cop's pay for twenty-five months last year partly because of public pressure. They don't want to be paying damages that a cop was responsible for. It didn't happen to a city patrolman, it happened to a Nassau County cop. They lifted the garnishee last December and the state settled for five hundred thousand."

"Make sure that doesn't happen." said Dad. Everyone's eyes went from my father back to the lawyer.

Mr. Smith put his hands on the metal bedpost. "You won't lose. You have everything in your favor. You were outnumbered one thousand to one. You weren't wearing riot gear, not even a helmet, and there must be a witness somewhere."

"See that," said Haggerty.

"When everything's finished, we'll sue the city. I estimate three million for physical suffering and two million for psychological damages."

Dad smiled. He tightened his arms. Larry reached over and put his hands on the tight, round bicep. "This," he grinned. "This did the job. You don't need a weapon when you have this."

There was a knock and one of the men moved his chair so that the door could open. It was Miss Marlboro Country. "It's after visiting hours," she said. "But, I'll let three of you stay."

The men, all eight of them, began flashing their badges like cameras. "This is official business, the P.D." said Haggerty.

She didn't know what to say. Everyone was watching her. "Then stop smoking."

"You guys with the smoking," said Dad in an annoyed voice, "it's sickening." He puffed his cigar.

Everyone laughed. My mother pulled the cigar out of his mouth and dropped it in a coffee container. It sizzled, and they laughed harder. Haggerty stamped his butt on the floor.

"For heaven's sake," said the nurse. "I'll get you some ashtrays."

Before everyone left, they made a big fuss over Louise and my mother. "How did Bill ever get you?" asked Haggerty.

"Everyone makes mistakes," said Mom, gripping Dad's hand.

"And where did Louise's beautiful blue eyes come from?" asked Smith. Louise blushed.

"Oh, we found her in a milk container," said Dad.

"You did not," said Louise, playing it up.

They laughed and said goodbye. We were one big happy police department family.

────────────

Vince, Larry, my mother, Louise, and I stayed behind in the hospital room. Everyone was excited. Vince had decided to organize a fund-raiser for Dad. "With all the doctor's bills," said Vince, "you might need some extra money."

He didn't mention the fact that Dad might also be out of work.

"I know somebody who owes me a couple of favors," said Vince. "We'll get the hall for almost nothing and the booze for half-price."

"Let's have Charlie say a speech," said Larry.

"I'd like to hear that," said Mom.

"This is just cops," explained Vince to my mother. "Just a bunch of cops acting crazy and drinking for a good cause."

"No speeches," I said putting up my hands.

"You just write a little something down about your Dad," said Larry rapidly. "Just that he's a good guy, a family man, it doesn't matter what, anything you say would have to be good." He looked at my father. "I'm telling the truth, too. Bill, I'm behind you all the way. If it wasn't for you I wouldn't even be a detective. I probably wouldn't even be a cop." Larry wiped his eyes. He was a mess of nerves. I remembered the story about him thinking his wife was trying to kill him. "Charlie, don't say a damn thing if you don't want to. You just have a good time, I'll take care of that. I'll pick you up at your house and we can drive in together. OK? Me and you will go in together? How does that sound?"

"Sounds good to me."

"If you don't want to, you don't have to."

"Sounds good," I said.

Vince took Larry's arm.

"Then it's all settled," said Larry. "You don't have to worry about a thing." His mouth was twitching like a rabbit's nose. "Let me get your number." He patted his pockets and said, "Who took my pen?" He spun around but there was no one behind him.

"It's the same goddamn number as mine," said Dad.

"Oh, oh that's right," he laughed.

"Give me a week to sell tickets, we'll have it November 8th, that's a Friday night," said Vince. He still had Larry by the arm. "We've got to get going."

Larry shook my hand, my father's, and Louise's. My mother got a kiss on the cheek.

"Joy," said Vince, "you make sure that character follows doctor's orders. I'm tired of working alone."

"Why should I?" called Dad. "As soon as I get better,

I lose my pay. That's some incentive for getting better. I think they're trying to kill me, if I don't get better I stay on the payroll and out of the courts."

"You just get better," said Vince. "And cut the crap."

———————

We sat around the bed on metal-framed hospital chairs that Miss Marlboro Country had dragged in. Dad yawned and then Louise yawned. "It's contagious," said Mom. There was a family feeling in the room. I'm sure they felt it. It was way past visiting hours so the nurses asked us to keep the door shut and our voices down. It seemed the bigger pain in the ass Dad became, the more the nurses like him. On his lunch tray he was getting extra dessert and juice. He had a name for all of them. There was VO-5, whose hair would have stayed in place during a nuclear explosion, there was Miss Daddy Long Legs, who was at least six foot one; I wondered how he got away with it.

"It must feel good to wear pants again," said Louise. She swung her legs back and forth an inch from the floor.

"Sure does." The closet door was open and his gown and bath robe hung on metal hooks. He folded his hands behind his neck. Under his arms, the curly hair was still black.

"Now you know how it feels to wear a dress," said Louise.

"In a couple of years you won't want to wear pants; you'll want to show off those legs."

"Va-va-va-boom," I walked across the room swinging my hips.

"Knock it off," said Louise.

"This may sound crazy, but I miss old Williams," said Dad.

"I should go down and read to him," said Mom.

"They won't let you in intensive care," said Dad. "I bet he never thought he'd end up like that."

"Maybe we could sneak down and see him," said Louise.

"I just want you to know one thing, if I ever get paralyzed or real sick like that," Dad said, pointing to the bridge of his nose, "I want you, Charlie, to shoot me right here. They say you never feel it."

"Bill, that's terrible," said Mom. "How could you say such a thing?"

"I wouldn't do it," I said.

"Just pull the trigger and put the gun in my hand."

"You're supposed to be paralyzed."

"Then smother me with a pillow, but don't ever leave me like some vegetable."

"Some of the Grey Panthers have signed papers so that they can't be kept alive by machines," said Louise. "But I don't think it's such a good idea. They may say you're braindead, but they don't know for sure. You might be reliving all the best parts of your life."

"I thought about smothering Williams one night. But, I couldn't do it," said Dad. "I just kept looking at him, thinking about it."

"You can't play God, too," said Mom. "You've got too much to do already."

CHAPTER
12

*L*ouise looked into her vanity mirror and smeared white pancake make-up on her face. She had teased her hair into a wild lion's mane of curls and held it off her forehead. On her lap was a Kiss album. The group Kiss was a mixture of ex-teachers and professionals turned rock stars who never appeared in public without their space costumes. Louise watched the picture on the cover and drew a black star around her eye. She was going to the Senior Center Halloween party dressed as the lead guitarist. With chalk, I drew pointy white teeth on the sides of her platform shoes.

"This is the big effect," she said, putting on red lipstick. She turned her head and stuck out her tongue. It was bright red from cherry Life Savers. "I'm going to buy some strawberry Kool-Aid and eat it out of the package. Then my mouth will really be red."

"It's really red now."

She clipped her shoes on and stood up. She was dressed in black except for a pair of white gloves. She began to growl, then opened her mouth and twirled her tongue around. The effect was frightening. "It's great, you're going to give them a heart attack."

"Thanks." She sprang and strummed an invisible guitar.

I knew Tracy was trying to avoid me. We hadn't talked since I had walked out on her Wednesday night. On Thursday, when I had called, I had gotten a telephone answering machine. "Hi, this is Tracy. As you can tell I cannot get to the phone right now."

"Tracy," I had said. "Cut the shit."

"At the sound of the tone, please leave a message and I'll call you back. Beep." I slammed the receiver down. Then I thought, maybe she bought it so that she wouldn't have to talk to Al. Good old practical Tracy. I called back and said, "Knock, Knock. Who's there? Duane. Duane who? Duane the pool I'm dwowning." Then I called back and said, "That was me, Tracy. When did you get the machine? It's a great idea, but please don't forget to call me." Later that night, I put on a Barry White album, called, and held the phone to the speaker. "You're the first, you're the last, my everything," he sang like the walrus of love.

She hadn't called back.

I drove Louise to the Senior Center. It was a new brick building, already covered with graffiti, in the middle of an experimental neighborhood for low-income families. It had failed badly. Half the houses were abandoned, boarded up, or burned out. "Don't walk home," I said to Louise, pulling to the curb.

She stuck her tongue out at me. It really was a spooky getup. "I'll call you."

There was a bunch of old folks standing on the sidewalk in front of the building. A couple of the ladies were dressed like gypsies, and there was a definite Abraham Lincoln. "See you later," Louise said, blowing a kiss.

The old folks began making a giant fuss over Louise. "Oh, now I've seen it all!" yelled a tiny woman in a red dress. Old Abe threw up his arms.

I walked around the lobby in Tracy's apartment rehearsing my lines. First, it was either me or Al. I stood in front of a veined mirror and tucked in my shirt in. Second, I pointed at the mirror, if you don't have the guts to tell him, I will. I tried to think of a third. Oh yeah, third, thanks for returning my call. This was it. I knew she was home because her car was in the lot and her light had been on.

If things went well I'd bring her to the Halloween party at the firehouse. We were guaranteed a good time. Last year's costumes ranged from a roll of toilet paper, a tampon, a rubber (all gross but funny) to Idi Amin and the Shah of Iran. Kevin had gone as a flasher. He wore a raincoat, the legs of a pair of pants, and flesh colored underwear with a salami attached. Most original costume went to Paul, who went as a six-foot fire hydrant and leashed his German shepherd to his ankle. I went to the elevator and pressed the button. Someone

had put new sand in the ashtray. I spun my finger around
in it.

The elevator doors opened and there was Tracy. She
was dressed as a cheerleader and held two red-and-white
pom-poms in one hand, her other hand held Al's. I took
a step back. Al looked at her, then me. He wore a black
T-shirt and had his hair slicked, fifties style. The guy
was bulging with chest and arm muscles.

I was blocking their way and didn't move. "Tracy,
I've got to talk to you," I said.

The elevator doors tried to close. Al stuck his sneaker
out. He had white socks on and his pants cuffed two or
three times.

"Is this him?" asked Al, freeing his hand. On his wrist
he wore a chrome-spiked dog collar.

"Yes. This is Charlie."

"Tracy, I've got to talk to you!"

They stepped around me and out of the elevator. Al
was about six inches and fifty pounds bigger than I.
"We're on our way out," he said.

"I just have to talk to her for a minute," I said. If he
said, no, I was going to say, Well, tough shit.

He shrugged and lumbered over to one of the plastic
couches and sat. When he spread his arms across the
top, he palmed each side.

Tracy rubbed her saddleshoes together looking at the
floor.

"I thought you were giving him the boot," I said.

"I didn't tell him," she whispered. She didn't smell
like herself, like musk. she smelled like French perfume. "I can't explain now."

"You owe me this."

"I'll tell you tomorrow."

"No."

"Charlie, not here."

"Tell him you forgot something and meet me at the apartment. I'll go up the stairs."

"OK," she said, taking a deep breath.

I walked to the side of the lobby then raced up the stairs, two at a time. Al had always been tall, but how the hell did he get so big? He must have been the fork-lift at his father's warehouse. If it came to blows, I'd kick him right in the balls.

I was able to beat the elevator. I trotted down the hall and stood puffing in front of the doors. Two, three, the doors opened. It was déjà vu. Al stood there next to Tracy. "Isn't this a coincidence?" He smiled. Al had a handsome Neanderthal look about him. His forehead shaded his eyes and his jaw protruded in an ape-like way. "But, listen," he said. "I don't have time to play games."

"Then you might as well know right now that she's finished with you."

"What?"

"You heard me." I began hopping around a little.

Al came out of the elevator and Tracy almost got caught in the doors. I looked up into his eye. "What did you say?"

"It's over. She wants out. She doesn't need a pimp."

I tried to dance out of the way but, he grabbed my jacket and lifted me against the wall. My shirt was choking me and his spiked bracelet was digging into my face. "Who's a pimp?"

"You, you fuckin' cock-sucker." I kneed him in the

balls. He didn't even blink. I tried it again and he hit me in the mouth, square in the mouth. My head smacked into the wall.

"If you don't watch your mouth, kid, you won't live to see twenty."

Over his shoulder I saw Tracy. She was holding her head, a pom-pom in each hand.

I could hear my father saying, "One of them spit right in my face. Do you know what that feels like?" I spit blood in Al's face. It splattered on his chin and he looked at me in disbelief.

I heard Tracy scream something as Al gave me a shot to the stomach with a knee or a fist. I couldn't tell. He pushed me away and I managed to remain standing. I glared right at him.

"You little prick," he said. "Tracy, open the door, let me wash this shit off."

Tracy dug around for a key in her skirt pocket and opened her door. He went inside. "Charlie, please get out of here," she said, standing in the doorway. "He'll kill you. He will, Charlie."

"You're staying with him?" Her face was distant. The lights seemed to dim.

She nodded.

I walked to the stairs, holding my mouth. My front teeth were loose and my tongue found a hole that almost went through my lip.

———————

I sat in the Buick holding a rag to my mouth. The rag tasted like grease. I pressed the electric window buttons and the glass around me floated down. The night air was crisp and wintery. I took some deep breath to clear my head. My heart was pounding away. The light in Tracy's apartment was still on. In the window beneath, a pumpkin's face glowed. I wasn't going to let him get away with this.

I got out of the car, opened the trunk, and pulled a breakerbar out of a bag of tools. It was two feet of metal and weighed about five pounds. I banged it in my hand. I was shivering and wasn't sure if I could use it.

A car pulled out of a parking space and Al's Corvette sat twenty yards ahead. The license plate glowed, "Koke kid." I thought about breaking the windows, or slitting the tires. Then, it came to me. I hopped in my car, started the engine, and put it in low gear.

I moved up slowly with the lights off until the Buick's bumper was touching the trunk of the sports car. I gave the gas a nudge and heard the fiberglass Vette body crack. I pressed harder on the gas and inch by inch moved forward, crumbling the Vette, driving its long, low nose under the car head. My engine was revving, tires screeching. Lights started coming on in the houses along the block. The Vette was getting smaller and smaller, the rear window shattered. The Buick lurched and plowed forward. I threw the shift lever in reverse. The two cars came apart, and I got the hell out of there.

I drove around the block and passed by once before I took off. The "Koke Kid" plate lay in the gutter attached to a shiny fiberglass panel. The Vette's trunk was gone, the gas tank was showing and the front was wedged under an old Oldsmobile, whose rear tires were barely touching the ground.

"Charlie, I'm sorry, but I can't do it." Mr. Beck blocked the doorway with a muscular green arm. He had on tattered shorts and his hair was dyed black. It was the best Hulk imitation I had ever seen.

"Just get Paul or Kevin." Behind him the fire trucks were decorated with orange and black crepe paper.

"Tonight, it's members only. The Chief gives the orders."

"Could I at least talk to them?"

"It's really crowded in there." He began shutting the door. "You're bleeding," he said. "You better get home and take care of yourself."

———————

In front of the Senior Center I pulled the pieces of the Corvette from the grill of the Buick. Luckily the front end wasn't damaged badly. The bumper had bent a little and the splash pan was crushed. I threw the fiberglass chunks in the back seat and began to realize how much trouble I was in. I knelt in the street and tried to straighten the bumper. I jammed the breaker bar behind the chrome and hung on it bouncing up and down. It didn't budge. I wasn't thinking about what Al or the police could do to me. I just wanted to know what I should do next. If I could have found a junked 1964 Electra I might have been able to exchange the parts. I considered going to the police station and turning myself in, but first, I had to tell Louise that she would have to find another ride home.

Inside the Senior Center the lights were low. On an orange spot-lighted stage a band in costumes played "The Monster Mash." "He did the mash," sang the lead skeleton. "It was a graveyard smash." The dance floor was packed with old people doing disco steps. Most of them had no rhythm and did something that resembled the Alley Cat. I spotted Abe Lincoln's hat floating above the mass. Tables with punch and food were set up around the walls, and there was a section of people following the song's beat by tapping their water glasses.

"Can I help you?" asked a woman knitting something pink. She wore a pointy hat and there was a star-tipped wand on the table. I couldn't tell if her skin was really grey or if it was makeup. "Don't worry, I'm a good witch," she smiled.

"I'm looking for Louise Patterson. She's my sister and I'm supposed to give her a ride home."

"Oh, Louise, our little cook. She's in the kitchen. Go to the back and make a left through those doors, then a right."

"Thank you."

"Where's your costume?"

"I'm a college graduate,," I said, but she didn't hear me.

I weaved through the dancers. I saw a lot of vampires, gypsies, and hobos. No one paid any attention to me. They were all having such a good time. I thought it was a shame that Tracy and I couldn't have come here. The band started playing "Blue Moon," and the seniors started slow dancing.

I pushed through the swinging doors and could smell something burning. Even with my sore lip, I had to smile. I went into the men's room and saw that my mouth looked as bad as it felt. My bottom teeth had almost sliced my lower lip in half. There was a small red mark where my tooth had almost come through. I gargled with water and spit blood into the sink. It stung like a bad burn. A guy wearing a tux with tails came in and hurried out. I had this terrible feeling that I was going to be arrested right in the Senior Center. The bathroom seemed to take a spin. I grabbed the edges of the sink and pressed my face against the tiles. "Please," I said, "please." I thought I was going to fall. What would Louise think if they found me on the floor? Slowly the room came to rest. I opened my eyes and stared at my reflection. My hair was a mess. I wet it and combed it with my fingers.

"Hey," I poked my head into the kitchen. Louise stood in front of a professional-sized stainless steel oven, holding a tray of cocktail franks wrapped in dough. She had on silver insulated mittens and looked like a cook out of a bad dream.

"Charlie." She balanced the tray. "I just made a hundred and fifty pigs in the blanket." The little hors d'oeuvres began sliding and she placed them carefully on the counter. There was smoke along the ceiling but the batch didn't look burnt. From around the refrigerator came a kid about Louise's age, dressed exactly like her, the same white face, red lips, and star around one eye. They would have been identical twins except his hair was shorter and he wore black framed glasses, the heavy duty unbreakable type. "This is Eddie," she said.

"How are you?" I came into the light.

"Charlie, what happened?"

"I fell, cut my lip."

"Where?"

"Outside. Too much celebrating." I tried to laugh.

She pulled off the mittens and gently touched my lip. "I just came by to tell you I can't give you a ride."

Louise told me to be quiet and pulled my lip down. "You're going to need stitches," said Eddie, looking over her shoulder.

"I'm sorry, I'm messing up your whole night."

"No, you're not."

I sat in a chair against the wall. Louise looked at my face and asked Eddie to wait in the hall. I wanted to cry but couldn't. "What's the matter," Louise asked. "Charlie, what's the matter?"

In the morning my mouth felt worse. My lip was twice its regular size and it throbbed. My front teeth were still very loose. Louise brought my mother into my room before I was out of bed. "Charlie, I had to tell her," she said. Mom became very upset, mostly about my teeth. She called the dentist and made me an emergency appointment for that afternoon. I was trying to think of a way to tell her what happened. How could I tell her about the Corvette? I hardly believed it myself. I told her that I had too much to drink and fell. "You better cut out the shenanigans," she said. "I've had enough of it with your father."

Louise and my mother drove the Buick to the hospital. From the window, I watched to see if they noticed the front end damage. They just got in and drove off. Mom had made me eggs but I couldn't eat them. I was too nervous. I was expecting the police at any moment. I kept walking back and forth from the side window to the front window. I thought I was going to be sick and ran for the back door.

I stood bent over in the garden and the feeling passed. It was one of those nasty November days when the dampness hung in the air and went right through you. I got a rake from the garage and figured I'd make a few piles. I started near the hedges where my father threw his cigar butts. My mother was always picking them up saying, Bill this yard isn't an ashtray. Dad said the tobacco was good fertilizer. The yellow, orange, and brown leaves were wet and heavy. I raised a sweat even in just my undershirt. A cigar butt stuck to the end of the bamboo rake and looked like a dried poodle turd. I knocked it off with the toe of my sneaker.

Raking leaves, cutting the lawn, and gardening were about the only real work there was to do around the house. I had had a neighbor who on Saturdays walked around his manicured lawn looking for, I guess, weeds. Around and around in circles he had gone, staring at the grass, every couple of steps bending, moving the blades with his hand. He lived alone and was in the house a week before anyone noticed his absence. The police broke in and found him slumped over one of those man-size frozen dinners.

In a short time, I had raked up a nice pile. A good pile to jump in. I remembered choosing it out with the other kids for first jump. We huddled and stuck out our fists. One kid, usually the oldest, counted out a rhyme on them. "One potato, two potato, three potato, four, five potato, six potato, seven potato more." If the counter's fist landed on your's when he said 'more,' you were out, and got to jump first. There was another one, the one I always said, when I counted. "Ink-ka, bink-ka, bottle of ink-ka, the cork fell out and you stink-ka. Not because you're dirty, not because you're clean, just because you kissed a girl behind a mag-a-zine." I looked at the pile and it seemed like a long time ago.

Tracy touched my shoulder and I almost jumped out of my skin. She had the Chinese jacket on over her uniform. "Charlie, we have to talk," she said. In her hand she held a crumpled license plate. "It was in the street," she said, handing it to me. It was the plate from the front of the Buick. I hadn't even noticed it was missing.

I dropped the rake on the pile and we went to the house and sat on the cement stoop. She leaned back against the door, and I leaned forward and folded my hands. I waited for her to say something. I had nothing to say.

"You shouldn't have done that. God, Charlie." She rubbed her leg and we both looked at our shoes. "Al called this morning. The car was totaled. He's not going to press charges. I told him your father was a detective and he got scared. The car had a stolen engine. He had collision so he's going to take the insurance money and forget about it. He's really doing it for me."

I looked at her face.

"I can't see you ever again," she said. "Even if this didn't happen, I don't think it would have worked." There was no anger or feeling in her voice.

"I never knew why I loved you," I said. "But I did."

She hugged me and I hugged her. "Charlie I'll always love you," she said. "But, you've got to start figuring things out." Her voice grew weak. "He could have killed you."

She took her arms off me and I showed her my lip. "My teeth are loose," I said.

"He got in the elevator with me and wouldn't get out. I'm so sorry."

"You're not going to stick with him, are you?"

"I'm not thinking ahead," she said. "I lied to you. I'm going to the Virgin Islands with him, not Bonnie."

The words were like the last blows of a long fight. I felt myself falling and falling, finally hitting the canvas.

"I should get going," she said.

I did not look up. I didn't feel anything until about a half hour later when I had raked all the leaves in a giant pile and the wind started blowing them around.

13

COPS WILL PROTEST 'FUND-HAZING'

Manhattan Supreme Court Justice Michael Chimera has scheduled a hearing for Monday over a statement written on November 3 by Inspector Andrew Kael, commander of the Public Morals Division.

"The Police Department is depriving us of our constitutional rights," charged four city police unions. Kael is urging the men not to attend a fund-raiser for Det. Patterson, who could be suspended without pay while under investigation. Vincent Tarentino, the fund-raiser's chairman, claims, "We would have sold more tickets without the statement. Now there's only one day left."

IN THE STATEMENT, Kael said he was simply voicing his feelings about the fund-raiser, to be held in a Crown Heights nightclub. "I did not order the men to skip the party. I assumed, however, that anyone attending must lack the good judgment and proper decision-making sought by the department." He went on to say, "It is a good way to evaluate the judgment of the personnel."

"Who does he think he is?" retorted John Haggerty, speaking for the Patrolman's Benevolent Association, the Lieutenant's Benevolent Association, and the Detective Endowment Association. "This isn't Hitler's Army. How we spend our money, and on what, is our business."

THE STATEMENT was "an obvious ploy to weaken Det. Patterson's credibility, who is one of the finest men in the Department," said Peter Gorman, president of the P.B.A. A protest has been planned for tomorrow at the 74th Precinct in Brooklyn.

There was an odor of whiskey around Dad's bed but no one knew where he got the booze or hid the bottle. It was the biggest mystery on the third floor. The nurses asked me to look around his room. When Dad went into the bathroom, I checked the closet, the nightstand, and under the mattress. Nothing. The toilet flushed and he came out dressed in jeans and a T-shirt. "So you fell?" he said again.

I had told him that I had tripped on the firehouse stairs and cut my lip. He zipped up his fly. "You didn't fall."

"I fell." I slipped into the bathroom and locked the

door. I opened the medicine cabinet and tasted his mouthwash: Listerine. I flushed the toilet and came out.

"You know it's not every day my son gets into a fight." he said. He buttoned up a shirt and looked out the window. He refused to stay in bed or wear a hospital bib. "Now tell me what happened."

"You tell my why you're drinking and where you're hiding the bottle."

"I'm drinking because I got a new strategy." He pulled the cord on the venetian blinds. "I'm going to stay sick and stay on the payroll. And, I'll give you a hint about the bottle. It's not in the bathroom."

Piece by piece I told him everything except the part about the Corvette and that Tracy was Al's mistress. I didn't want Dad to think too badly of her. Maybe she and I could work things out. I explained that Al was twice my size. "I kicked him in the balls and he didn't even flinch."

"In other words, you missed."

"Yeah."

"So, then what did you do?"

"What could I do?"

"Let me tell you a little story," he said, looking at Williams' empty bed. The old man had died. Dad had tried to go down to the morgue in the middle of the night. They stopped him in the basement and there had been a bad scene with one of the guards. Dad wouldn't talk about it or explain what he was trying to do. "In high school we used to run mile races. It was four laps around the track. I was the fastest guy in the school. I knew it, everyone knew it. Then, in my senior year, a

guy from the track team set a new school record. I never
got timed but I knew I could beat this kid and no one
believed it. I'm only six foot and he's six three and he's
got the legs of a giraffe. So I go out to the track after
school with a few of my buddies and I tell him I'll race
him for ten dollars, that was a lot of money. He ran
first, in little shorts and track shoes, and almost tied
his fastest time. Now, all of my friends are there and
the team is standing around and I have long pants on
and old sneakers with cardboard stuck in the bottom."
He looked at me. "Honest to God, cardboard. So, no
one thinks I'm going to win. My friends tell me to save
my strength. Don't waste yourself on the first two laps.
I pull my shirt off, line up, and they yell "go!" and I
lost. I lost by two seconds. I could have won easily but
I held back saving myself for the last lap. There's one
thing I learned. You don't save nothing." He opened
the blinds, and slatted sunlight shone across his face.
"Give everything one hundred percent and don't look
back because if you do, you'll start getting scared and
start slowing down and then they've got you. Don't be
afraid of tomorrow." He laughed and fumbled nervously with the curtain cord. "I mean, the damn thing
never comes anyway."

"So you think I should have killed him?"

"Whatever was necessary."

"Well, I wish the whole thing had never happened."
I thought about the crushed Corvette. "I'm going to
that protest on Wednesday. I'll do whatever I can."

"Thanks," he said. "Let me see your lip."

———————

I ate dinner with Louise. More or less. I just pushed
my food around. I had no appetite. Louise wasn't talk-

ing to me. The day before I had told her the true story about my lip. Everything. She had said losing Tracy was probably the best thing that could happen. "Charlie, you don't need any girl who would do that," she had said.

"How do you know!" I had snapped. "You're thirteen years old."

So tonight Louise was giving me the silent treatment. I told her I was sorry.

"There's nothing to be sorry about. Why would you tell a kid that you're sorry anyway? Why should you care what a kid thinks?"

"Louise, come on."

"Whenever I try to help you, you say I'm too young to understand."

"I'm sorry."

"Will you stop saying that? You're not sorry."

I went up to my room and lay on the bed trying to put things in some kind of order. Nothing made sense. How could Tracy never want to see me again? I couldn't believe it. I imagined her in bed with me and panicked when I couldn't remember her face. I opened my dresser and pulled out an envelope stuffed with cards, letters, and little things she had sent me.

On a narrow six-inch strip were four black-and-white photos of Tracy and me that had been taken in a fifty-cent booth at Woolworth's. The first shot had caught us both off guard. I had my eyes closed and Tracy was trying to manage a smile. She looked as if she was going to be sick. In the other three, my face was buried behind her hair and she was laughing with her mouth open. I had been giving her a hickey. The pictures made me feel worse.

I opened a card that had a picture of two people holding hands walking on a beach.

> Dear Charlie,
>   Happy two month aniversary! We've come such a
> long way together, sharing so many happy times. All
> the times we shared together were so perfect. You've
> opened my eyes to a lot and there's always more I'm
> learning when I'm with you.
>   Happy anniversary!!! I hope you enjoy my gift.
>
> With all my love,
> Tracy xxxooo

She had given me expensive after-shave. I said thanks
and kissed her, but I thought it was a terrible gift. I
wanted something that would last. My relatives always
gave my father after-shave because they didn't know
what to get him. After Christmas, he gave the bottles
to the neighbors. You can only use so much after-shave.

It had been her idea to exchange gifts on every stupid
anniversary. One of Tracy's great habits was keeping
track of every little thing that barely mattered. She had
a bulging scrapbook that held almost every moment of
her life. She'd say things like, "We've made love exactly
ten times this week." I enjoyed it, though. It was very
flattering. On that anniversary, I had given her a gold
charm in the shape of a record album. Cut into the
metal was the word "Hit Parade." It was a corny thing
and not really her style, but I liked it. Tracy wore it
maybe twice.

On our four-month anniversary, I had taken her to
the Jones Beach Theater to see "Damn Yankees," star-

ring Joe Namath. It was an outdoor theater. There wasn't a breeze and the gnats ate us alive. But, after the play, we danced to big-band music in the tent near the beach and I don't think I've ever had a nicer time.

I read a letter she put under my windshield wiper the other day.

> Dear Charlie,
> I'm sorry things ended up this way. You are a very considerate person, a real sweetheart. Maybe we can remain in touch, I hope, but it may be very hard to do that knowing the way we feel about each other.
> I should have told you about Al right from the beginning, but I thought if I did we would break up in a fight and it would be harder that way. Well, I was wrong. I'm sorry that I broke up with you so abruptly, but I had to, because I wasn't being fair or honest with you. I guess what I found hard about our relationship was you going back to school and me going to work. Because you didn't work we couldn't go out on the town or do the things I wanted, and we couldn't agree on our future.
> I hope everyone at home is well. I really hope that you write me back to let me know how you are doing and how you are feeling.
>
> Love,
> Tracy

On the edge of the bed I sat with the letters and cards on my lap. I tucked them in the envelope and slid them back in the drawer. Knowing that she didn't need me as much as I needed her made me feel terrible. The letter was full of lies. In one sentence she lies and the next tells me she wants to be honest. Did she ever believe we had a future.

That night I woke up sweating. I had dreamed that I was choking Williams. My father was trying to stop me but he couldn't pry my fingers off the old man's neck. I lay awake for a while, then got dressed and went down to the kitchen.

My mother was sitting at the table next to an ashtray crowded with cigarettes, a crumpled pack in her hand. She hadn't smoked in years. "What are you doing?" I asked. She stared at me and her eyes scared me. They looked as if there was nothing behind them, as if she wasn't thinking about anything at all.

She got up real fast and put her coffee cup in the sink. It was three in the morning and she was dressed in black knit pants and a lavender blouse. "Just couldn't sleep," she said.

"I couldn't sleep, either."

She washed and dried her cup and hung it with the others.

"Are you OK?"

"You mean because I'm smoking?" she said. "Well, I can have a few bad habits, too. Everyone else around here does."

"No, I don't mean the cigarettes," I said, wondering what types of bad habits she thought I had.

A year ago she had found a box of rubbers hidden in my closet. Not four or five, but over a hundred. Paul had worked for a drugstore and had stolen them. I had never used one, but I figured someday they would come in handy. Finding them seemed to shake her up more than any of the crazy stunts I had pulled. She must have told my father and he must have laughed. "Your father may think it's funny," she said one night. "But I want those things out of this house." She pointed at the closet. At that time they had been under a pile of old *Look* magazines for about six months and I didn't know what she was talking about. I asked her what things? "Don't humiliate me," she said and walked out, slamming the door. I gave them to Paul the next day and tried hard to explain, but she never believed me. She must have thought I was screwing every girl in town.

She poured coffee, the one thing we both didn't need, and lit another cigarette. "Tonight your father got down on the floor and started doing pushups. 'Maybe I can have a stroke.' That's what he told me." She played with her cigarette in the ashtray. She pounded the glowing end until it was just about out, then took a drag to start it up again. She had stopped smoking when she was carrying Louise. "And I'm sure he was drunk." She tapped and the head fell off the butt. "If you know where's he's getting it from, tell me."

"I don't. I even searched his room today." It had always been my father and me and her and Louise. It was my father who signed my report cards, my father who made me breakfast on Sundays, my father who came up to the school on parent-teacher night. When she went to Disney World with Louise, I hadn't even been asked to go.

"We were sitting down in the sunroom," said mom, finally putting out her cigarette, "and he asked a nurse if his wife had come out of surgery. The poor woman went to find out. Charlie he thinks it's all a joke. But it's not funny anymore. No one is laughing."

"I don't think he wants to believe he had a heart attack. You know, he's afraid of getting old. You remember when he started going grey." He had given Mom a tweezer and told her to pull them out. There were only a couple. But, then, they seemed to be coming overnight and in a year he went from black to grey.

"I signed something tonight. He's going to start seeing a psychiatrist. I had to do something. I can't just sit there day after day watching him kill himself."

"He'll never do it." I could hear my father yelling, Get that shrink out of here.

"They're going to handle it discreetly. Your father will think it's just an interested physician." After a minute she said, "I'm trying to do the right thing."

I told her that I was going to the protest and would do anything I could to get his job back, without any idea of what I was planning to do. She didn't say anything and I began to feel uncomfortable. "Mom, there must be something I can do." She brought the cups to the sink. I wanted to tell her how bad I felt about Tracy but, when I had dated her, I felt my mother never really approved. I'd ask her if she liked Tracy and she'd say, she's fine. But, do you like her? I'd say.

"I don't think she's right for you, but she's fine otherwise."

Tracy was Jewish. Maybe my mother thought I would get her pregnant and have to marry her.

"And college," said Mom, looking into the sink. "How's that going?" By her voice I knew that she knew it wasn't going well.

"Fine." College used to be the only thing she and I had ever really talked about. She wasn't against my going away to school. She never said it, but I felt she thought the community college was a mistake. "I've got a lot of other things on my mind."

She nodded and dried the cup.

The city sky, hung heavy with the threat of rain, faded from white to gray as evening approached. I drove past the precinct slowly in the battered Buick. The protest was scheduled for five P.M. but there were already well over a hundred men standing on the sidewalk. Over half the crowd wore police uniforms, their dark blue slickers flapped as the wind came down the treeless block. There wasn't a parking spot in sight, so I stopped in the street and looked for a familiar face. A few men came around to the window. The car had become my father's trademark. I opened the window and told them I was Bill's son.

"It's Bill's son," one of them shouted.

John Haggerty tapped on the passenger-side door. I popped the lock and he hopped in next to me, breathing heavily. Although he was fat, he looked as hard as an apple. Only his face, clean shaven and red from the weather, was fleshy and soft. "Glad you could make it," he said. "How's your father doing?"

"OK," I said, thinking about the pushups and the drinking.

Haggerty explained what he wanted me to do. "Just blow this." He handed me a chrome whistle. "We'll give you the signal." He opened his door.

"Where should I leave the car?"

"How about right here."

I shut the engine off and followed him through the crowd. All the men greeted Haggerty with, How ya doing, or, Hey big Johnny. He introduced me to a few

guys. I saw the men from the hospital, and Larry, who
shuffled his feet with his hands stuck in his pockets.
"What the hell we waiting for?" he asked me as if it
were a secret. "I'll tell you, some of these guys are
creeps."

Haggerty motioned with his eyes and we headed up
the steps and stood in front of the dark green doors.

There was no traffic on the street. Orange police bar-
riers were set up at each end of the block. On the opposite sidewalk, in front of a row of fake red-brick houses
barely three feet apart, the neighborhood people gathered. There was a circle of Hasidic Jews in overcoats
and fedoras. None of the men paid them any attention,
but I felt their presence soundlessly shouting defiance.
Some black teenagers danced in a jerky robot way to
music from a suitcase-size radio that a thin kid held on
his shoulder. I listened closely and could hear Kool and
the Gang sing, "Can't get enough of that funky stuff."

"The natives are getting restless," said Haggerty,
rubbing his hands together. "But, I don't want to start
until the TV crews get here."

Bicycle traffic developed on the empty street. One
kid, wearing a sweat shirt that said, "Flashy Flash," did
wheelies on his sting-ray, riding on two tires only when
he made the turns at the corners. Three heavy women,
house dresses blowing below their coats, marched down
the street and opened webbed patio chairs. They sat in
the midst of the dancing kids and the bicycle traffic.

Now, there were over two hundred men standing in
small groups. They had spilled into the street and the
kids on bikes weaved through them fearlessly. In every
man's hand was a whistle. Dad, probably watching the

news waiting for a report on the police protest, seemed a million miles away. I could see my mother with him, her long fingers around his heavy hand. I remembered her vacant eyes the night before.

No news crew or press came and it was getting dark quickly. "Could I have everyone's attention?" said Haggerty in a voice deep with authority. Quiet spread through the men and they pressed toward the steps. "We're here to show our strength." He held up his fist. Everyone's arm shot up. I raised my fist.

"And if Commander Kael doesn't like it or feels that we're violating a city ordinance then I say, let him call the cops."

The men dropped their fists and clapped.

"There is going to be a fund-raiser next week for Detective Patterson whether this department likes it or not. I hope you will attend. Chances are you know him or know of him. He is a twenty-one-year veteran and would be working right now if he had not had a heart attack nine days ago at a departmental hearing. For the next twenty-one minutes, Bill's son, Charlie Patterson, will lead us in a whistle-blast salute." Gorman, who was watching his watch, nodded at me, and I gave the first blast. A second later all the men blew and the air was electrified with screaming whistles. It was earshattering. It lasted for ten seconds.

It had begun to drizzle, and the men stood silently waiting for the next blast. No one spoke. The radio across the street was off. The youths leaned motionless against the parked cars, hands in their pockets, ankles crossed. Again I blew. The mist seemed to make the whistles louder. During the silences my ears felt as if they were filled with cotton.

After the tenth whistle blast, the block was jammed with people who had come out of the houses and apartments to investigate the commotion. On the other side of the barrier, Hasidic Jews gathered. Their number grew like a black shadow. Squad cars jammed the side streets. Instead of the cops standing guard, they came and blew their whistles. The Buick sat in the middle of the mass and I imagined the day of the storming and what it must have been like to push through the crowds to get the Jews off the car.

Peter Gorman lowered his hand and I blew again, and the men blew again. The whistles shrieked scornfully at the precinct house and the stormy sky. As each blast passed, I was filled with a feeling of brotherhood and solidarity. The Buick and I were links to my father. The last blast came and the cops and some of the spectators clapped and cheered. Haggerty said, "Thank you." That was all that was needed. I had a feeling that something important had just happened. The solemnity of the protest made the men linger and talk in whispers. Haggerty shook my hand and I told him that I wanted to give a speech at the fund-raiser. "Let me just say something about my father."

"I'm sorry I didn't ask you," he said.

I must have shaken a dozen more hands before I got in the Buick. For the first time in a month I felt some kind of purpose. In my head I was already writing the speech. Larry came to the window. "Can you believe this," he said. I shook my head. "I'm picking you up on Friday, right?"

"Yeah."

I started the engine. I wanted to get to the hospital. I wanted to tell Dad what had just happened.

CHAPTER

14

*T*HE *"Patterson Fund-Raiser" sold out two hours after* the protest. Detectives and policemen who had never met my father or even worked in Brooklyn shelled out thirty dollars for a ticket. The protest had made the papers. A small column on page twenty-one quoted John Haggerty: "We're standing behind Det. Patterson. I don't care what the consequences are. They think they've seen a storming, now they'll see a rampage." I cut the clipping out and took it to the hospital.

Dad learned of my speech from Vince and offered to help with the writing. We faced one another, using the breakfast tray as a desk. I had brought a pad, two pens, a thesaurus, and a dictionary. Dad was in better spirits.

All day Thursday his phone had not stopped ringing and he had yelled to Miss Marlboro Country, "I need a secretary, not a nurse." Today he wore blue pajamas with black piping. His clothes were back in the closet. There were no traces of alcohol on his breath. I wondered if his soberness and new attitude had anything to do with the psychiatrist.

"You've got to use words that got power," he said. The thesaurus had been Dad's idea. He opened it and read, " 'Proud.' You got 'honored,' 'gratified,' 'prideful,' and 'self-respecting.' We work these words into the speech and the guys will think you know what you're talking about."

"It doesn't work that way."

"That's what *you* think."

He composed a speech loaded with big fancy words. It was terrible. I kept quiet. He was having a ball. Adjectives described adverbs, sentences were joined with *howevers*, *hereafters*, and *therefores*. The first sentence was, "My father, a man of undivided integrity, who tried to reconcile a confrontation, and was thus faced with alienation from his job of twenty-one years, wants me to thank you for coming." Quite a mouthful.

———————

Louise was lying on the living room rug, her head propped on her hands. Eddie, opposite her, was in the same position. They were playing Scrabble. The maroon-rimmed board was almost filled with the lettered wooden cubes. "That's a double-word score and X is on a double-letter score so that's," Louise lowered her head, "forty-eight points," she said.

"What kind of word is *xebec?*" asked Eddie squinting through his glasses.

"An old one," said Louise. "It's a boat. You can challenge me if you want to."

"Don't bother," I said. "If she uses it, it's a word." Louise was a notorious Scrabble and Boggle player. I think she must have studied the dictionary. I found myself grinning at Eddie. It was the first time since Louise was a little kid that she'd brought a boy home. She chose her letters from the box and placed them on her wooden block stand. After studying them for a moment, she arranged the word *zircon*.

Eddie sat up and placed the letters c h i r onto the word *tweak*. I had no idea what the word *tweak* meant. "Chair," he said gravely. He had an awfully old face for a young kid. His straight black hair was cut barbershop style, as if he always said, "Just give me a regular."

I stood there towering above them and realized they probably weren't talking because of me. Eddie lifted his glasses off his thin nose and dropped them. "Well, I got work to do," I said, sounding so much like my father it scared me. I tapped the pad. "I'm making a speech tonight."

"Did you finish it?" asked Louise, sliding *zircon* onto the board. Eddie held his forehead.

"Yeah, but it needs heavy duty editing." I climbed up the stairs. "Just tickle her and she'll blow the whole game."

My desk was covered with dirty clothes. Since my father was in the hospital my mother was on a slowdown and it was every man for himself. I had two days of clean underwear left and no clean socks. I flattened the blankets on my bed and lay down. I began crossing out almost every other word in my father's speech. I wanted it simple and personal. I wrote and rewrote. There was much to say. I remembered the pot of stew for Ben Goldstein and the time he bailed out a criminal he had arrested. "It's a violent job," I wrote and was already at a loss for words.

———————

Larry came for me at six o'clock in a ratty '67 Ford. The quarter panel on the passenger side was rust-eaten all the way to the gas cap. I wore a black suit, a cheap, last-minute off-the-rack from Times Square Department Store, bought the day before my Uncle Scott's funeral a year ago. It was a bad way to learn that I had grown two inches. Oh, it doesn't look bad, my mother had said. But, I felt like a Long Island yokel going to the big metropolis. I could hear them asking, "So, how's the harvest coming along?"

I climbed into the car and slammed the long door shut. Larry didn't look too much better. His worn maroon jacket clashed with his blue pants and his fat bib tie wasn't tucked completely under his collar. Larry's wife had left him, and the police department had recently taken away his gun and transferred him to desk duty. The story goes that when he had been cleaning his gun, it misfired and just missed his wife. "They sold seven hundred and forty tickets," he said, pulling away from the curb. He had a profile like an eagle. His thinning black hair was combed forward and then curled back. It must have taken a lot of time. There was never a piece out of place. "The hall can hold only five hundred, but who's going to give us a summons for over-occupancy?"

I had expected Larry to be a speed demon but he drove so slowly that he was a menace. On the parkway entrance he made a full stop. Horns sounded as he crept into the traffic. The old Ford had accelerating power, but Larry nursed the gas pedal. In the first lane he averaged forty miles an hour and talked a mile a minute. Mostly he told me stories about himself and my father that I had already heard. Stories about cases, like the prostitute who took off her clothes in the squad car. "She's rubbing her tits, Charlie. Saying, 'Aw, come on fella's let's make amends,' and your father says, 'You'd better get dressed, you're attracting flies.' " Then he told me the story about the junkie. "He had his eleven-year-old sister out selling her pussy for him, and he's beating the shit out of her anyway on a regular basis, and your father's questioning this dude in the station house. Your old man takes out a pair of scissors from his desk drawer, big shears used for trimming photographs, and he grabs the guy by the lip." Larry pulled out his lip. "And your father asks me, 'Larry, do chickens have lips?' I swear on my mother-in-law's grave, this guy shit his pants."

Cars and trucks were passing on our right at sixty and the faster Larry talked the slower we went. I interrupted him and said, "You better speed up."

"What's the rush?" he asked. "We're early."

We talked back and forth for a while about the news coverage and how well Vince was handling everything, and then Larry sped up and said slowly, "You heard that they took my gun away?" The needle climbed to sixty-five. "I guess your father told you, right?" I said "yes," and his face became grim. "My wife, Estelle, thinks I tried to shoot her. She called the department and told them I was losing my mind. We've been married for five years and I've never raised my hand to her, never once. And we've had some beauties of arguments. She's Italian and has that temper. But no one knows that, no one knows that she's out to get me. She's got herself a boyfriend, a hotshot car salesman. She brought him to the house, had him over for lunch. She thought I was working but I got my tours mixed up and came home early. I found them eating bacon, lettuce, and tomato sandwiches. And she was wearing my football jersey and a pair of drawers. That's it, and she tells me that he came to make an offer on the Ford. Who would want this piece of junk? He says he'll give me three hundred for it and runs out the door." Larry slowed, and I felt very sorry for him. My father had told me that he was making the whole thing up, that there was no boyfriend. I wanted to tell him about Tracy. "And then," he said, "that night, I'm cleaning my gun and it misfired. The bullet blew a curler right off her head."

"A curler?"

"She wears these giant plastic pink curlers to bed every goddamn night, just like her mother. An inch lower and it would have taken the top of her head off."

No one believed Larry. It had happened at four in the morning. Who cleaned a gun at that hour? "You know, I had these big plans," said Larry. "Lots of kids, a summer house, a big dog, all the shit that I never had, and I almost had it. I got the dog and the house anyway, but fucking Estelle walked out on me. And I don't even know if they'll let me stay on the force. I don't mind the desk work. It doesn't take much to make me happy."

Three years ago my father told me that he had a new partner whom he had to get rid of. "They shouldn't let guys like Larry on the force," he had said. "You have to have a certain temperament or you'll crack up." I looked at Larry, at the fast food containers on the floor, at the overflowing ashtray and wanted to put my arm around him. "Maybe you should get off the force and do something else," I said.

"What? Are you kidding me? Where am I supposed to get a job with unlimited sick time, benefits out my ass, vacation, and a damn good salary. And, besides, policework runs in the family. My old man was a cop in Chicago." Larry concentrated on the road for a while. We went slower and slower as if we were heading up a mountain. "You know your father's worried about you," he said. "Says you're losing weight and getting real cranky. He tells me a lot of things. I've been bringing him a bottle of Scotch. Dewars White Label, only the best and we have some real deep conversations."

"Larry, what the hell are you doing that for? Don't you know he's had a heart attack?" I was yelling. "Are you trying to kill him?" Larry—one nut helping another nut. Of course, Larry. I was mad at myself for not thinking of it.

"Hey," he said. "We were partners."

"I don't give a shit what you were."

"Charlie, come on." I kept my face to the window. It wasn't all his fault, but Christ, couldn't the guy have a little sense? "He asked me, Charlie. Man to man, your father asked me to do him a favor and you know how many favors he's done for me. You know he saved my ass. I know, I'm sorry, it was wrong, but . . ." He searched for words.

"It's OK," I said. "Just don't bring him anything else."

"I promise," he smiled and held out his hand. He would have continued to apologize and promise, shaking my hand all the way to Brooklyn.

"Enough," I forced a laugh. "Forget about it."

Larry and I walked past stores protected by silver-and-black riot gates. The metal cages that opened accordian-style were secured with big chrome locks. Next to the parking meters were pails of garbage and bags and boxes. In many of the dark doorways cigarettes glowed and eyes flashed. Above, people looked down from open windows, heat spilling into the cold night. "Where is this place?" I asked. The street was deserted. It didn't look like there was a party on the block.

"It's a short walk," said Larry.

He stopped and turned around. "You're cool, aren't you, Charlie?"

"Yeah." I wasn't sure what he was talking about.

Larry ducked into a doorway and leaned against a brick wall. "I feel like I can trust you." He took out a brown vial and, using a short plastic straw, snorted some coke up his nose. "You ever do this shit?" he asked.

"Once in a while. Actually no."

"I'm a fucking coke fiend," laughed Larry nervously. "I'd lose my job if anyone found out." Larry waited for me to say something. "Shit, they'd hang me," he said.

Maybe I was naive, but I was so shocked I couldn't say anything.

"Me and you, we should hang out sometime," he said.

I followed Larry up a narrow stairway. Every inch of the walls was sprayed with bizarre colors. The names and scribblings seemed to be struggling for space. Every ten or so steps an unshaded light bulb illuminated the madness on the walls. Larry had just snorted more coke. I wondered how it looked to him.

I figured the hall would be a dive but at the top of the landing Larry opened the door to an elaborately trimmed room. Chandeliers hung from the high ceiling and thick velvet drapes were pulled across the windows. The bar was three deep with drinkers. At a few of the tables covered with white cloths men sat laughing and talking. "Nice, isn't it?" asked Larry.

Vince emerged from the bar area and came around the tables. "Hey, a suit," he said. Behind him I noticed a carpeted podium that held a long table and a microphone on a lectern. A wave of uncertainty left me staring beyond him. It was a combination of my butchered speech and the fact that I had received a C in high school public speaking.

We went to the bar and Vince handed me an overflowing beer in a cup that said, Nathan's Hot Dog, The Original Foot-Long Frank. I was introduced to the men. "How's your father doing?" they asked. "Is he still a crazy bastard?" asked a fat loudmouth holding two beers. A few men gave him a hard stare.

I told them that he was getting better everyday and that they should go visit him. "Nassau County is only a couple of exits on the parkway."

"I still can't understand why Bill doesn't retire. When I get my twenty in, it's goodbye New York, hello Florida," he waved.

"It's become a matter of principle," I said.

The hall was filling fast. I finished a few cold ones at the bar and watched all the activity. There were all types of men there. A three-piece tailored suit, gold cuff links, and tie clasp circle, stood with the ski sweaters and knit pants crowd, who had their arms around the T-shirt and jeans gang. I noticed Larry sitting at a table with a highball and a back-up. Every minute or so he gestured with his hands as if explaining something. But there was no one else at the table.

"You're going to say a few words?" asked Vince, more as a statement than a question.

"Yeah." I patted my pocket and felt the folded papers.

"Gentlemen," said Vince into the microphone. "Gentlemen, at the bar, get your drinks and find your seats." There were some shouts, "Aw, let them drink, Leave 'em alone, Get one for me." Chairs scraped loudly on the tiled floor, and men wound between the tables, holding drinks above their heads.

I sat in the middle of the table on the podium, between John Haggerty and Peter Gorman. The tight suit was making me sweat. I ran my tongue along the soft scab on the inside of my lip. The beer had opened the cut. The lights in the hall dimmed and some men said, "Owoo, Ahaa," like children watching fireworks. A spotlight in the back of the room came on and found its way to Vince's face. "Could I have some quiet," he said. A minute later, the only noise was the hum of ceiling fans.

"In case you don't know, I'm Vince Tarentino, Bill Patterson's partner." His voice boomed around the room. I loosened my tie and unfolded my speech. "Can you hear me in the back?" There was a chorus of "Yeahs," and a loud, "Unfortunately." The men laughed. "I'm going to do the introducing tonight," said Vince. "We've got some powerful speech makers here so I'll leave that for them. Our first speaker tonight is John

Haggerty, the D.E.A. president."

The clapping stopped when big John said "OK, OK, you're going to spoil me" into the microphone. "You men here tonight show three things." He held up three fingers. "One, support for Bill Patterson, who lies, at this very moment, in a hospital recovering from a heart attack. A heart attack that, and there's no doubt in my mind, was not caused by his 3,603 career arrests, his two honorary awards, or many court appearances. It was caused by internal pressure." The audience clapped. "And you show courage," shouted Haggerty, holding up two fingers. "Kael feels that, and I quote him, 'you men lack the good judgment and proper decision-making sought by the department.' Isn't that some shit?" A few hooted and cheered. "And again I quote our fearless leader, whose only collar is the one around his neck, 'It is a good way to evaluate the judgment of the personnel.' Well, I say, and he can quote me, you men are the finest of New York's Finest." They clapped again. "And I say he lacks the good judgment and proper decision making that Bill Patterson used on the seventeenth of October, when the Hasidic community stormed the seven-four." Men rose one by one, clapping and whistling. Haggerty raised his hands and stepped back to the table like a prizefighter. He never got to number three.

Gorman didn't speak clearly, and the guys yelled, "We can't hear you." "I was saying," he cleared his throat, "although we cannot strike we can act. And tonight is a fine example of action. In the coming trial, Bill is going to need all the support you men can muster. Let's remember him in our prayers," he paused and there was silence, "and carry his spirit in our hearts."

After the clapping subsided, Gorman took the seat next to me. Sweat dripped down his forehead and he gulped his drink. There were two more similar speeches and then Vince went to the microphone and waited for silence. Some men were dashing to the bar for a refill. "Our next speaker is our guest of honor tonight and knows Bill Patterson in a way that we never will. I'd like to introduce Bill's son, Charlie Patterson."

They clapped, and the spotlight hit me in the eyes. I stood and made my way around the table. "Tell'em Charlie," said Haggerty.

I stood in front of the lectern and quiet spread through the hall. I smoothed out the folded papers and gripped the stand. I swallowed and read, "My father, a man of integrity, tried to reconcile a confrontation and now faces alienation from his job and . . ." I looked into the light. In the blackness, the men waited. The speech was all wrong. "My father wrote this today," I explained. The men laughed. "What I want to say . . ." My voice crashed around the room and my foot started tapping the floor. "Could you turn off the light?" I said.

"Shut it off," someone yelled, and there was darkness. Slowly, I was able to see candles at the tables and men's faces, all watching and waiting.

"What I want to say is," I searched for the words, "that my father is like my best friend." I caught my breath not believing I had said something as corny as that. "He taught me everything. He taught me how to ride a bike, how to shake hands, how to," I thought, "do just about everything. He taught me right from wrong." I dug my fingernails into the wood and listened to the quiet. "My father's old fashioned," I said, "My mother says he's from the old school. He called his father Sir until my grandpa died a couple of years ago and he told me one time that he never loved anyone more than his mother until he met my mother. My father has a lot of anger in him but he's got a lot more love." I began to breathe more easily. "It is true that he hates, but he hates only people who will hurt him or his family. He doesn't hate religions or races. I know he's in a lot of trouble, and he's worried about keeping his job. He doesn't want to retire. He loves his job, so don't let them take it from him."

The men stood clapping and clapping. "We won't," they yelled. "Don't you worry!"

I was drunker than I could ever remember and was going to Manhattan at seventy-five miles per hour with Larry. I had the window open and sucked the rushing cold air trying to clear my head. After the speeches the guys had brought me shots and beers and mixed me a few concoctions with names like Arebarbubas and Whambaslambers. I did a three-stage drink called, A Hop, Skip, and a Jump, and Get Naked, with the guys cheering me on. It was like drinking three glasses of fire, and when I woke up, Larry told me the party was over and he was giving me a ride home.

Larry watched the road with glazed cue-ball eyes. He was also flying from who knew what, and in the back seat, there was a passed-out guy whom we were supposedly driving home. They had carried him through the hall and rolled him down the stairs. We didn't even know where he lived. About a half hour ago, before Larry decided to cut across two lanes of traffic and drive over the center island of green and shrubs that divided the parkway, I had tried to check the guy's wallet. I had turned around and left my hand hanging in midair. The guy was lying on his side like a baby, his shirt rolled up over his pregnant-looking beer belly, with his hand holding his holstered .38 special that was attached to his belt. I turned slowly and sat low.

The speedometer was bouncing from seventy to eighty. I was sober enough to dig around in the crease of the seat for the safety belt and suggest that we call it a night.

"We're almost there," said Larry. He finished a bottle of Miller and tossed it in the back. It bounced off the guy's hairless gut and clanged against the other empties. I buckled up and watched the guardrail whiz by on the left. "And besides," said Larry, "it's early."

"Then, slow down."

"Oh, sorry." Some nervousness that the drugs had smoothed returned. "We got any more brews?" The needle dropped to fifty-five, fifty, forty-five. Headlights were coming up fast.

"Not that slow," I yelled. A little white import, not bigger than a refrigerator on wheels, swung around us, the horn sounding like "D-i-i-i—ck."

Larry leveled off at fifty and moved into the first lane.

"Don't get me killed," I said, giving him a beer.

"Killed?" He twisted off the bottle top. "I kill you, your father kills me. Right?"

"Let's not find out."

"Well, one thing I'm going to do is get you laid, parlayed, relayed, and delayed," he said, taking a slug.

"Just worry about yourself." I didn't want to get laid. Plenty of times at the firehouse I had had my chance with a hooker named Coral. I guess she was about forty and, from the look of her body, was someone's mother.

It was real weird the way it always happened. She'd come in and hang at the bar for a while sponging up free drinks, rubbing guy's crotches, trying to kiss them. Everyone had a big laugh and pushed her away. Then, she'd zero in on a shy guy, usually this guy Spear, nick-named that because of the shape of his head. Coral would start undressing him and he'd try to put his clothes back on as fast as she pulled them off. Every-body would be yelling, "Go for it, Spear." With a little help from his friends, Spear was dragged into the men's room and got a freebie right on the floor in front of the urinals. Coral always took the top. I guess because the floor was so cold and not very clean. If she gave Spear a blow, she'd spit the sperm in the sink, and the fire-men would whisper, "I'm not using that sink any-more." After Spear's free ride, most of the married, and one or two of the single, guys lined up in front of the door. She did them each for five dollars. On line they'd be pushing and yelling like kids waiting to go out in the playground. Afterward everyone ignored Coral and they threw the glass that she had used in the garbage.

"I got this chick on the side," said Larry. "Her name's Goldie, and I was supposed to meet her tonight. But, she got sick of me. I met her on the New Jersey Board-walk, and I fell in love with her. She had this blonde hair and one of those up-turned noses. This chick wasn't ruined yet. She was still clean. She was so fine I would have eaten peanuts out of her shit, I loved this chick that fucking much. You ever love somebody like that?"

"I don't know about peanuts," I said, flashing on Tracy. "But , yeah, I loved someone like that."

"I might even have to kill her," he said too seriously. "I can't get the cunt off my mind. She had her phone number changed and now I've got nobody to call and every time the phone rings I get this fucking rush. She was the only one who ever called me." The crazy talk was sobering me up. Larry's eyes were opened fiercely. "The police department thinks they are so fucking smart. But look." He opened his coat. There was a gun on a shoulder holster.

"I told you that," muttered the guy in the back. I leaned over the seat. He was still asleep, but his arms were over his head.

"You like oldies?" Larry plugged a tape in the 8-track player that was built into the radio. He switched tracks by pressing the fine tuner. "Big Girls Don't Cry" came on and Larry sang "No, they don't cry-yi-yi, they don't cry."

Soon, we were somewhere in the city and Larry ran red lights and sang, "She talks too much, she worries me to death. Yeah, she ta-aw-aw-awks too much, she talks too much." He did a roll of drums on the steering wheel. I watched the street signs, trying to figure out where we were, and opened another beer. I didn't know a damn thing about the city and it pissed me off. Besides class trips to the Museum of Natural History and Radio City Music Hall in a yellow school bus marked School of the Most Holy Eucharist, I had been to the city only three or four times. On Louise's tenth birthday, I took her to see a Broadway play. I remember walking uptown holding her hand, ready to fight off muggers, pushers, prostitutes, crazy madmen, and pickpockets who worked in gangs of three and four. It was a Long Island surburban phobia that kept my friends glued to the town bars and local movie theaters that specialized in horror flicks.

A cop on horseback trotted across the street, and Larry said, "I should run that beast over and put it out of its misery." He honked his horn and sped by.

I told him I had to take a leak.

On a dark side street, we got out and pissed. I had to go badly. In a doorway, I ran a stream against the window, and it drained all the way to the curb. Before I could get my dick in my pants, Larry grabbed me around the shoulder. "I fucking love you and your old man." I zipped up and he twirled me around. He was strong for a skinny guy.

"You're OK, Larry," I said, hugging him.

"Charlie, you're the fucking best." We stood holding each other like two lovers. "That speech you gave had me crying."

"My father really cares about you." I said. "So do I."

"I'm gonna get you a cute little piece of ass." He laughed, and I saw that his front teeth were fake. Bridge work held everything in place.

When we got in the car the guy in the back was sitting up. Booze and sleep kept his eyes half closed and the hair on his head was standing like the fur on an angry cat. Larry started the engine, smiling, watching the guy's dazed and bewildered face in the rearview mirror. "Where the fuck am I?" he asked, rubbing his eyes. His voice sounded friendly.

"We were giving you a ride home," I said.

"How long have I been out?"

"A good hour."

He thought about this and nodded, "You're Patterson's kid, aren't you?"

"Yeah."

"I worked with your father over in robbery squad back

in the sixties; name's Bruce Porter." I told him my name and then Larry introduced himself.

"We're going to get a little sea food," said Larry. "A couple of bearded clams. You up for it?"

"Run that past me again," said Bruce, leaning forward to listen. He was somewhere in his late thirties or early forties. The hair around his ears and sideburns was greying.

"We're gonna get some slit," he said, pulling into the street. Larry was growing tense and the night was losing its momentum fast.

"You'll drop me off in Queens afterward?"

"Sure."

"What the fuck." He sat back and closed his eyes.

We cruised the Times Square area. I saw the building that dropped the ball on New Year's Eve and remembered reading that they would change the white lights to red and drop an apple this year. Every December thirty-first, I counted off the seconds, listening to Guy Lombardo's Royal Canadians play "Auld Lang Syne," led by Guy Lombardo's brother, who looked just like him. Guy was dead. And all the people in the square acted like raving lunatics, climbing on each other's shoulders to get a better view, hoping to get on TV, and I watched them with my family, relatives, and friends also waiting for the goddamn ball to drop, never yet having a real girl friend to kiss on the mouth, so I usually stood there with a bottle of champagne ready to pop the cork, aiming it off to the side so that I didn't give anyone a black eye. Four, three, two, one, pop. May old acquaintance be forgot and la-da-de-da-da-daa, may old acquaintance be, I shake my father's hand and kiss my mother on the cheek, I give Louise a punch and a hug, my aunts peck me on the face, leaving traces of lipstick, my uncles shake my hand firmly saying, Happy New Year, Happy New Year, Happy New Year, and then, I clink glasses with my friends but this year they'd be at the firehouse watching the goddamn apple drop on the donated TV, and Ralph at Princeton had a steady girl, so he wouldn't be around. If I didn't get back with Tracy, I'd be popping another cork this year. It was pretty goddamn depressing. Yeah, the night was losing it fast.

I breathed in the city air. The smell of reefer, sausage meat from the Greek take-out counter, beef shishka-bob on sticks, and, yes, even chestnuts roasting on a charcoal pit, drifted in the window. People roamed up and down Forty-second Street. Cars flowed by slowly, like thick blood. Larry snorted more coke, using a rolled match book cover. He opened his eyes wide and smiled. A woman in a short yellow dress and a short rabbit fur coat crossed the street unsteadily on high heels. She stared into our car like an animal blinded by head-lights. Larry pulled to the curb in front of a fire hydrant and she came to the window. She reminded me of one of the Supremes gone bad. "You boys going out?" she asked.

"Yeah," said Larry. "How much for some head?"

"Fifteen for a blow job, thirty for anything else, or I could give," she smiled and looked at me with her ruined brown face, "you all a little something for fifty."

"Count me out," I said, as though it was no big deal and as if my next sentence was going to be, I'll pick some up in the morning.

"Me, too," said Bruce.

"What the hell is this?" shouted Larry.

"Honey, you look like you need to shoot a load,"

said the woman smiling fingernail-size teeth the color
of coffee stains.

"Nah," I said, wondering if she really saw something
in my face. "But, you go ahead, Larry."

Bruce and I got out with Larry bitching and groaning
and trying to talk me into it. "A measly fifteen dollars," he said. "And I'll pay." I kept up the no's and
nah's. The woman climbed in the front, ripped stockings and all. "I'll meet you back here in an hour," said
Larry.

"Baby, you best not take no hour," she said.

———————

Bruce and I watched the car pull into traffic, the square
red taillights glowed in the night, blending with the
others. "Some character," said Bruce. It was a still night,
but cold, and it came right through my cheap suit. Bruce
was tall, with thin arms and narrow shoulders that
melted into a fat belly. Street people passed, giving us
the once-over.

"We might as well have a look around," said Bruce.

Hands in our pockets, we headed up the block. I spied
a small man squatting in a lighted doorway eating
Cheese Doddles. Around his mouth, his grey beard was
orange. A cocoa-skinned Puerto Rican girl wearing jeans
and a high school sweater hooked my arm. "What do
you need tonight?" she asked. I spun and pulled away
and she rebounded using the same line on someone else.
I walked backward, watching her bounce from one
potential john to the next. She was full of electric energy,
eyes flashing, her little ass springing in stride with the
fast-paced passersby. How long could she keep that up?
It couldn't take long to burn out in this scene. I bumped
into someone, the guy gave me a blank stare. I caught

up to Bruce. He was standing in front of "Peep-O-Rama! New York's Largest Peep Show." Orange neon flashed "Adult Books, Movies, Sexual Aids, Private Booths, Live Peep Show." Men sidewinded into the door like crabs.

"Some crazy shit goes on in these joints," said Bruce. I followed him in the door.

Disco music blared in the brightly lit yellow room. Magazines lined the walls and filled table upon table. There were about a dozen men browsing as if it were a garage sale. "It's not a library. No trying, just buying," shouted an old man behind the cash register. I paged through *Close Encounters of the Lesbian Kind.* A lot of girls fingering and sucking each other. I closed the book. Already, I had lost Bruce. For a second all the unfamiliar eyes seemed to look up from the smut and peer at me. I walked to the back looking for Bruce. Rows of black booths advertised sexual scenes. "Little Dinah. Nothing Could be Finer" showed a young bleach-blonde dressed as little Bo-Peep. She was sucking on a dildo the length of her arm. I slipped into the booth feeling like a low-life piece of shit and fished a quarter from my pocket.

A white light flashed and a fuzzy movie began. I stood at attention, thinking the walls were sticky from guy's jerking off. The plot was simple. Poor little Bo-Peep had lost her sheep and found a twelve-inch dildo, which she shoved up every place possible. I don't think I've ever felt so low.

I emerged from the black booth and rescouted the place for Bruce. I had had enough and I wanted to go but I didn't want to be out on the street alone. I followed arrows up a carpeted staircase. The second floor was crowded with men, all types; suited businessmen holding briefcases, some Chinese guys with, honest to God, instamatic cameras around their necks, some Superfly-looking dudes, and a bunch of Long Island high schoolers, probably with wallets full of fake proof borrowed from their older brothers. There was a little guy with an ice cream vendor's change machine on his belt who kept yelling, "Can't do nothing with paper money." Around the walls were glass doors with girls behind them in bras, panties, and garter belts. When a man entered a booth, the girl drew the curtain. Bruce, if he was still in the place, was behind one of the doors.

I waited there watching the women. They must have been working on commission because they were putting on a good show. One caught my eye and she slid her hand in her panties then licked her fingers.

I went over to her window and she opened her legs as if inviting me in. Black pubic hair stuck out of her white panties and looked as hard as wire. A rash of pimples coated her inner thighs. She smiled enticingly, showing rotten teeth, and I bolted down the stairs and out into the night.

Five minutes later, Bruce showed up at the fire hydrant and we waited for Larry. "This city sucks," he said.

"Boy, did she love it," said Larry. "And she had some nice little tits." He stopped at a light at Broadway.

"She was just a fucking whore," said Bruce.

Larry shut up fast. There was no use in bullcrapping. It just made things worse. He turned down a street, went too fast for the bumpy road, and pulled over. "You want to see the asshole of the world?" he asked.

The three of us got out and looked through a plywood barrier of a construction site. The excavation was deep and dark. Larry threw an empty bottle over the fence. We listened for it to break, nothing.

"That's a hole and a half," said Bruce.

We began throwing all the empties over the fence listening for them to break. Bruce threw his high in the air, heaving his heavy body off balance. We didn't laugh or talk. We threw as if we had to throw. Larry began breaking bottles in the street. They smashed loudly, the yellow glass splattering across the road. When there was nothing left to throw, we got back in the car and left.

CHAPTER

15

I kneeled next to the toilet in my underwear trying to heave Friday night into the bowl. I had a hangover and a half and there was a burning sensation in my stomach. It felt as though I had swallowed a lit pipe. Everything seemed worse because the bathroom was a mess. The plastic garbage pail shaped like an oyster shell was overflowing with tissues, shampoo bottles, rolled newspapers, and cigarette butts. Now my mother was even smoking in the bathroom. No one had even put the toilet paper in the holder. It lay unraveled and soggy from the shower that leaked around the base. What the hell was going on?

I curled on the rug in front of the sink and pressed my face on the blue tile floor. It felt good. Bathroom floors are always like ice. The phone began to ring and

I listened, hoping someone would answer it. It rang and rang. I yelled, "Will somebody answer that?" The caller didn't give up. Where was everyone? It had to be my father. He was the only madman I knew who would let it ring thirty times. I got up, charged down the stairs into the kitchen, and grabbed the phone.

"Hello."

"Charlie, why didn't you answer the phone?" It was my mother.

"Because I was busy."

"Are you all right?"

"There's not even a clean towel in the bathroom." I must have sounded like a two-year-old but I felt so bad.

"I'm at the hospital." she said. "And no one can find your father. His clothes are gone so he must have . . ."

"Oh God," I moaned.

"Charlie, would you go out and look for him? They want me to stay here in case he comes back. You know where he goes."

"Where?"

"He could have had another heart attack."

"OK, don't worry. I'll find him." She was still saying something when I hung up.

I poured myself a glass of orange juice and washed my face in the kitchen sink, above the dirty breakfast dishes. I wasn't very worried about his heart. I was wondering just who the hell he thought he was pulling this shit? My mother was the one I was beginning to worry about. Even the kitchen was a mess. The counters were cluttered with dishes, canned goods, and old newspapers, and last night's greasy frying pans were still on the stove. The fat had hardened and turned white. I never remembered the house in worse shape.

I filled the sink with hot water and added a squirt of
Dish-Brite dishwashing liquid and the stupid TV commercial song ran through my mind, "Hands that do
dishes as soft as your face." I could see the typical
housewife holding her hands to the fake sunlight. Could
my mother be worried about dishpan hands?

I filled the drainboard with plates that I could see
myself in, and decided I'd check Kelly's Bar and Grill
and then Pete's Pub. Maybe Larry had taken him out. I
let the dishes soak and found Larry's phone number in
our telephone directory.

"Hello, Larry?"

"What do you want from me?" he yelled and hung
up.

I called back. "Larry, it's me, Charlie."

"Charlie who?"

"What do you mean Charlie who? Charlie Patterson."

"Oh, yeah, sorry, I was sleeping. It takes me a few
minutes to collect my marbles."

"Have you seen my father?"

"No."

"Well, if he calls, tell him to go back to the hospital."

"I thought he was in the hospital."

"He's escaped."

"How?"

"How am I supposed to know? Maybe he tunneled
out."

"That was some time we had last night. You had a
good time, right?"

"Yeah, Larry, a ball. Listen, take care."

———

I parked the Buick in front of Kelly's. It was across the street from the mini mall. The Saturday shoppers were out in full force, so I was lucky to get a spot. The sidewalk in front of Sal's Pizza was crowded with bikes. I wondered where Louise was. I hadn't seen her since the Scrabble game.

Kelly's was an English-Tudor pub that specialized in businessmen's lunches. Dad loved their Reuben sandwiches. I'm going to grab a Reuben, he'd say leaving the house, and come home six hours later with mustard slopped on his shirt. The noon whistle sounded, one long blast from the firehouse. I imagined Paul pressing the button with a satisfied look on his face. It was such a small town.

I ran across the street, remembering the night my father was almost hit by the car. He had punched a man for me. For me, because I wouldn't. It almost didn't matter if he was right or wrong. Someday I would tell him about the Corvette. I pulled open the heavy wooden door and walked into the dark bar. Red lights in cut-glass lamp shades glowed above the mahogany bar. A white-shirted bartender with a red, veiny nose polished glasses with a cloth napkin. "Help you?" he asked.

I described my father and asked him if he had seen him. "He comes in here for Reuben sandwiches all the time," I added.

The bartender looked up. "Bill the cop, hell, yes. That's your old man, that son of a bitch?"

"Yes."

"He was here this morning. I had to open the door to let him in."

About then I started getting real scared. I asked him how my father looked.

"Well, he's lost some weight. No, I can't say he looked good."

"Thanks." I walked out, ran across the street, and got in the car.

I cupped my hands and peered in the window at Pete's Pub. Dad stood at the end of the bar next to Scotty. They were laughing at something, and Scotty waved his white sailor's cap in the air. The bar was lined with men with heavy eyes, and a couple of days' beard on their faces. What the hell could he be laughing about? I swung the door open.

The only voice in the place was my father's, and about the only thing moving was the curling cigarette smoke that trailed above the men. The bartender looked me over as I passed down the narrow room.

"Charlie," said Dad. "What a coincidence, I've been in here twice in a month and both times I run into you!" Scotty rasped out a laugh and pulled his cap to his eyebrows. "Have a drink."

"What do you think you're doing?" I asked. Half his shirt tail was out and his belt had missed the front two loops.

"Me? What do you think *you're* doing?"

"Dad, everyone's worried about you." He pulled me to him. His breath came fast and smelled like potato chips and beer.

"Your mother tried to sign me into the funny farm." He released me. "The nut ward. She thinks I'm crazy. What do you think?" He lifted his thick beer mug.

"She didn't sign you . . ."

"Twenty-two years of marriage and she signs me into the loony bin. Let me tell you something, no one is locking me in a psycho-ward." His face shook. "I'd rather die right here in this shit hole."

"It was just counseling. She was trying to help you."

"That's what my kids told me," said Scotty, sticking his face between us. "But you've got to catch the bear before you sell his skin. We'll help you daddy. They had me over in Gardener's Hosptial drying out before I could blink an eye. And," he clicked out his front teeth and laid them on the bar, "One of those goddamn winos knocked my teeth out." Dad and I looked at his row of teeth attached to a pink plastic retainer. Scotty picked it up and snapped it back in his mouth. "I used to have a nice smile. A smile was my umbrella," he laughed. "And I'll tell you this, beware of chefs who wear nurse's uniforms. They cook in the bedpans." Scotty's watery black eyes shone and he waited for us to say something.

"This is a whole different story," I said.

"Well, I say there's a hole in your story," said Scotty, smiling his fake teeth. He was a clever old guy.

"You want to really laugh," said Dad. He rummaged through his coat pocket and handed me a crumpled cocktail napkin. "Read this."

There was a couple of jokes and a drawing of a guy trying to tie his left shoe with his right one on a chair. "No, I don't want to laugh."

Scotty snatched it from my hand and read, "How do you get a one-armed Polack out of a tree?"

"Wave to him," I said. It was an old joke.

"What did the Polack name his pet zebra?"

"Spot." They were very old jokes.

"Hey, Charlie, you're pretty damn good," said Dad.

"Let me read him another one," said Scotty.

Scotty, having our attention, took his time. He finished his beer and lit a smoke. "What happened to the Polish terrorist who tried to blow up a car?" I thought and pulled at the hard gum under the bar.

"You don't know this one," said Scotty. "He burnt his lips on the exhaust pipe."

No one laughed. "That wasn't on the napkin," said Dad, seriously. "You read him the ones on the napkin."

"How many pieces does a Polish jigsaw puzzle have?"

"One," I said. "Let's get out of here. I have the car outside, and Mom's waiting at the hospital."

"Give him another one."

"What do you call a dozen empties?"

"Let's go," I said.

"A sad case," yelled Scotty.

"Randy," called Dad.

The wiry bartender lifted his black leather cap and stroked his long brown hair. He took his boot off the sink and walked slowly down the bar on the creaking wooden flooring. "I got you this time," he said taking my father's mug.

"And get him," said Dad, pointing to me.

A man in a baggy wool sweater and painter's pants slid quarters into the jukebox. There were dried leaves clinging to his back. Afternoon sun came through the cloudy windows and dust floated in the shafts of light. My father leaned on the bar, head hung, his weight on his elbows, one foot on the brass rail watching Randy fill the glasses. "Read him another one," said Dad.

"That's all there is," said Scotty.

I was worried about his heart. He had been drinking at the hosptial but not this heavy. Thank God, dirty as Pete's Pub was, it was warm. I dragged a stool over and told him to sit. Dad sat and the bartender brought over headless mugs of Schaeffer. "You know this guy?" he said to me with a wink.

"I think so," I said.

"Then you're on the house."

"I'm not going back to the hospital," said Dad, when Randy moved away and Scotty shuffled to the men's room. "We'll have a couple more and go home. I'm going to sleep with my wife tonight." He shrugged his square shoulders like a kid. In his face, I could see mine. We had the same lopsided smile.

"The hair of the dog that bit you," Dad said and had a swallow of beer. The jukebox played "House of the Rising Sun" and Dad rubbed my shoulder and began to sing, "There is a house in New Orleans, they call the Rising Sun, and it's been the ruin of many a poor boy . . ."

On my tenth birthday Dad bought me a lemon-colored Gibson folk guitar. It was one of the best money could buy, and when I went for my ten free lessons at the music shop the guy who owned the place always asked me if he could play it. I handed it over proudly and a little embarrassed because I had such an expensive guitar and didn't even know how to tune it. The first song I learned was "House of the Rising Sun" and although Dad really couldn't hold a tune, he'd sit there for an hour singing it over and over while I struggled with the chord changes. I still have the guitar and I'm not too bad at some songs. I started singing with him. "The only thing a gambler needs is a suitcase and a trunk and the only time . . ." A couple of guys at the bar joined in singing real low. Dad hugged me and I put my ear to his chest to try to hear his heartbeat.

Five Schaeffers on an empty stomach had given me a nice glow. Drunk, hung over, and drunk again in less than twenty-four hours was probably a new record for me. I followed Dad into the house. Turning the handle of the pantry door, he weaved and bounced off the wall. Laughing, holding his bumped head, he almost fell into the kitchen. He looked around like a prisoner coming out of a dark cell. Louise put down her half-eaten tuna on toast that was neatly cut into quarters. She had chocolate milk above her lip. "Dad, everyone is looking for you," she said.

"Here I am." He kissed the top of her curly head.

"He was at Pete's," I said.

"You're drunk," she said, smiling.

"He's not drunk," said Dad, stuffing a triangle of toast and tuna in his mouth. "Charlie's not allowed to drink."

"X–Y–Z," giggled Louise.

"What?"

"Examine your zipper," she said pointing at my fly.

"He's advertising." Dad slapped me on the back as I zipped up.

I dialed the hospital. My mother came on the line, and the switchboard operator clicked off.

"Charlie, did you find him?" she asked.

"Yeah, he's home."

"Let me talk." Dad pulled the phone out of my hand. "Honey, I've had enough," he said. "And I don't need head treatment, I'm not crazy yet." Pressing his forehead against the refrigerator, he listened for a moment. "No choice," he whispered. "Who the hell has a choice? Nobody ever gave me a choice, but what the hell difference did that make? You just come home. No, I'm not going anywhere."

Dr. Hall, five foot five and round as Humpty Dumpty, followed my mother into the house. Above his wire-rimmed glasses, his forehead stretched to the back of his head. Everything about him spelled egg. Dad had been lucky to get Dr. Hall. The fat little man was the heart specialist at three Long Island hospitals. "He's upstairs sleeping it off," my mother said.

"Sleeping what off?" asked the doctor.

"The excitement," I said before my mother could answer.

"Charlie, you don't look well," she said taking off her long coat. The shirt she wore was tucked neatly into her pleated pants. She seemed to have gotten taller, or perhaps thinner. "Louise, why don't you start supper."

"There's nothing to make," she said.

"Then go out and get some chopped meat. There's money in my purse." After hanging her coat on a hook in the hall closet, Mom shut the door with a bang. "I'm sorry to keep you waiting," she said. "But things have been a little hectic around here."

"I understand," said the doctor. My mother towered over the little man and he nervously picked lint off his tweed jacket that couldn't possibly have buttoned around his stomach. When they started up the stairs, Louise and I followed.

———————

In a voice usually used on kindergarten children, Dr. Hall asked my father how he was feeling. Dad lay across my parents' king-sized bed. "Joy," he murmured.

"The doctor's here," she said.

"Hello." He opened his eyes and sat up. "Hello, everybody," he said.

Leaning his pudgy head over the bed, the doctor shone a thin silver flashlight in Dad's right eye. "You've been drinking?"

"Yeah, and I'm real sorry about that. But honest to God, it couldn't be helped."

"Just lie back and let me listen to your heart." He clicked off the flashlight and Dad fell back and bounced on the bed. My mother kneeled with one knee on the bed and unbuttoned his shirt.

"What you should be listening to is my head. Right, Joy? It's real sick. It's not working right. Someone left it out in the sun too long and now my brain is crawling with maggots. They're going to come out of my ears some time tomorrow after lunch." He stuck his fingers in his ears. "I'm holding them in right now."

"Bill, stop it," shouted Mom. I started backing out of the room, thinking about those maggots. One time at the docks I had seen a big carp lying on the sidewalk with its dried-out scaly skin moving slightly. I thought I was seeing things and gave the fish a kick. It was hollow and the white maggots flew across the pavement.

"I'm sorry," said Dad. "But, if I'm crazy, I might as well act crazy."

The doctor put his stethoscope in his ears and moved the silver receiver on Dad's hairy chest. "That's enough of that talk," said the doctor loudly and chuckled.

"It's not funny," said Louise.

"I know that," the doctor sing-songed. Louise started crying and bolted from the room. I looked at my father's ears, half expecting to see little white worms come crawling out. My mother held his hand, watching the doctor's face. From his bag, the doctor pulled out a device in a leather case and began putting wires into

the leads. "We're going to get your heartbeat on tape.
It's a portable EKG." Four suction cups were stuck to
my father's chest with glue that looked like vaseline.

"I'm not going back," said Dad.

"You don't have to." The doctor strapped the machine
around Dad's neck and under his shoulder.

CHAPTER
16

*A*gain, Dad pounded up the stairs and I sat up in bed. It was eleven A.M., and he had been banging doors, playing the radio, and going up and down the stairs since nine. My door swung into the wall, chipping a small piece of plaster. "Charlie, you getting up today?"

"I might as well, you won't let me sleep."

"I'm used to getting up at five o'clock." In his hand he held a couple of letters and under his arm the heart monitor hung like a woman's handbag. The black wires crept inside his vinyl hunting vest that he wore half-zippered over a white undershirt. From a side pocket, he took out his reading glasses and unfolded the letter. I imagined the little needle recording his heartbeat, bumping up and down. It was hard to believe he had a weak heart. Last month he had carried my neighbor's refrigerator up two flights of stairs. My father had strapped the thing to his back and it rose like a small building.

"I found the mail," he said. "Doesn't sound too good." He waved the letters. "If I lose the case they could take this house. They'll sue me up the ass, and I don't even get a lawyer."

"You can't worry about that now. You've got to worry about getting better." I pulled my legs up and he sat at the bottom of the bed.

"I told you once you'd get everything when I die," he said. "But I may not have anything to give you."

About six months ago, after a day of guzzling beer, my father had eaten chicken with his head a few inches out of his plate. It was a Saturday, the night of Louise's eighth grade variety show. "You're not going in that condition," my mother had said angrily. "You'll be a spectacle as usual."

"I'm going," he had muttered. "I wouldn't miss it for the world." After supper he had sat in the recliner and fell asleep. Mom and Louise left for the show without him. I could have gotten him up, but I felt sorry for my mother. An hour later, he woke and raced up the stairs and put on a suit. I told him the show was just about over but he went anyway and fifteen minutes later he was home again, drinking beer. Sitting at the kitchen table in his suit and shined shoes he had said, "When I die you're going to get everything, every damn thing. No one else is getting a dime."

Now, he sat at the end of my bed looking out the window. He opened a letter and read, " 'Protection does not apply to any cop or city employee guilty of misconduct or abuse of authority.' Looks bad, Charlie."

"Dad, don't worry. You've got everyone behind you. The whole police department." I told him about the fund-raiser and he wanted to know who was there and how the speech went. "Oh, everyone loved the speech," I said. "And there must have been over six hundred guys."

"Come on, I'll make you breakfast." He stood up and rubbed his hands together.

I sipped coffee and gave Mom the main section of the paper in exchange for the Long Island pull-out. She flipped through the first few pages, then started clipping out coupons. Every Monday was double-coupon value day at the Foodtown Supermarket, and she tried to cash in on the savings. Dad leaned against the cabinet, still looking over his mail. "I'll have to sue the city one way or the other," he said. "That's exactly what I'll do." He went to the cabinet above the stove and took out the Scotch.

"Bill, put that away." My mother got up. "It's not on your diet." She had taped his low sodium, low cholesterol diet to the refrigerator. "It says right here, 'no alcoholic drinks.' "

"I've never had a better reason to drink in my entire life." He screwed off the cap. "The more erratic my heartbeat is, the better my case is." He tapped the machine.

"Don't start drinking," I whined.

"Don't you have school today?" he asked.

"No."

"Why not?"

"I took off."

"He's quit," said my mother. "He'll start again next semester." I felt like a rug had just been yanked out from under me. "Charlie, I called the college. It would be impossible to make up the work you've missed."

"Why didn't you tell me you knew."

"Do you want me to kick you in the ass or do you want to kick yourself in the ass for the rest of your life?" asked Dad.

"Nobody's kicking me in the ass," I said flatly. He filled a juice glass with booze and seemed to size me up. "You're the one who's in trouble. I'm not getting sued and thrown off the police force."

"Listen, big man, if I want any shit out of you I'll knock it out of you."

"You'd love to hit me, wouldn't you?" He glared at me, and Mom stepped between us. "Go ahead and hit the only person who gives a shit about you."

"Stop it." She gave me a shove.

"Charlie, you're the one who's sick," said Dad, drinking the Scotch. He made a face and swallowed.

"No, you're not sick." said Mom, grabbing the bottle and capping it. "And you're not going to stand there drinking right in front of me."

"Forget it, Joy." Dad finished the glass and ripped the diet off the refrigerator. "Just forget the whole thing, the doctor, the diet, my heart, me, because you don't know how I feel." He pulled some grey hairs out of his chest. "Did you feel that?" he demanded. "Did you?" My mother tried to say something, and I muttered, You're out of your mind. "So from now on," he shouted. "I'm the boss of my body. I'm the only one who knows how I feel."

"Then go ahead and drink." She stormed inside and

put on her coat. "But don't expect me to sit by watching you kill yourself. Drink, drink, drink." She opened the back door. "Go on, drink." She left.

"I will," he yelled.

At the counter, Dad poured two shots. "Come over and toast our futures." He lifted his glass. "We'll have a party. It might be the last party I ever have." Holding the bottle by the neck, he marched in place. "Boom, boom, ba, ba, boom, boom, boom," he said imitating a base drum. "Come, Charlie, celebrate." He marched over and handed me my shot.

Years ago my father had marched with the police department in the Saint Patrick's Day Parade and I had seen him on TV. It was drizzling, the announcer called it, "Perfect weather for the Irish." My mother kept saying, "Your father is going to catch pneumonia." When a rowdy gang of blue uniforms could be seen coming up Fifth Avenue, the announcer said, "Here comes New York's finest, New York's proudest." Dad was out in front, sopping wet, waving his nightstick. He was on for only a second but I'll never forget how happy he looked. Now, he stood marching in the kitchen holding the shot and the bottle. "I don't want it," I said.

Still marching, he drank my shot, uncapped the bottle, and took a swig. I noticed a tiny red light on the side of the heart machine. "As stupid as you may think it is, I'm the only one who knows how I feel. And I don't feel anything anymore."

Looking at the floor, the empty Scotch bottle behind him, he asked, "Did I ever tell you about Georgie LaRosa?" He had, but I said No. "Well, he thought he was a tough son of a bitch. And he was, damn he was.

We grew up together. He lived on Avenue A and 10th Street, fourth house on the . . .? Anyway, Georgie could lift a car, one end at a time, onto the sidewalk, and I saw him do it. Put handkerchiefs on his palms and did it like it was nothing. You show me a guy who can do that and I'll give you a hundred dollars. And I'm talking about a car, not one of those piece of shit imports." The radio was blasting, "Strangers in the Night," and Dad's face reminded me of an old black-and-white photograph.

"Why don't you sit down?"

He let go of the cabinet counter and sat across from me at the kitchen table. Leaning in the chair like a cowboy in front of a saloon, the back of his head resting against the wall, he said, "So I hadn't seen Georgie in fifteen years and he shows up at a bar on my beat. What the hell's the name of the joint?" He squeezed his temples. "Eddie's over on Flatbush Avenue, and do you know, Chuck, he was the fattest fat slob I've ever seen. It made me feel bad seeing him like that. A big fat nothing. But you don't know what I'm talking about. You have to get old to know what I mean." I knew what he meant. He came forward on the chair and got up. "Come on, get up, I want to show you something."

We stood in the kitchen, and I knew he was going to show me some kind of boxing move. "Now, remember that time that kid socked you?" He put up his fists.

"Yeah, I remember." It was still a sore spot. Our car had gotten bombed by snowballs, and Dad had jammed on the brakes and said, "Go punch one of those kids in the nose." I was only a kid myself and tried to hold onto the seat as he shoved me out of the car. I chased one kid down—actually, he didn't run very far. But, before I could even make fists, I had the beginnings of a nice black eye. "That was about the rottenest thing you ever did to me," I said, sitting down again.

"That's because you've never done in-fighting. Fights are won by body punches." He bent at the waist and leaned over me.

"Knock it off." I tried to push him off but he leaned all his weight into me. His fist landed softly in my side.

"That's a kidney punch," he said. Another fist shot into my stomach, almost taking my wind. "That's the payoff."

"Don't you hit me again," I growled.

"Holy Jesus," he said. "I'd never hurt you. I'm just trying to show you something." He stood and stuffed the empty Scotch bottle in the garbage. "You should be happy. Really, Charlie, do you know, I could never fool like that with my father. And he never tried to show me anything. The only thing he ever did for me was get me a job in a lumberyard and I had to hand over every penny that I made and he never gave me a cent back. Do you see what I'm saying?"

"Yes." The only thing I remembered about my grandfather was that he had given me a dollar every time he came to the house and the story he told one holiday about my father climbing a tree and refusing to come down.

"Do you want anything?" asked Dad.

"No," I said, thinking he meant something to drink.

"There isn't anything you've had your eye on?"

"I wished I knew what I wanted," I said. I wanted to get away, go someplace new, but I felt as though I had fifty feet of chain on each leg and I was getting awfully tired of dragging them around. I missed Tracy, her smell, and the way she put her arms and legs around me in bed. I missed the way she listened to me, and watching her get ready for work. The last thing she put on was her uniform, so she'd walk around the room for an hour in a bra and bikini underwear. Yes, I missed her. But, Al floated around my memory of her like a terrible odor. They were in the islands now, perhaps going back to the hotel room for a lunchtime quickie. The Corvette had not been much of a victory. "I know what I want," I said to Dad. "Let me have that shot."

He smiled and got a bottle of Canadian Mist out of the liquor cabinet. "This is nice smooth rye, we're out of Scotch." He twisted the cap, tearing the gold tax-seal and poured two shots. The red light on the heart machine was still glowing.

"A toast." I raised my glass. "Here's to the places I'll never go to and to all the women I'll never know."

"And here's to the man in the moon," Dad laughed and we clinked glasses.

Half the rye was gone and we had toasted to health, wealth, happiness, President Carter and his brother Billy, to John Haggerty, Tracy, may she get what she deserves, Bobby Sands, and the I.R.A. It was one o'clock in the afternoon, and Dad weaved to the front door. "Where the hell is your mother, anyway?" he asked loudly. "Don't you ever marry a woman who runs. They're the worst. It's the only way your mother can get under my skin." He came back into the kitchen and sat down heavily.

I heard the back door open.

"Anybody home?" It was Larry.

"Come on in," called Dad.

"There you are." He came in slowly, a little crouched as if he was walking in a low basement. "I've been looking all over for you. I went to the hosptial and there was some broad in your bed who never heard of you." On the lapel of his green leisure suit was a D.E.A. pin with the paint worn off to the brass. The pants and jacket fit him like old slipcovers. The knees and elbows bulged even when he had nothing in them. Under his arm was a brown bag. He opened it and pulled out a bottle of Scotch.

"What are you standing like an old lady for?" I asked.

"My back is out. I had to call in sick." Larry lowered himself in a chair. "I took a bad fall." He put a cigarette in his mouth and the end danced up and down. "I was feeling real low so I went down to Long Beach last night figuring I'd take a walk on the boardwalk. I was a little fired up." I looked under his nose for traces of white powder and it was there right in the crease of his left nostril.

"Well, what the hell happened?" Dad brought him a glass.

"So I'm walking trying to think things out with me and Estelle and I fucking walked right off the end of that boardwalk. I swear to Christ, it must have been fifteen feet and that sand is hard this time of year."

"You're some piece of work," laughed Dad.

"It's not funny," said Larry, blowing his big nose one side at a time into a crinkled yellow handkerchief. "Hey," said Larry stuffing the snot rag back in his top pocket. "You should be proud of this kid. Bill, I mean it now, proud. That speech he gave didn't leave a dry eye in the place."

"I wrote it," said Dad.

"No," Larry looked from my face to Dad's. "Nah, nobody could have wrote that. Charlie, you just said that, right?"

"No, he wrote it."

Dad started nodding. His face said, "Yes I know it's unbelievable."

"Well," he puffed his cigarette and watched me. "Well, it was something," he said, catching on. "And then I took Charlie to get laid."

"You got laid?" asked Dad.

"No, I just got drunk. Larry got laid."

"No, I just got head," he grinned. "And a little of this." He squeezed invisible breasts.

We sat at the table doing shots, chasing them with Carling's Black Label. It was cheap beer, probably the cheapest beer you could buy, something like ninety-nine a six-pack, but Dad and Larry had a big discussion about how good Black Label tasted. "But, you really can't tell until you've had a few," gulped Larry.

"My old man drank this," said Dad. "I'd bring back the bottles every week for him and give him the money and not get a cent back. He was so tight, he squeaked." Larry kept looking at the wires and the heart machine. "And you know why they call it Black Label?" asked Dad, turning the recyclable aluminum can in his hand. Larry shook his head.

"Because the label's black," he said.

The conversation went around like that for a while. Crushed cans were filling the garbage and the Scotch went down to the middle of the label. Larry took a deep breath and sang the Schaeffer beer jingle in burps and belches until he was red in the face. And my father did two shots of Mist in a row and I wondered how his heart felt about that. Larry went to the bathroom and came back a little more bent, his nostrils looking like igloo entrances. Dad was too drunk to notice. I just leaned back and laughed. I had a glow that you could have read by. "What the hell is that thing?" asked Larry.

"It's a hearbeat recorder. They want to see how I'm beating. The badder my beat, the longer I get to stay on sick leave." Dad rolled up a newspaper and gave the machine a smack. "That's one heart attack." he said.

Larry laughed.

My father stood holding the rolled newspaper. "You take the neck from some old bottle," he sang and smacked the machine again. He did a soft shoe shuffle and sang, "You take the legs from some old chair."

"You know, the doctor told him to stay in bed," I said.

"And from the horse you take the hair," he swung around and stumbled. "You take the hair." Wack, he hit the machine.

"And he's not even allowed to drink," I laughed.

"And when you put them all together, with a little bit of wire and some glue." He did a shuffle step and Larry cracked up.

"He's going to kill himself," I said. "Did you hear me?" I yelled.

Side step, shoe tap, "I'll get more loving from that goddamn dummy." He pointed the paper at me. "Than I'll ever get from you." He bowed and smacked the machine. Larry clapped.

"Don't be a stupid ass." I got up and put him in a chair.

"Than I'll ever get from you," he sang again.

———————

For a long time we sat there with nothing to say. The Scotch was at the bottom of the label and the Mist was half gone. Larry was looking at his hands and making faces by moving his mouth and squinting his eyes. Dad was falling asleep. Every minute or so his head dropped a little lower. The refrigerator motor kicked on, and Larry said, "Hey, am I bleeding." He touched his nose and looked at his hand. "I'm bleeding." He went over to the sink. I got up and leaned around him. I couldn't see any blood. "Look at this," he kept washing his face and rinsing his hands off.

"You're not bleeding." I said. He checked his nose a few more times.

"I thought I was bleeding," he laughed shakily.

"Everything's fine. You're fine."

———————

Larry tried to explain what had happened. "It's Estelle, she's got me going crazy," he said, draining the last of the Scotch into a glass. "Oh, she's a smart one. Don't let her fool you."

Dad began to snore. He was sprawled on the table as if someone had shot him in the back.

"It's a plan," explained Larry. "I've seen it on TV a million times. She's trying to get rid of me. I know what's going on." Looking at his reflection in the chrome on the side of the toaster, Larry combed his thinning hair. "I'm going go pay her a little visit. She's at her mother's." He stood up and shook a little like a dog coming out of a swimming pool.

"I understand about your bleeding," I said.

"Well, I don't," he laughed. "I don't understand anything anymore."

"A regular wood-sawer," I said as Dad's snore grew loud.

"Hey, Bill, I'm gonna get on the road," Larry whispered in his ear.

Dad roused and lifted his head, half his face red from lying on the table. "Who?" he said drunk and half asleep.

"Me," said Larry. "I'm gonna split."

Dad sat back in the chair and smiled. "Put an egg in your shoe and beat it," he laughed. "Charlie, give him an egg."

————————

The afternoon wore on. Louise would be home soon. I went into the living room, sat down, and put my feet on the coffee table. From the window, I saw Larry sitting in his car behind the wheel. His head was hung in sleep. What a long day. Even minutes standing in front of a time clock couldn't compare. I closed my eyes and wondered where my mother was.

"Charlie, there's pills in the refrigerator. Would you get them out for me?" called Dad.

I went into the kitchen. He was sitting in the same chair. There were a million things in the refrigerator. "On the bottom shelf," said Dad, pointing. He reached for the Mist across the table, but I beat him to it.

"Pills and booze? What are you crazy?"

"Damn it, don't be a smart ass, because I'll knock you right on your ass."

"I'd love to see the day."

"Will you get me the goddamn pills?" The color drained from his face and he held his left arm. "I might be having a damn heart attack," he moaned.

"You stupid fool." I slammed the bottle on the counter and looked through the whole refrigerator cursing him under my breath.

"You couldn't find the nose on your goddamn face," he said. The color of his face and lips were white. I was scared.

"They're not in here," I yelled.

"Check my coat pocket."

I found the pills in his dungaree jacket. The pocket was stuffed with Polish joke napkins from Pete's Pub. It was a small yellow bottle, almost a vial.

"You brought this on yourself," I yelled racing back into the kitchen. "You and your goddamn drinking." The child-proof cap opened with a jolt and the tiny pills showered on Dad's chest and lap. With two fingers he picked one off his shirt and put it under his tongue.

"These things feel like they're blowing the back of your head off." He rubbed his chest.

I searched our phone index for the doctor's number. Dad took another pill and began putting the rest back in the bottle.

I dialed and told the nurse that my father was having a heart attack. I was switched to another line. On his knees Dad crawled under the table looking for the pills. The heart monitor dragged along the floor.

"Is your father one of my patients?" asked a man.

"Yes, Bill Patterson."

"Is he conscious?"

"Yeah, he's right here."

"Ask him where the pain is."

It seemed like a dumb question to ask someone having a heart attack but I asked anyway, and Dad said, "They're all over the freakin' kitchen."

"Where's the pain?" I yelled again.

"It's gone." he came out from under the table.

"He says it's gone, but I think he's lying."

"Give me the phone," said Dad standing.

Relieved, I handed him the phone.

"It was a false alarm," said Dad. "Just gas. This diet you have me on is giving me gas."

"Gas?" I said.

"You shut your trap," he said, covering the phone.

"No, he's been drinking and eating crap all day," I yelled hoping the doctor would hear me. Dad back-handed me across the face, hard enough to open the cut on the inside of my lip. I tasted the blood and stood there almost not believing he had hit me.

Dad hung up the phone and we stood there staring at each other.

"You're really sick. You know that?" I said. I didn't want to fight. I wanted to get away from him.

"I didn't mean that." He opened the freezer and took out an ice cube. "Put this on there so that it doesn't swell," he held out the ice cube.

"You're just so stubborn sometimes." I took the ice cube and threw it in the sink. "I just don't want you to die." I was holding back tears by then. Dad tried to put his arm around me, but I pushed it away.

"Do you think I want to die? I don't want to die." He looked so sad, but, still, I didn't let him hold me. I didn't want to hold him.

In the den Dad slept on the couch with his shoes on. I watched the afternoon movie on the edge of a chair waiting for Louise to come home. She walked to and from school now because she claimed the boys on the bus were too wild. It was a thirty-five minute walk. On TV, Clint Eastwood spit on a dog's head and mounted his horse. He adjusted his hat so that it shaded his face just above his twisted cigar and rode off. He was the baddest guy in the West and rarely had to say a word. In his new movies he was playing the good guy and talking up a storm. There was something scary about

Clint Eastwood playing a broken-down rodeo bum, or
a happy-go-lucky car mechanic whose best friend was
four-foot orangutang. A commercial came on.

About a half hour later I let Louise in the front door.
She was red from the cold. "I would have picked you
up but I didn't want to leave Dad alone."

"You should have seen it," she said, throwing her
books in the corner. She wore designer jeans that didn't
fit correctly because she was so skinny. I felt kind of
sorry for her. I mean, the whole point of wearing them
is the fit. "This one kid, Byron Hubert, he's the only
boy in my ceramic class, dropped this mug he was
making. It broke in about a million and one pieces, and
then he just went crazy. He broke everyone's project,
threw them all over the place, and Mr. Barnhart grabbed
Byron by the hair and pulled it so hard that Byron wet
his pants and started crying."

"Did he break your project?"

"Yup."

She had been making a two-foot ceramic greyhound,
the kind that you put on the floor in front of a fireplace
as a decoration. I had bought her the paints.

"Byron had been smoking angel dust or something.
At least that's what Dee said." She took off her coat
and flopped onto a chair. "I'm not making anything
nice anymore, because someone always ruins it."

I remembered a morning I had gone to Jones Beach
with Louise. It was before the clean-up trucks made
their rounds so there were beer cans, food wrappers,
half-eaten sandwiches all over the sand. We walked
down to the water and there were chicken bones going
in and out with the waves. Nothing was nice anymore,
not even the beach.

"I think Dad had a heart attack today." I said.

"You're kidding?"

"No, I'm not. He got stinking drunk with Larry and passed out."

"You're kidding me."

Louise and I went into the den and watched Dad sleep. One foot rested on the floor and his hand was extended as if he was asking for something.

"He looks bad," she said.

"You should have seen how white he got. He scared the hell out of me."

She loosened the laces of his shoes and pulled them off. Dad didn't wake. "He doesn't look right," she said.

"He has to sleep it off."

"I know, but he doesn't look right."

"He's fine," I said and covered him with a blanket.

"You've been drinking, too, right?" Louise bit her index finger. It was a new habit she had. She gnawed at it so much that the skin was raw and red. I didn't say anything, but when our eyes met she took her hand away from her mouth and put it in her pocket.

My mother came in the back door holding a half gallon of milk and a box from the bakery tied with red and white string. "Why is Larry sitting in his car?" she asked.

"He's probably sleeping," said Louise.

"Where's your father?"

"Sleeping."

I had convinced Louise that telling Mom about Dad's heart attack would do no one any good. She watched me. "They finished two bottles," I said.

Mom sighed and took off her coat.

Louise worked out the knot on the cake box and Mom said, "It was marked down to half price."

"Where were you?" I asked.

"At the church and then shopping."

Next to the stove, five pork chops had defrosted and lay in a pink puddle on a white styrofoam tray. They were supermarket chops, not butcher chops, and the meat was ringed and veined with fat. "They should be juicy," said Mom.

"I'm not hungry," said Louise.

"Well, I'm cooking them anyway," said Mom, lifting the tray and pouring the bloody water into the sink. The windows above the counter were dark and I could see her face in the glass.

"Thanks a lot, Mom," I said.

"What?" She went and opened the oven.

"You know what I'm talking about."

"No, I don't."

"You know, leaving the way you did. Leaving me here all day with him. Thanks a lot."

"No one made you stay, Charlie. You didn't have to stay." She set the stove and shut the oven. Her answer felt like Dad's slap in the face.

Louise helped her set the table. I sat in front of my clean plate, shining silverware, napkin, and milk glass, and again listened to the story about Byron breaking Louise's project. "And I'm not making anything else," Louise concluded.

"Of course you will," said Mom, arranging frozen french fried potatoes on the toaster oven tray.

"Why should she?" I said. "Don't you think people get sick of trying? I mean, not everyone can sit in church all day."

"We'll have a good meal," said Mom. "That will make everyone feel better. And we have a nice cake for dessert." She forced a smile.

I think even Louise wanted to tell her that the whipped cream had turned. But we didn't say anything.

———————

Silence hung over the table like a storm cloud. Dad had recovered quite well and sat ripping apart a catsup-covered chop. Louise, sticking to her word, had eaten only two forkfuls of applesauce. I peeled a crispy layer of fat off my meat. Mom watched with an apology on her face.

"So, how was your day?" asked Mom.

"Fine," said Dad. "What type of day did you have?" He held out his hand as if holding a microphone and pretended to adjust a dial on the heart monitor.

"Fine."

"And you, little girl?" he asked like a reporter.

"Fine," said Louise.

"Well, there you have it, folks. It was a fine day for the Pattersons."

No one laughed.

"But," said Dad. "There was news. Charlie over here dropped out of college."

"You did?" asked Louise.

"Yeah, I was failing everything."

"Everything?" she repeated, holding a crumpled napkin, her blue eyes waiting.

"Yeah."

"Wow." Her mouth hung open and she looked at me until a small smile crept across her face. "I never heard of anyone failing everything."

"Well," Dad slapped me on the back, "now you have."

"How did you expect me to concentrate with all the shit that's going on around here." The word *shit* hung in the room and Dad grabbed it.

"Don't curse. So help me, God, I don't care how old you are, don't use that language in front of your mother and sister."

"How did you get so far behind?" asked Louise.

"I don't know."

"He doesn't need college, anyway," said Dad. "I can get him a job doing security work at ten dollars an hour. One phone call and it's done." Dad lifted his bloody-looking chop and ripped the gristle from the bone.

I lifted my chop and put it down. I couldn't take a bite. Without excusing myself, I got up and left the kitchen. My father said, "Hey, you didn't even start eating yet." I went up the stairs.

I fell on my bed and a moment later bolted into the bathroom and started puking. The worst part was, Dad was coming up and I had left the door open.

I sat on the tile floor leaning over the bowl. He walked in slowly and rubbed my shoulder. "You all right?"

I nodded.

"I'm sorry," he said.

"About what?"

"About today, about smacking you."

"Just leave me alone," I moaned. For a second I thought he would leave, and I almost said I was sorry. But, he sat on the edge of the tub and folded his hands.

———

I went out in the yard to get some air, but wound up driving Larry home. He had sat in front of the house, sleeping, with the ignition on. "You wouldn't think a battery would go dead that fast," he said, getting into my father's car.

I started the Buick and pulled out of the driveway. It

was around six o'clock and we hit traffic on the Southern State Parkway. I put on the heat and the motor whirred and blew hot air that tasted like the engine. I was getting a sick feeling in the pit of my stomach again.

"There's just too many people," said Larry, waving at the traffic.

I opened my door and vomited on the concrete road.

"Are you OK?" Larry held my arm as if I were going to topple out of the car.

The car in front of me moved up and the driver behind us beeped.

Larry opened his window and yelled, "Can't you see he's sick."

I shut the door and told Larry that it had passed. "I'm just a little sick inside," I said, giving the car the gas.

"What did you eat today?"

"Nothing."

"Then, you have to eat something. All day nothing? For God's sake, Charlie, no wonder you're sick."

The traffic stopped again. On the car bumper in front of us was a sticker that said, "Have you hugged your child today?"

"I'll get you something to eat," said Larry. "I don't have much food. In fact, actually none. But, I saved some little things in jars and a couple of cans. You can drive? You're not going to die on me?"

"You call this driving?" I asked, inching up, wondering if the guy in front of me had hugged his kid today. Maybe he was on his way home and the little guy was waiting in a pair of Star Wars Pajamas. Then, again, maybe someone had put the sticker there while the driver was in the supermarket. I thought I was going to be sick again and pulled up on the shoulder.

Larry stayed in the car and I walked up and down. All the people in the cars crawled by watching me step around the weeds and black puddles.

"It passed," I said, getting back in the car.

"Good," said Larry. "Good." He looked at me with shiny coke eyes. On his lap was a chalky zip-lock sandwich bag. He zip-locked it, and I tried to pull back into the traffic.

———————————

Larry lived on a dead-end block in a newly developed area. The trees between the sidewalk and the curb were thin, leafless saplings supported by metal poles and protected by round chicken wire fences. Every house had a brown sod lawn as thick as carpet and cement stoops with wrought iron railings. The end house, next to a small forest that tried to hide a super highway that led to Jones Beach, was Larry's. I pulled into the driveway, and Larry opened his eyes.

"Home again, home again, jigity-jig," he said.

What separated Larry's house from the others on the block was fake animals. On his front lawn, a line of plastic yellow ducklings stood motionless, forever following their white-feathered mother. Behind an evergreen, a cement deer stared with painted eyes, and on the side of the house, nailed through their paws, were chipmunks. Larry got his keys out and we climbed the stoop.

"I like the animals," I said.

"They're all fake," he said picking up some junk mail. The traffic behind the trees sounded like the ocean.

I followed him into the living room. The couch had sheets and blankets on it and there were clothes hung over the furniture.

"I'm sleeping down here now because of Estelle. You wouldn't believe how sneaky she is. I'm going to have all the locks changed. A few days ago, I found her in the kitchen. I threw all the food out." He turned on a light. "She was poisoning me. That's why she was always making me tuna fish. It's that much easier to mix in." He went into the next room.

"Nobody believes you," I called after him. "All that coke is making you paranoid."

"I know that," he said, returning with two cans of Black Label. "But, you believe me?"

I went over to the window and looked out. It was getting dark. "I guess anything's possible," I said. "I mean, I want to believe you." I opened my beer and faced him. "But, why would Estelle want to kill you?"

"Because I'm in her way. It's as simple as that. She's screwing around, coming home with wet panties. Charlie, do you understand what I'm saying. Some slob shoots a load in her and I got to lie in bed next to her listening to all that goo ooze around in her. And she knows I can hear it." Larry pulled off his jacket. His leather shoulder holster fit tightly. The gun, over his heart, gleamed. I pictured Larry and Estelle in bed. Her body curled in a tight ball, wet between the legs, and Larry with his hands over his ears. Maybe Estelle was fooling around. Tracy had done it easily enough.

"And lately," said Larry. "I've been thinking about doing her a favor—blowing my brains out." He stood in front of shelves that held little ceramic boys and girls. He picked up a pink-faced girl holding an umbrella. "I sat with the gun to my head for an hour. I must have done every angle possible. In my ear, in my mouth, right up under my chin." His spider-thin fingers unhooked the holster. He threw the gun on the couch.

"You don't want to be dead," I said, not knowing what else to say.

"I think I do," said Larry. "I'm being put off the force. Put out to pasture with a three-quarters mental disability pension. I got the letter yesterday." I told him that I was sorry. "Just don't tell your father," he said.

I followed him into the kitchen. He opened the brown refrigerator that matched the stove and dishwasher. There was nothing on the shelves except a six-pack of Black Label and a box of Arm & Hammer baking soda. "Me and Estelle used to pack this thing like there was going to be a famine."

The kitchen table was covered with newspapers. On a chair was a dead potted plant. Everything, even the can opener and the rooster plaques on the wall, matched the brown refrigerator. I could almost feel Estelle in the room. I imagined a small, dark woman pressing the buttons of the blender. Larry stroked his hair back the way he always did and sat. The skin on his face tightened. His wrinkles could have been cut in with a razor.

"You have a nice house," I said. The words sounded hollow. "You really do."

"It is, isn't it?" Larry looked around. "Estelle had nice guinea taste. Everything in our bedroom is red: red sheets, red carpet, red drapes. She said red was the color of love. Me? I think it's the color of blood. It wasn't bad though. We went out every Saturday and bought something for the house. Just like two kids trying to fill a doll house. We got a nursery upstairs, but no baby. I got a work room downstairs and never even hammered a goddamn nail. It makes me cry when I think what my father could have done in that work room."

He gulped his beer and held the can with both hands. "Que sera, sera," he said.

"Maybe you should try religion. Start going to Mass." Larry waved the idea away.

"The Lord writes straight with crooked lines, that's what my mother says." I looked at him and had a strange feeling. It was as if Larry was already dead.

"Your mother likes that religion," said Larry. "But I could never get into it. Sometimes I think why doesn't He show Himself. What's all the mystery for? And if there's a God, there's only one thing I'm sure of! I'm going to roast in Hell. I was never a good son until it was too late. Now I love my mother, now I miss her, and she's dead and buried right on top of my father, in the same grave. I still haven't had the name put on the stone. Near the end, I had to put her over in Grace Hills Nursing Home. When I went to visit her, she called me Stanley. Stanley's my kid brother, who's dead. He was twenty-two, fresh from Vietnam, a hero with two medals, going to college on the GI Bill." Larry snapped his fingers. "A bike accident on the parkway. I thought people don't fall off Electra Glides." Larry tried to laugh. "And Charlie, that parkway was cruel. It was just like a grind wheel and he fell right here." Larry pointed to his chin. "My mother never recovered from it. She called me Stanley and asked me how Larry was. I said, don't you remember Larry died." Larry finished his beer and looked at the table.

"So what happened? What did she say?"

"Nothing. She just called me Stanley right to the end." He crushed the can. "I wish I was Stanley," he said.

We sat drinking in the quiet house for a while. My stomach felt better and I was getting a buzz. That kitchen was so full of dreams it almost talked to me. Next to the wooden spice rack on the counter hung a handstitched dish towel that said, "Larry & Estelle." Stuck to the front on the range oven with small magnets shaped like tea kettles and cups were notes on yellow-and-white lined paper. One said, "Larry, Please contact the bank (or me). We have to make some decisions about the money. Stell." In front of yellow curtains and a windowsill crowded with miniature glass animals was another potted plant hanging on a hemp rope. It was dying and some leaves had fallen into the sink.

"I'm coming down fast," said Larry. "Crashing is the only thing bad about flying." He took a brown envelope out of his top shirt pocket, the type most people get their pay in, and stuck his finger in. He rubbed the cocaine on his gums and snorted a little off his thumbnail. I remembered reading somewhere that if you squeeze a coke freak's nose he would scream in pain.

"Well, I'm circling the airport again." He smiled. "A couple of years ago the P.D. sent me to school for drug control. The instructor called coke the champagne of social and recreational drugs. So, for me this is like going to a party and the gym at the same time." We both laughed. "They made us memorize ten names for cocaine and I already knew them all." Larry laughed too hard. "Let's see, coke snow, nose candy."

"Blow," I said.

"Right, blow." He put up four fingers. "Superblow, white lady, snowbird, stardust, crank, Bernice, whiff, that's eleven. Yesterday, I heard some dude call it paradise. What about you, Charlie, you want to try some paradise?" He threw the envelope across the table.

"No, thanks."

"Come on, take an icy trip with the snow queen to the crystal heights of pleasure." The look on his face was scaring the shit out of me.

I got up and walked out the back door.

"Hey, it's cool," he said, coming after me. "You're better off without it. I was just joking around. You don't want to take anything that's going to take you up, any-way."

I breathed the still, fall air. In the sky a few stars shone and the moon glowed above the electrical wires. In a few days it would be full. The yard, a patio and a parking-space-size square of grass, was fenced in. Next to the house were two garbage cans and a coiled green hose with an aluminum sprinkler attached to the end. Four bamboo poles stuck out of the ground, supporting shriveled tomato plants. We sat on the redwood picnic table. "I really can't blame you," continued Larry. "Coming down is the ultimate bumaroo. That's why I never want to come down. But, but . . ." he shook my shoulder. "I don't want to be up here, either. Do you get that?"

Larry turned on the water and hosed off the patio with the sprinkler. There were no trees anywhere to be seen, so there was really nothing to wash off. The spray just hit the concrete and streamed into the grass. Larry worked the water back and forth. A dog barked some-where, and a plane with blinking lights passed under the clouds.

"When you're up in a plane looking down, you see how crazy it all is," I said. "All these neat, straight streets, row after row, and tiny houses with swimming pools the size of pinheads."

"You're too young to think that way," said Larry, shutting off the water. "But it's the fucking rotten truth. And there's no fucking way out of it. You want to hear the way it is?" he shouted. "OK, here it is. Pop. You come out between some legs, get slapped in the rear end, and cry your eyes out. OK, right?" I nodded. Larry dropped the hose. "Then it's learn, learn, learn, learn. You learn to walk, to talk, to shit in a toilet, to spell, to say please, you learn what happened on December 7, 1941, if they still teach that, and then you learn to stand on your own two feet, and that if you don't eat the dog first, he's gonna eat you." Larry munched his mouth and swallowed. "Now you got to learn to get back between those legs again, so you can lean on somebody because if you stand too long on your own two feet, you'll fall right on your face. So now you got to work, work, work, work, because now you got someone leaning on you, and this little lady and you have kids that have to eat, eat, eat, eat. So, now you are going crazy," Larry spun around on the patio. "Going crazy for them, and some asshole with a shitty little suped-up van shows up and picks that daughter right off the vine, just when she's getting ripe, and takes a big fat bite out of her. And your son, your only god-damn son, with his man-size dick, tries to wrap himself up in some legs, just like you did. So, it's bye-bye, sonny boy. And now, if, and I say if, your old lady hasn't left you, she's all dry and used up from those two kids and all that working and leaning and you're not getting it up anymore and probably shooting blanks anyway, and you got this shitty little house with a shitty little yard and you sit in them. Just sit like two goddamn stuffed peppers with the filling falling out and the skin drying out." He began to moan. He walked to the end of the yard, holding his head. He screamed so loud the dog that was barking stopped and I imagined the plane falling out of the sky. Larry clung to the fence and I hugged myself.

CHAPTER
18

The next day I didn't get up at all. Throughout the afternoon my parents came into my room and I pretended to sleep. At suppertime Louise brought me a plate of tenderloin and potatoes. "Wake up," she said, placing it on a metal folding tray that she had carried up from the living room. There was a set of them that we never used. The legs were gold colored. The top, black with purple flowers, snapped to the legs.

I sat up, but wasn't hungry. I wasn't going to let her bring supper for nothing.

"How you feeling?" asked Louise. She pulled a fork and knife out of her pocket and placed them next to the plate. "We had flurries today," she said. "But the snow didn't stick."

She sat on the edge of the chair like a sparrow lighting on a branch. "Are you going to eat?" she asked.

"Yeah." I swung my legs out of bed and pulled the tray over. I looked at the slices of red tenderloin and knew I couldn't eat them.

"Aren't you going to ask how school was?" Louise pulled her legs together and bit the corner of her index finger.

I watched the way the light went through her curly hair. I could have slipped my finger inside each curl. When she was a little girl, my father had called her Orphan Annie.

"I'll tell you anyway," she said. "Eddie tried out for the wrestling team and was cut. He says he doesn't care, but I know he feels pretty bad about it. He bought a lifetime membership to the spa over in the mall. He thinks I'm going to be really impressed with his muscles, but I don't care."

"Guys are like that," I said.

"And do you remember Mr. Atkins, the English teacher? He wants me to write for the school paper. He says I have a natural gift."

"Do you still have that piece you wrote about the bowling ball?" I hadn't thought of it in years. I remembered Louise reading it to the family at dinner and my father clapping.

"I'll go get it." She raced out of the room before I could say anything, and a minute later returned with a folder full of papers. She sat, licked her finger, and paged through the old notes and assignments. I knew she was doing it because she wanted to cheer me up.

"Here it is." It was written on big, yellow, lined paper,

neater than some examples in a child's workbook. She
wrote it in second grade in a special class called T&G
(talented and gifted). " 'A Day in the Life of a Bowling
Ball'," she read. " 'Oh no! Now I'm gonna get it! He's
throwing me down the alley. Boom, bang, ooff. Wow,
now I'm in trouble. Oh boy, here come the pins. I'm
gonna get the biggest headache in the United States of
America. But, wait! I'm going in the gutter. Plop. Saved.
Well, that's my life so far. But, wait! Don't go already.
I've got more to tell you. Oh, here I go into the ball
return. And I'm scared of the dark. Up, up, up, roll and
back to my friends. But, no, here I go again. No. you
can't do it. He's putting me down. Do you think I convinced him? No, he's just drying off his hands. Whoa,
here I go. Boom. A strike. Those pins sure are hard.
Does anyone have some aspirin?' " Louise laughed and
folded the paper. "I was such a cornball," she said.

"The teacher called the house when you wrote that
and wanted to know if you had any help."

"It seems pretty dumb now."

"I like it. It's still good."

"What's the matter?" asked Louise. "I mean really."

I just looked at her, feeling bad about being in bed
and her bringing my supper.

"Mom says you're not really sick."

"I don't know. I threw up yesterday and I feel awfully
tired."

"And that's all?"

"Maybe I'm just not looking forward to anything
anymore. I can't see the point to anything. I got involved
with Tracy and look what happened. I don't even know
if I'll ever see her again. Everything's no use. And it

hurts to talk. I feel so tense." I rubbed my jaw. It felt
as though I had a football helmet on and the chin strap
was too tight.

"Charlie, you'll find another girl."

"No, I can't explain it, but it's not just Tracy. It's
everything. Just looking at Dad makes me so sad. I can't
stand it. And I'm afraid to cry but I feel like it all the
time. Do you remember when Grandpa died? That was
the first funeral I ever attended and I didn't cry. I
couldn't. That's the way I feel about Dad. I want to cry
but I can't. Dad doesn't even care if he lives or dies.
And Larry. Louise, you don't know about Larry."

"You must have been only a kid when Grandpa died,
and Larry's crazy. Everyone knows that."

"Larry's not crazy, but you don't want to know what
he knows. And you're right about Grandpa. I was just
a kid. I can't even remember Grandpa. I can't say he
ever told me one important thing. One time I remember going fishing with him in a rented rowboat. We
couldn't stand because it was very tippy and Grandpa
took it only a hundred yards from the dock. It started
raining and he fished my pole and his, lifting them up
and down. I sat with his raincoat over my head. He
caught two flukes and I watched him gut them. You
don't know about the day he died. You were just a baby.
He was sitting on the lawn in a plastic patio chair dead,
all afternoon dead, and Mom told me to keep quiet so
that I didn't wake him. And, then the automatic sprinkler went on and he was sitting there getting drenched.
But what else? There's got to be more to Grandpa than
that."

"There is," said Louise, her eyes big. "Don't you
remember the way he gave us hard candies from his

pocket and the way he turned the sound off on baseball
games and pretended to be the announcer. You told me
about that."

"But, I want more. Don't you understand what I mean.
He lived his whole life and that's all we have. Remember how close I was to Ralph. We did all that blood
brother crap, and now he's at Princeton, too busy to
answer my letters."

"Visit him. It's only in New Jersey."

"I couldn't and I can't eat this," I said.

She moved the tray away. I got into bed and closed
my eyes.

———————

I had been in bed three days when my mother brought
a priest home. Dad and I were in my room watching an
afternoon game show called "The Family Feud." The
color TV was another thing that had been carried up
from the living room. It sat on my dresser in front of a
charcoal drawing of the Beatles. On the wall above my
bed was the framed *New York Times* headline, "82 Are
Hurt, Including 56 Officers, As Hasidim Storm the 74th
Precinct." I had put it up a couple of days after the
Storming.

On my night table was a cold bowl of Campbell's
split pea soup with ham and bacon. It was my favorite,
but I still wasn't eating. As my mother came in the
door, Dad opened another beer. The heart monitor had
been removed. I had asked Dad what the results were.
"I'm alive," he answered, "and kicking." Bubbles rose
inside his bottle and a woman on the TV show tried to
answer the question, What do people do on rainy days?
"Watch TV," she said, pulling on her dress. "Watch
television," yelled the host, and a screen flipped over,

Watch television. The woman and her family jumped up and down.

"On rainy days I don't do a damn thing and I don't have to feel bad about it," said Dad.

"Someone's paying us a visit," said my mother with false cheerfulness. A priest stepped in front of the television. "This is Father Michael."

"Everyone except your mother calls me Father Mike," he said.

"How are you?" Dad stood and shook the priest's hand.

I pulled my arm out from under the blankets and we shook hands.

"He's not feeling well," said my mother.

"Not feeling well?" asked Father Mike.

My mother put a pillow behind my head. I looked at my father, wondering if he was in on this chance visit. He looked away.

"I must have a bug. Yesterday I was running a fever."

The priest scanned the room for a place to sit, looked at the bed and asked, "Can I sit here?"

"Reminds me of an exorcisim," said my father, and we all laughed.

Father Mike, in his neat black suit with that small square of white on the collar, looked very out of place in my messy bedroom. My mother shut the television off and the priest crossed and uncrossed his legs like a man who had something very important to say. Dad finished his beer and slipped the empty bottle behind his chair leg. The baseboard radiation rattled as the heat came up.

"I like to visit our parishioners," said Father Mike. "Joy is one of our most active parishioners."

"She's a saint," said Dad. "And believe me, I should know."

"I'm sure she will be," said Father Mike.

I started seeing flashes of my church. I could hear the priest say, Born in Christ, Body of Christ. The sound of the bells, when the priest raises the cup of wine and turns it to Christ's blood, came back to me. Father Mike asked me something. I closed my eyes and listened to the church organ whining, and the people praying. Holy, Holy, God of power and might, blessed is he who comes in the name of the Lord. And I remembered fainting on line waiting for communion and waking looking straight up at the high round ceiling, Christ nailed to the cross, and the stained glass windows.

"Hey," said Dad. "Wake up."

I opened my eyes.

"Do you still attend Mass?" asked Father Mike.

"Whenever I went to Mass," I said trying to remember. "I could never understand the priest. I couldn't concentrate."

"Where did you sit?"

"Mainly in the back."

"Well, sit in the front," he smiled and looked at my mother. "All problems, even big problems like the nuclear arms race, can be solved if we look hard and long enough. And most of the time," Father Mike pulled white rosary beads from his suit pocket and pressed them in my hand, "the answer is right in our lap."

Dad looked into his lap and said, "Not with me. I'm not trying to be sacrilegious or anything like that, but with me everything's out of my control. My life is in one of those big roller coaster cars. It was dragged up by one of those big greasy chains and then let go. And it's a rotten ride, Father. The turns will snap your neck."

"Oh, come now." The priest smiled with nothing to say.

"Would you like anything, Father? Coffee, tea?" asked my mother.

"Oh, no, no thank you."

"What kind of wine do you drink, anyway?" asked my father. "I've been wondering that since I was a little kid."

"We don't drink the wine, we drink the blood of Christ."

"Oh, come on, you know what I mean," Dad winked at him.

"Bill!" snapped my mother.

The priest put up his hands showing that he was willing to answer all questions. His black eyes beamed with the knowledge that there was no question that he did not have an answer for. "At dinner I enjoy chilled Cabernet Sauvignon."

"You mean you don't drink that Mad Dog 2 plus 2," laughed Dad.

"No." The priest folded his hands.

I wondered if the rosary beads glowed in the dark. I held them to the light over my bed.

"I'll show you how to pray with them" said my mother smiling. Outside a car roared by with a bad muffler and a sputtering engine. It backfired loudly and my father jumped.

"So what do you think of those Jets?" asked Father Mike.

Dad and I looked at each other, then to my mother, who watched the priest.

"The Jets," he said.

"That was a car," I said.

"No, the New York Jets, the football team." The priest smiled and waited for us to join him.

"Boy, oh boy. I must be on cloud nine," said Dad. Mom smiled.

"No," said Dad. "We haven't been following football this year. Anyway, we're Giant fans. Right, Charlie?"

"Right." I said. Really, I had never been a fan of any team.

Dad and Father Mike talked football for a while. The games and teams Dad referred to were twenty years past. Dad told stories about losing bets and lousy coaches. "Nobody gave you a better show than scrambling Fran. The Giants didn't win much then, but they sure gave you a game. And big number forty, Joe Morrison. When they gave him the ball, he always got an honest four yards. There wasn't a defense in the league that could stop him. In those days when you played a game you knew it. There was no artificial turf or special glue-tipped gloves for the receivers. Remember when I lost my paycheck on the Giants-Colts game? They lost in the last thirty seconds."

Father Mike looked at his hands, and my mother nodded. "Well football is still a good game," said the priest. "To change is to grow."

The slatted sunlight reflected on my dresser. Children shouted outside. The yellow school bus would be flashing its lights. The two young mothers on the block, one with black hair and in jeans so tight her ass seemed to be screaming, "Let me out," and the other in bib overalls and construction boots and, most likely, a red or blue bandana holding her hair up, would grab their kindergarten babies by the hand and rush back to their houses.

"Sports are a beautiful release," concluded Father Mike. "I play tennis twice weekly and I've been told I have an awesome serve. Do you play?" he asked, his eye on me.

"No." I pulled the blankets up and moved my feet to the wall. The priest's weight on the blankets was hurting my toes.

"You should learn. I could teach you." He liked the idea.

"That sounds wonderful," said Mom.

"He doesn't have a racket," said Dad. I knew he considered it a sport for fags. He liked handball.

"Use one of mine," said Father Mike.

"But, I'm sick."

"You'll be better soon. Your mother tells me your temperature is normal. You just need some fresh air." He stood. I wiggled my toes. It was a small room for four adults and Father Mike leaned against the wall as if he were in an elevator. "Then it's all settled," he said.

I nodded looking at the white sky outside the window. Tennis lessons with a priest I needed like a kick in the balls. I had nothing to worry about, though. It would take more than a miracle to get me on the court. I was having trouble getting to the bathroom.

CHAPTER
19

My mother brought me cereal in a small bowl and sat next to the bed. It was early morning. The frost on my windows was thick. She helped me sit up. I felt very stiff and not hungry at all. My mother did not look well. The wrinkles around her eyes were dark and pronounced. The cereal was already soggy. Raisins and a freshly sliced banana lay just under the surface of the milk.

"About Father Michael," she said. "I'm sorry. He didn't understand. I don't know what I expected him to say. He wants to come back, but I told him perhaps a professional would be better." My tall mother was all bunched inside her bathrobe. She seemed to be shrinking. "Should I feed you?" she asked.

"No." Tears were making my eyes swell, But I couldn't cry.

"Louise told me how you felt, everything hopeless and futile, but, my God, you're a young man. You can do anything you want. If you want to take a trip somewhere just tell me. Your father and I have a little money saved. I was thinking maybe you could go and visit Ralph. He called me just yesterday and invited you."

"He called?"

"Yes, while you were sleeping." I knew my mother had called him.

"I don't want to go."

"Why? You could see the campus and meet," she hesitated, "his fiancée."

I almost tipped the cereal over.

"Yes, he's getting married. And you know you'll never meet the right girl if you don't look. She won't fall out of the sky."

My father came in just as the sun hit the windows. He opened the blinds and turned the television on. He had the mail in one hand and a pint can of Schaeffer in the other. "How you doing, Charlie?" he asked softly. "You feeling better?"

"A little." I propped myself up.

"The police department is backing down," he said. "They still haven't set a date for my case, because they have no case." He snapped open the beer and caught the foam in his mouth.

Dad flipped around the channels until he found "Candid Camera" and sat in the folding chair. He leaned until the chair back rested against the wall. On television Allen Funt asked a little girl if she wanted to be a movie star. "I don't know," she said. "I'll have to ask my father."

Dad handed me a letter in a flesh-colored envelope. In the corner next to the Holiday Inn Globe logo, it read, Freeport/Lucaya/P.O. Box 760/Grand Bahamas

I read my name and address on the envelope. It was Tracy's handwriting. I took a breath and waited. Allen Funt asked the girl how much money she wanted for her first movie. "About ten or eleven dollars," she said.

Dad laughed.

The possibility that the letter was good news was slim. It was probably one of her guilt trip letters, written next to the pool with one hand down Al's suit. I opened it as if fearing a letter bomb.

> Dear Charlie,
>
> Al and I did not work out (I'm not going to explain). I left him at Paradise Island and managed to get a job waitressing at the Holiday Inn in Freeport. I had nothing to go home to. Leaving Al meant losing my apartment.
>
> The tips here are guaranteed and I'm already taking scuba lessons. You would love it here. You still mean a lot to me and I think of you all the time. I am straightening out my life, learning a lot about myself.
>
> Love x o,
> Tracy
>
> PS: I know this is out of the question, but if you wanted to come down, I could probably get you a job as a waiter or (if worse came to worst) a dishwasher.
> PPS: Write back, OK?

So, Tracy had done it. She was in the islands. I remembered her calling me a dreamer. Maybe she had it all planned. I was numb. "Fucking Tracy," I said.

"What," asked Dad.

"Nothing."

"What are you grinning about?"

I was imagining Tracy underwater swishing her long legs, her curls floating around her head. I could see Tracy on the sand, Tracy in a lounge chair beside the pool, Tracy collecting pieces of coral on the beach, Tracy and I having a barbeque under the palm trees.

"Who's the letter from?" Dad tried to peek over my shoulder.

"It's just an advertisement." Dad thought Tracy was worse than a nuclear disaster. Deep down, so did I. After you get burned you're less anxious to go near the girl who set you on fire.

"I know damn well it's no advertisement."

"It's private."

"Well, then say that. Don't lie, goddamn it." He got up and shut off Allen Funt who was about to drive a car with no motor into a gas station.

———————

That afternoon, I got up, took a shower and dressed. Boy, I was weak. My legs felt like spaghetti. At supper everyone was all smiles.

"I'd like to know what was in that letter," said Dad.

———————

It took a couple of days for me to get my strength back. I had lost nine pounds. Every pair of pants I owned was falling off me. My father moved the television back to the living room and sat there drinking in front of it. For him, there was nothing to do but wait. He didn't say it, but he was afraid of the Supreme Court. He didn't want to believe that they would get him on the stand. "My defense is," he said during the commercials, "that there is no case. Number one, there were two thousand of them and four of us. Number two, any action I had taken was appropriate. It was a life-threatening situation." He was able to list twelve reasons.

I heard him but had stopped listening. I had Tracy and the Bahamas on my brain. I was working on a letter to Tracy. It was awfully hard. I told her I just couldn't leave for good right at the moment, so I would go down for a couple of weeks and feel things out. It would give us time to patch things up. I didn't tell her about getting sick.

The truth? Fear crouched inside me like a little man. He kept telling me that Tracy would leave me again. Do you really think she's not screwing around? She's working at the Holiday Inn. All the rooms are on the house. Where is she getting the money for the scuba lessons? Are the tips that good?

I read her letter over and over. I walked around the neighborhood fingering it in my pocket. She loves me? She loves me not? I had no idea.

I started stopping in the diner to hide out and kill time. My mother was on a new kick. I called it "The Get Charlie Back in Shape and Drive Him out of His Mind Exercise Plan." Mom cut off my coffee and I wandered around the kitchen in the morning with a cup of herb tea like a heroin addict in withdrawal. She squashed all the father-and-son drinking jamborees. Twenty dollars went down the drain for *Miss McBride's 21-Day Shape-Up Plan*, a natural movement exercise course specializing in toning every part of the body.

With arms and legs like pipe cleaners, I was in no position to protest. So, in the living room, with my father snickering, my mother and I sat tailor-fashion doing head droops and spine stretches. All the movements were demonstrated by the author. Miss McBride wore a lumpy bra, baggy danskin leotard and fishnet stockings. Let me tell you, that old gal was as flexible as a Gumbie doll. My mother was also a natural. After two days she could hook her ankles behind her neck. I refused to do the "Spine lift." It was supposed to eliminate "Dowager's Hump." It looked like air humping. What the hell was dowager's hump anyway?

Late one afternoon, I ducked into the Diner for my daily fix. Most of the help was new. Only the Greek with the toupee, and Maria remained. I sat at Maria's station. We had gone to school together and liked to swap memories and gossip. She told me who was in what college, who was pregnant, who was burntout, and so on. Poor Maria had gotten fat. She wore her high school ring on her pinky. Once she had had her teeth wired together. The joke was that the A&P had had to lay off six cashiers and a stock boy.

Maria pushed out the swinging doors, came around the counter, and squished into my booth. Something was up.

"I got a letter from Tracy today." She sat back and wound her long black hair around her hand.

I ran my fingers around the edge of my own letter.

"Well, do you want to hear what she said?" She folded her arms over her bosom. Bigger tits I've seen only on old Italian women.

"Of course I do."

"She left Al and she's in the Bahamas and she's not

coming back. And," said Maria, moving closer, "she invited me down."

"Really?" I could see Maria and me on a plane going to see Tracy. The thin man and the fat lady. "Did she invite anyone else?" I asked.

"You mean, you? No, but she asked about you." She pulled out the letter from her uniform pocket and unfolded it. Same stationery as mine. "Do you see much of Charlie?" read Maria. "Does he still come into the Diner?"

"That's it?"

"Well, she said some personal things to me about Al."

"What?" I was ready to rip the letter out of her hands.

"That, I can't tell you. I'll tell you this, though. He's a creep." She slipped the letter into one of her bulges. I knew sooner or later Maria would tell me. She thrived on this sort of crap.

"Are you going down to see her?"

"I think so. She says she might be able to get me a job."

I bit the top of my fingernail off. I wondered if Tracy was making a commission on the people she brought down. How many letters did she write?

"Tracy told me not to tell anyone, so mum's the word, OK?" Maria pushed out of the booth. "The pineapple cheese is fresh this morning. I could cut you a big piece."

———————

I hopped down the walk in my socks to get the paper. The neighborhood was still asleep. Only Mrs. Bell stood down the block, waiting for her poodle to select a tree. I picked up the paper and started for the house. On our front door, just below the window, someone had spray painted a big, black, six-pointed star. On the blue shingles, between the living room windows, it said in white paint "Never Again."

I walked across the lawn, stepped into the garden and touched the paint. It was still wet. Mrs. Bell, poodle in arms, came down the sidewalk, staring at the house.

"I've read about this sort of thing in the papers," she called. "Has your father seen it?"

I charged into the house. "Dad!" I yelled. "You're not going to believe this." I ran up the stairs.

Dad was in the bathroom, shaving. Half his face was lathered. "What?" he said.

"You better come out and see this."

"What, for God's sake?"

My mother was making her bed. She lifted a sheet and let it fall like a parachute. "What is it, honey?" she said.

"Someone spray painted a Jewish Star on the house."

The three of us pounded down the stairs and out the door. The back of my father's neck was already getting red. My mother had on a blue dress and her hair was twirled on top of her head. She must have been getting ready to go to Mass. Dad's shoulder's looked huge. They came out of the corners of his T-shirt like weathered rocks.

We went out the front door. Dad walked slowly to the center of the lawn and turned around. "That's beautiful, really beautiful," he said.

"It's a disgrace," called Mrs. Bell from the sidewalk. The dog squirmed in her arms and she gave it a wack on the nose.

Mom said nothing. She touched the star on the door and came away with a black spot on her finger.

"If we clean it now, it will come off," I said.

"Leave it there," said Dad.

Louise pushed the door open and came out. "Oh wow," she said.

Dad called the police, and two detectives came. They stood in front of the house with my father. They were both big men, the type of guys who could never buy a suit off a rack. I knew them both from nineteen years of living in the same town. Detective Martin had a short Johnny Unitas crew cut and a square, hard face. Detective Davis was older and going to flab. He stood next to my father, stamping the dew off his shiny shoes.

"Well, it finally happened out here," said my father. The men looked at him. "I'm on the job in the city," he said out of the side of his mouth.

"No Michelangelo," said Martin.

"That's for sure," said Dad, and they all laughed.

Behind them, on the sidewalk, neighbors gathered and listened to Mrs. Bell. "I saw it early this morning," she said. "And I said right then and there that it's a disgrace."

In the kitchen Mom made coffee before anyone could say "Automatic Drip." I poured myself a cup. She didn't notice. The detectives sat at the table. Dad offered them bacon strips on a grease-soaked paper towel. "Help yourself," he said.

"I'm trying to watch my cholesterol level," said Martin, crunching a strip. "But what my wife doesn't know won't hurt me."

Dad brought down a bottle of Crown Royal Whiskey from the liquor cabinet. He opened the blue box, untied the gold cord, and slipped the bottle out of its felt pouch. "Special occasion," he said and winked at me.

"That's the good stuff, all right," said Martin. His hands lay on the table like two baseball gloves.

My father and the detectives did a shot without a toast. Mom leaned on the stove watching them.

"It went down like buttermilk," said Davis.

"It won't come off with just a cleaner," said Mom to no one. "And if we use anything stronger it will take the paint off the door."

"We're leaving it on," said Dad. "Passover is coming. That Angel of Death will go over like the goddamn Concord."

From the top of the refrigerator, my mother took an Entenmann's cake. We always had one somewhere. She trusted Entenmann's. She cut the strips of apple strudel and the men helped themselves, especially Detective Martin, who dunked it in his coffee.

"You know," said Davis. "I've seen a lot. I got my years in. I've seen *KKK* on houses, cross burnings on front lawns, even a few Nazi signs on a temple, but I've never seen nothing like this." He loosened his tie.

"It's the J.D.L.," said Dad. "It's got to be. Who else got the," he looked at Louise in the doorway, "the you-know-what."

"Best we can do is take a report. Ask around. Somebody must have seen something." Martin leaned back in his chair. I imagined the legs snapping like toothpicks.

"It's probably revenge," I said. "It's probably the Hasidim."

"Hasidim?" said Martin, coming back on all four legs.

"That could be," said Dad. "I was involved in the storming over in Borough Park last month."

"Then we'll send reports over to the city," said Martin.

"Well, you don't know. It could have been anyone. A bunch of rabbis out drinking."

"I doubt it," I said.

A report was filled out, and Dad signed in three places.

Dad stood on the lawn with Mr. White from two doors down. Mr. White was an accountant and wore wing-tip shoes and pin-striped pants on his days off. Dad polished off his beer and threw the bottle with other empties that lay in the garden. "You know this sort of thing wouldn't happen if people could sit down and talk," said Dad. "Do you know what I'd say?"

"What's that, Bill?" asked Mr. White.

"Life's too short for all this crap," he said.

A truck with the CBS letters and the black eye logo on the side pulled into the driveway. A van parked behind my Corvair. I tried not to look at my car. The top was almost gone. The seats were covered with leaves. The tires were going flat. The body was rusting away. The words *collector's item* haunted me for a moment.

A familiar looking newscaster was assisted out of the van by the driver. She wore a red dress and her hair in a flip curl. "Welcome to newsbreaker territory," said Dad, his hand extended.

"Hello, I'm Beverly Reed from the Channel Two News Team." She took his hand.

"There's the news," said Dad, looking at the house.

A television crew began setting up on our front lawn. Dad rushed inside and put on a black turtleneck sweater and a maroon sports coat.

The spectators grew into a crowd. Neighborhood kids joined their parents and ran around yelling, "Gotcha last." Mrs. White came wearing her fur coat, carrying her husband's London Fog raincoat and pipe. The sky grew dark, threatening rain.

The lawn was getting torn to bits. Dead autumn grass became uprooted and stuck to my shoes. There was a problem with one of the cameras. The technician spread the parts on a blanket and worked on his knees. "Made in Japan?" said Dad.

The man nodded and cleaned the lens with a production wipe. He wore a wool cap that said "Go Islanders."

"Buy American and you wouldn't have these problems," said Mr. White.

"You can't buy this camera in the United States," said the technician, snapping it together.

"That's because no one would buy it," said Dad.

"Could you get me an extension cord?" the man asked getting up.

I jogged back to the garage and swung open the door. On the back of the Buick stood two cans of spray paint, one white can and one black can. The tops were off. I looked out at the camera truck and at the cans again. My father had balls the size of the planet Mars. Standing on the lawn saying, "Beautiful, really beautiful," and breaking out the Crown Royal. I put the cans on a shelf with others and stuck the hedge clippers in front of them.

I gave the cameraman the extension cord and plugged it into the house. Louise and my mother had cornered Beverly Reed. "I feel like I've just been walked on," Mom said. "Those criminals defaced my property, my home. Do you own a house?"

I could feel myself growing angry. Dad stood lecturing the neighbors. "This is a sign for all of us," he said.

He deserved an academy award.

"We have to talk," I said, grabbing his arm.

"What the hell is it?" he asked.

I tugged him to the side of the house. "Who do you think did this?"

"That's what you dragged me over here for?"

"Who did it?" I repeated.

"Look, you know what I know?" he pulled away, looking around anxiously. "Why don't you comb your hair? You're going to be on television."

"Dad, I know who did it."

"Who?"

"You."

"Walk with me," he said and put his arm around my shoulder. "I was going to tell you, anyway. You'll keep your mouth shut?"

"Yeah. Do you think I'm going to rat on my father?"

"Would you do something for me?" He pulled a dime out of his pocket and whispered the favor in my ear.

I climbed the back fence in our yard and ran out to the next street. On Ocean Avenue I crossed in the middle of traffic and trotted up the block. I thought about the news tonight. My family standing in front of the house, and the words "Never Again." Louise wearing too much eye makeup saying something like, "I studied the Holocaust in school." Mrs. Bell yelling, "It's a disgrace," and all the neighbors commenting, "They're a very nice family. Bill is always there when you need him."

I went into the 7–11 store. This month's motto was, "Oh, Thank Heaven for 7–11." It was always the same in 7–11 stores. Beer and soda were on one wall, there was a magazine rack, paperback novels, a couple of rows of potato chips, corn chips, pretzels, then the counter, with two registers, and dirty magazines under the counter. When I was a kid I loved the stand with the cardboard roof filled with toys, and I liked putting my head in the deep freezer where the pops and ice cream sandwiches were, then blowing smoke out of my mouth. Today, I bought a Hundred Thousand Dollar candy bar for fifty cents. I paid a girl who had wide hips and buck teeth. "It's a crazy day," I said.

"You telling me?" she said.

I hung around outside for a while eating the candy bar. A few cars came. No one I knew. Yes, I'd keep my mouth shut. What else could I do? Fingering the dime, I went to the pay phone and called my house. It rang a half dozen times.

"Miss Reed, please," I said, disguising my voice.

"Oh, OK, just a minute," said my mother.

I heard the receiver bounce on the counter.

"Yes?" said Beverly Reed.

"Miss Reed?"

"Yes. Who is this?"

"I'd like you to know that the J.D.L. put that on that house. We are responsible."

"Who is this?"

I hung up, my heart racing.

I sat at the curb in front of the store for a while. I didn't want to go home until it was over.

CHAPTER
20

N.Y.C. DETECTIVE'S HOUSE DEFACED

N.Y.C. Detective William Patterson was outraged yesterday when he discovered his Long Island home had been painted with a Star of David and the words "Never Again". Through a phone call to newscaster Beverly Reed, the Jewish Defense League claimed responsibility. The incident is believed to be linked to the Hasidim–Police Melee in Borough Park, Brooklyn, last month. Detective Patterson faces the grand jury. He is accused of assaulting a Hasidic resident during the clash.

The outraged protestor, Sidney Cantor, has brought the accusation against Detective Patterson. The clash occurred as 2,000 Orthodox Jewish residents of the area marched to the 74th Precinct to demand better police protection following the robbery-murder of an elderly Jew.

Mr. Cantor himself faces assault and harassment charges stemming from the incident. Charges of police brutality brought by others who participated in the protest were dismissed earlier by the department's Civilian Complaint Review Board.

Yesterday Detective Patterson remarked, "I am a victim in this vicious circle. Now my wife, son, and daughter are also victims. It's got to end here."

I knelt on a paint-splotched dropcloth and began sanding the black star off the door. Dad, wearing a painter's cap, a cigar stuck in his teeth, poured blue paint into a rolling pan. Although the color was correct, it would never match. The shingles had faded. If Dad cared, he didn't show it.

"Just paint it," said Dad. "You don't have to sand the whole thing off." He took off his jacket. The sun had been popping in and out all day.

"Did you have to use black paint?" I asked.

"Why don't you tell the neighborhood," he said.

"Tell who what?" said Larry. He sat on the stoop, picking his teeth with a blade of grass. He had come over to help and hadn't touched a brush. The pants he wore were spotted with paint from many jobs. On his head was a cloth hat like my father's. Larry wore it with the brim up and looked like a hillbilly.

"Tell nobody nothing," said Dad, giving me the eye.

I pried open a can of white trim paint for the door. "Here, why don't you make yourself useful," I said and handed Larry a stirring stick.

Larry looked into the creamy white paint and swirled it around and around. "Did you build this stoop?" asked Larry.

"Twenty years ago," answered Dad. "Still as good as the day I poured it. It'll be here a lot longer than I am. That's for sure."

"That's not true," said Larry. "Nothing ever leaves. It just changes. One thing goes right into the next thing, then into the next thing." Larry stirred faster.

"What are you making? Butter?" I took the can from him and set it in front of the door.

"When you die, you're nothing but fertilizer." Larry picked up some dirt. "Man, I'm telling you that people are in everything and everything is all mixed up with everything else." He examined the dirt. "Who knows what could be in here. Maybe my brother is in here. Maybe some bird ate grass that he fertilized, flew over, and took a shit, right here in this dirt."

"You're talking crazy," said Dad.

"Am I?"

"Birds don't eat grass," said Dad. "Cows eat grass, and believe me I've never seen a cow fly over and take a dump."

Larry didn't laugh. He looked at the dirt.

"Larry, people have souls," I said.

"I don't believe they do," he said. "Do you know how long eternity is? Forever and ever and ever, right? Well, that's how long I'm gonna be in hell if I got a soul. What kind of God would make me suffer forever and ever for a bunch of crummy mistakes during my shitty little life?"

We had stopped painting.

"And if there is a God, wouldn't He have a sense of

humor? How could He throw me in hell? I'm funny, right? Look at me, Charlie. I'm funny, right? Ain't I?"

"What the hell did you do that was so bad?" yelled Dad.

"I tried to kill my wife," he shouted. "She was the best thing that ever happened to me and I tried to kill her. And I missed. Isn't that funny?"

"Please, Larry, stop." I tried to grab his arm. He stood.

"That's why I know we just go into the dirt and change into something else. And if you don't like it, tough."

My father and I looked at Larry.

"You think I'm crazy, right?" He stuck his hands in his baggy pants' pocket and backed away. "Well, I'm just starting to figure things out." He moved away like a man made of rubber.

We watched Larry take off in his car, then went back to the painting. I didn't know what to say and I'm sure Dad didn't know. I didn't think Larry was crazy. "You shouldn't think about stuff like that," I said.

"Stuff like what?" asked Dad.

"Like this whole life serving no purpose except becoming plant fertilizer."

"No, you shouldn't." said Dad. "It's like juggling with grenades."

"But if you don't think about things, you might as well be dead," I said.

"When you were a kid, you asked me what happened to dead people. I told you they buried them. Boy, oh boy, I never saw a kid so scared. You kept saying, 'What happens to them after that?' " Dad wet the roller in the mixing tray. "I never answered you. I couldn't."

"Why didn't you tell me that I'd go to heaven?"

"I don't know. I really don't."

I finished painting the door. Maybe I was imagining it but I swore I could still see the star. Dad said he couldn't see it, but his eyes weren't the way they used to be.

I began painting the trim around the front windows. Dad stood in the garden working the roller up and down. "I've been wondering," he said. Overspray had dotted his face and hat with blue spots. He took his cigar out and spit. "What was in that letter from the Bahamas?"

I thought about lying, but was too tired. "I was invited down there by Tracy. She's working at the Holiday Inn."

"You're not going, are you?"

"I've been thinking about it." There was nothing keeping me at home. The television commercials said, "There's no better time to go to the Bahamas than now." United Air Lines was running a discounted fare, $199 for a round-trip ticket. I could afford that. And as far as Maria goes, it could have been a coincidence that she had also been invited and promised a job. Maybe there was a big demand for waitresses. I had to write Tracy soon. I'd go right after my father's case was settled.

"What about your car?" asked Dad. "You just can't leave it sitting like that."

My car was quietly falling apart at the curb.

"I could junk it," I said.

"Junk your first car? With some work and a new roof it would be as good as new."

As a testimony to his words, the Buick sat, shining, in the driveway. The bodywork was flawless. Good as new.

"You just have to get back on the track again. You and I both." He dipped the roller. With one stroke he covered the word "Again."

John Haggerty drove up in an unmarked city police car. Dad dropped his roller and crossed the lawn to greet him. Haggerty, clean shaven, wearing a trenchcoat over a blue suit, said, "I'm here to take some pictures of the house for the Gold Shield Newsletter." He took a large camera off the front seat of the car and slammed the door.

"You're too late," said Dad.

"No, no, this is perfect," said Haggerty. "Let's get a few of you and Charlie in front of the house holding paint brushes, then I'll tell you some news."

We posed for two pictures.

"That's enough," said Dad, dropping his brush on the drop cloth.

"Just one more."

"No," said Dad. "I'm sick of this whole thing."

In the kitchen Haggerty said, "I'll tell you all of our protesting wasn't in vain, Bill. You're going to be cleared. They're afraid to bring you to court. After what the J.D.L. did to the house, they're afraid to touch this thing. They're going to dismiss the charges on Cantor and his merry men. The thing's gotten too big."

My father's mouth hung open. His plan had worked and he looked as if he couldn't believe it.

"You mean, when I get off sick leave I can go back to work?"

"That's what it means."

Dad hugged my mother. He lifted her a couple of inches off the floor and they turned around.

"Doesn't seem to have a bad heart," Haggerty joked.

Mom didn't seem as happy as she could have been. I honestly wasn't too happy, either. If I had not known about the damn graffiti, I would have felt that Dad had won a victory. Now he had just used the system to beat the system. Maybe my mother knew about the graffiti.

This time, *I* got out the Crown Royal and poured shots.

"To you, John," said Dad, raising his glass. "And to you, Charlie." There were tears in his eyes.

"That star on the door broke this case wide open," said Haggerty. "Everyone feels sorry for you now."

"Plus I'm innocent," said Dad.

"Of course," said Haggerty.

"It's not a question of guilt and innocence," I said. "The only people who were guilty were the kids who killed the jeweler. Everything else was just a chain reaction. Do you think my father wanted to be in the middle of that riot and do you think the Hasidim were planning on ripping apart the police station? No, it just happened."

I guess I had been talking too loud because the kitchen was awfully quiet.

"Well," I asked. "Am I right?"

"Let's just thank God it's over," said my mother, crossing herself. "It's been a rough time for all of us." She looked at me.

"Charlie went through a bad time," said Dad.

"I went through a bad time? What about you? What do you call that?"

"That's another story," said Dad.

"So what are you going to do with yourself?" Haggerty asked me.

"Not too much," I said.

"Going to follow in your father's footsteps? We got a police test coming up." He put his shot glass down, and my father refilled it. "You get on and I'll get you into a nice area."

"First, there's college to finish," said Mom.

I could hardly breathe. College? Me struggling through accounting again? I didn't want to be an accountant.

"A cop," I said, trying to laugh. "Me, a cop?"

"You could take the test," said Dad. "It couldn't hurt."

"Oh, come on," I said, trying to meet my father's eyes, but his face seemed to turn to wax. I got this real sad feeling. The Bahamas, I thought, I'll go to the Bahamas.

"At least you'd have job security and a twenty-year retirement," said Haggerty. "Right, Bill?"

EPILOGUE

*It was raining that night. We skidded on the slip-
pery roads and didn't say anything. Dad drove fast, but
it was too late. Larry had done it. My father wiped his
eyes. I had nothing to give, no tears, nothing. I was just
becoming angry as hell.*

"Did you know Larry really loved you?" I asked. "He
looked up to you. He would have done anything, anything for you. Maybe if you had showed him something."

"Don't say things like that now," said Dad.

"You don't want to hear it because you know it's the
truth. He was always worried about you."

"Please, Charlie." My father's voice was breaking.

I held my head. There was so much spinning around,

it felt like it was going to explode.

Police cars lined the dead-end street. Dad double-parked and stuck an "Official Business N.Y.P.D." sign on the dashboard. The house was roped off with an orange ribbon. A few neighbors stood under the street-light watching the house as if they expected it to lift off like a rocket. We ducked under the ribbon, and Dad flashed his badge at a couple of cops. "You got enough light here, or what?" said Dad.

A floodlight illuminated the front stoop and another hit the side of the house. The cement deer behind the bushes appeared blinded. The little plastic chipmunks nailed to the shingles had shadows the size of dogs.

In the living room a couple of men, probably detectives, stood around exchanging small talk. The room was neat. The couch, where Larry had been sleeping, was made up. The blankets were tucked under the cushions carefully.

"You never can tell with some guys," I heard someone say.

I wanted to ask where Larry's body was, but the words wouldn't come. I went through the house peeking into each room. I needed to find something. Where was the grief? It was all too neat. No one cared then, and no one cared now. My insides were twisting. I remembered a story about a man who had killed himself in the bathtub so that he wouldn't make a mess. I nudged the bathroom door open, nothing.

From the bedroom window I saw my father standing outside on the patio rocking on his heels with his hands stuck in his back pockets. The pink bug lights shone off the house and onto his face. It was white.

I went down the stairs and out the back door. It was

drizzling steadily. The sheet that covered Larry was wet
and had become transparent. He sat half on the picnic
bench with his face on the table as if he were praying.

The detectives had moved into the yard. They stood
in a small circle, smoking butts and drinking steaming
coffee in 7–11 go-cups. I wanted to get Larry out of the
rain.

"Let's move him into the house," I said.

Dad went right over and lifted the sheet. Larry's hair
and face were red.

"Nobody touches him until the city police get here,"
said a cop.

"I'm the city," said Dad, showing his badge.

No one moved.

"Are you going to stand in the rain like a bunch of
jackasses?" said Dad.

When we moved him, there was a lot of blood. Even
the rain puddles were red.

———————

On the way home Dad handed me a clear plastic bag.
"Open it," he said. "And empty that shit out the window. Those bastards were going to write this stuff up.
Everyone would have thought Larry was just another
coke freak."

I poured out the bag of cocaine. In an instant the white
crystals blew into the night and disappeared.

———————

Larry's death went into Dad like a ghost. White-faced
and a drink in his hand, he sat at the kitchen table. My
mother tried to help. At dinner she told him not to be
afraid.

"I'm thinking. Is that all right with you?"

"Don't be afraid to feel," she said.

My father got up and went out the back door.

"He's not as strong as he looks," she said.

Two days later the funeral was held. My mother refused to go, saying, "I went to an early Mass and prayed for his soul. Bill, go with Charlie and let me do it my way." My father blew up at her, but in the end she won and sent us off like two boys on the first day of school.

"Your mother is getting strange," said Dad when we were in the car. "She gave me fifty dollars of my own money and told me to take you to a nice lunch. I asked her what a nice lunch was and she said, 'One that comes with soup.' Is that what you want?"

"No, not really."

"I didn't think so. If we go to lunch we'll go some place where we can get a beer."

Dad was nervous and cranky. He had sat for hours at Larry's wake drinking red wine from tiny plastic glasses. The funeral parlor either ran out of wine or cut my father off and he got nasty with the manager. There was a bunch of men who tried to calm him down. Just don't touch me, he had said when someone took his arm. I managed to get him out of the wake. All the way home he complained about the wine. "Shitty, cheap screw-top wine and they run out. Wine-o wine at a cop's wake. Ten years ago you wouldn't have crap like that."

The church was way out on Long Island. Dad drove slowly with an unlit cigar in his mouth. It was a weird day. One of those cloudy days when the leaves seem to blow all by themselves.

"You know, I'm supposed to go back to work in two weeks," said Dad.

I knew it. Everyone in the family was counting the days. What was I going to do? The application for the police was due in two days. I had it half filled out. I was qualified. I had finished high school and did not have a criminal record. I had ten toes and ten fingers. I wasn't flat-footed. I had a clean driver's license.

For a week I walked around thinking that Tracy could save me from making any decisions. I pictured us in the Bahamas with tans as dark as mahogany. But she had returned to New York. I had seen her at the drug store buying pearl nail polish and a Fifth Avenue candy bar. She had a hell of a tan.

"What are you doing here?" I had asked. "You're supposed to be in the Bahamas."

We talked outside the store in a drizzle. Cars swished by, people rushed past. I wanted it all to stop. I wanted her to look at me.

"Why didn't you call me?" I asked. "When did you get back?"

"Charlie, I've been busy. A million things have happened. I'm in a completely new line. I'm washing hair now and taking a course at the community college so that I can cut. There's a lot of money in cutting hair."

"And that's it. That's it. You have nothing else to say to me."

"I didn't want to call you. Look at you, you're so angry you're trembling and you were yelling at me just then, you were yelling."

I told myself to be calm.

"I'm afraid of you," she said.

"You should have called me."

She pulled a card from her purse. "That's good for a free wash and blow. If you use it on a weekday I should be able to get you a free styling."

I took the card. It said "The Head Hut". On the back

it said, "Free Wash and Blow."

I grabbed her coat. I wanted to punch her, but she broke away.

"You're sick," she screamed.

I wanted to run after her and make her say she was sorry. But she got into her car and closed the door.

I threw the card at her. It flipped through the wind and landed on the wet pavement.

"This has got to be the place." said Dad, pulling to the curb. On the church steps three cops in blue uniforms stood holding their caps in their hands. Dad put his cigar in the ash tray and ran his hand through his hair. "You going to be all right?" he asked.

"I'll make it. What about you?"

"Who knows?" he said. "Who the hell knows?"

Only the first twelve church pews were full. In front of the altar was a polished redwood coffin. Dad and I decided to stand. I could picture Larry's bloody hair and face, but I wanted to remember him alive. Eyes closed, I tried to see him and the only thing I saw was the rotten-toothed hooker he had picked up in the city. Almost everything Larry and I ever did came to me. But not his face, at least not alive.

I couldn't understand the words the priest was saying. They were echoing too much. Dad stood rocking slightly, with his arms folded. I held the back of the last pew. The sermon, or whatever it was, went on and on until organ music began. Some men lifted the coffin and it came right toward us with the mourners following.

Dad grabbed my shoulder and we went out the doors and down the steps. "Let's walk somewhere," he said.

We left the car and headed up the block, neither of

us knowing where we were going, neither of us looking back.

"I don't know what I want to do anymore," said Dad. "And let's forget about the police test. You don't want to become a cop."

"I know," I said.

We came to a fork in the road and began walking to the water. We passed some small bungalo type houses that had nets hanging over the front fences to dry. Behind the houses a shallow muddy canal led to the bay. The air smelled fresh and good.

"How can I go back to it now?" asked Dad. "Just answer that one question. I'm past it. Larry and that goddamn fiasco knocked all of the fight out of me. Poor Larry. Remember, you asked me why I never did anything to help him?"

"Dad, I was wrong that night. I was upset."

"But that was a damn good question. I knew Larry was cracking up. We all knew it. For God's sake, he shot a curler off his wife's head. I mean, what the hell do you have to do to get help?"

"It was as if we were all waiting for it to happen," I said.

There were a lot of pot holes in the street. Dad and I zigzagged around them. "I wish I knew what to do." I said.

"Maybe we could go into business," he said. "I don't know, maybe a gas station. It's a lot of hours, but when I retire I'll have nothing but time. We could get a loan and I'm a halfway decent mechanic."

I didn't say anything.

"What's the matter? he asked. "Don't you think we could make it?"

"I don't think you'll ever retire. It's in your blood."

"It's out," he said. "You wait and see."

At the end of the block the canal met the channel. On a peninsula was a small bar and grill, painted white, called The Navigator Inn. It was built on a bulkhead right over the water. We crossed the white-shell parking lot and stood on a worn wood dock. The tide was rushing into the channel. It was clean green water.

"Don't you think you could work with me?" asked Dad.

"I just don't believe you and I don't feel like dreaming right now."

He took his gold shield out of his front pocket. A chain attached it to his belt loop. I'll prove it," he said. He unhooked it and drew his arm back.

At the last moment I grabbed his wrist. The gold caught the light of the day and shone in his eyes.

The strength drained from his arm and I let go.

———————————

Dad sat on the old splintering dock and hung his legs over the water. He held the badge with his fingers and turned it end over end.

"When the joint opens we'll have a nice lunch and a beer for Larry," he said.

I sat next to him. The sun was high and made the water look like silver.